Readers love
JOHN INMAN

Sunset Lake

"I loved this book and didn't want it to end. It had everything: humor, mystery/suspense, and romance all rolled into one!"

—Joyfully Jay

"Well, it has finally happened. I have been rendered speechless by what I must say is one of the most exciting and exceptional murder mysteries on the market today."

—The Novel Approach

Chasing the Swallows

"It's so well written, its descriptions so starkly believable and filled with hurt feelings that I never once doubted the raw, immediate lives John Inman was laying out before us."

—Scattered Thoughts and Rogue Words

Scrudge & Barley, Inc.

"In spite of all of the fantastical activities, there is an odd realism to the narrative, and a cinematic quality to the prose that suggests it would make a great film (as if)."

—Prism Book Alliance

"While this isn't the first retelling of the well-known story in my library, it's probably one of the best I've read... a lovely, lovely book"

—My Fiction Nook

By JOHN INMAN

Chasing the Swallows
A Hard Winter Rain
Head-on
Hobbled
Jasper's Mountain
Loving Hector
Paulie
Payback
The Poodle Apocalypse
Scrudge & Barley, Inc.
Shy
Snow on the Roof (Dreamspinner Anthology)
Spirit
Sunset Lake
Two Pet Dicks

THE BELLADONNA ARMS
Serenading Stanley
Work in Progress
Coming Back

Published by DREAMSPINNER PRESS
www.dreamspinnerpress.com

TWO PET DICKS

JOHN INMAN

Published by
DREAMSPINNER PRESS

5032 Capital Circle SW, Suite 2, PMB# 279, Tallahassee, FL 32305-7886 USA
www.dreamspinnerpress.com

Two Pet Dicks
© 2016 John Inman.

Cover Art
© 2016 Paul Richmond.
http://www.paulrichmondstudio.com
Cover content is for illustrative purposes only and any person depicted on the cover is a model.

ISBN: 978-1-63476-790-3
Digital ISBN: 978-1-63476-791-0
Library of Congress Control Number: 2015918432
Published March 2016
v. 1.0

Printed in the United States of America
∞

This paper meets the requirements of
ANSI/NISO Z39.48-1992 (Permanence of Paper).

For those readers who like a little bit of silliness with their romance.

Chapter One

Hı. My name is Maitland Carter.

"Hey, you! Cuddleumpkins! Get your bony white ass out here and give me a hand!"

Sorry about that. That's my partner, Lenny Fritz. He's black and proud. And noisy.

Before we go any further, let me clear something up. Yes, we're the two dicks in the title of this little masterpiece. But don't get the wrong impression. We're not *dickhead* dicks. At least I don't think we are, although I might know a few people who would disagree with that assessment. We're not anybody's pets either, in case you're wondering. No, we're just dicks. As in private investigators.

For pets. Lost pets. Get it?

And while we're in the process of clearing things up, let me clear up something else. When I say Lenny is my partner, I'm referring to his position as my *business* partner only. While we are most certainly as gay as geese, the two of us, we are not lovers.

Don't get me wrong. We've had sex now and then. And when I say now and then, I mean every chance we get. But mind you only under the direst of circumstances. Like when we're mutually horny and maybe between boyfriends and quite possibly on stakeout, and it's late at night and there's nothing else to do but watch some fatass bulldog sneak out of his enclosure with the intention of playing hide the Milk-Bone with the cute french poodle up the street, whose owner happens to be a client who is paying us good money to keep her precious Fifi's hymen in place until she pays the stud fee on an animal worthy to impregnate the mutt. Yes, there are people who will actually hire people like us to do that.

So to recap—stakeouts are boring. Anything to alleviate boredom is a good thing, right? Thusly, in our quest to alleviate that boredom, Lenny and I *may* have hid the Milk-Bone a few times ourselves. In fact, we most certainly did. But we're men. What do you expect?

Let me answer that question for you too, if I may. As far as men go, here's what you can expect: Straight, homo, fruitarian, or Jehovah's Witness, it all boils down to one thing. Men are ruled by their peckers and have no more sense of restraint than a swarm of whiteflies chowing down on every hibiscus blossom that crosses their path. Or a horny bulldog going after a french poodle. Trust me. I see it every day. After all, I'm a dick. I mean, private investigator. I understand the human condition. At least I tell myself I do.

Lenny and I stand six feet tall. We both weigh in at one seventy-fiveish on a good day and we both have all our teeth and those teeth are fairly even and straight. My hair is red and curly and Lenny's is black and frizzy. His skin is a rich umber and mine is vanilla cream. There's not an ounce of fat on either one of us except quite possibly between our ears. If you're interested, Lenny is circumcised and I'm not. In both instances we're rather impressive to behold, if I say so myself. We've been told we're good-looking dudes, and while modesty forbids me to praise my own appearance, I can certainly attest to Lenny's, for he is indeedy-do a good-looking dude. I wouldn't be porking him in the stakeout van if he wasn't, and I assume that goes for him with me as well. He admires my red hair, he says, and I admire the way he goes into an orgasmic meltdown with such enthusiastic fervor his come can fly right through the van's side window and hit a mailbox four feet away.

But enough about us. Let's get on with the story.

Lenny hammered on the storefront window with both fists, rattling the glass and making an unholy racket. He was standing outside in the pouring rain, and he didn't look happy. I figured if he pounded on the glass any harder, the rain outside would be inside, and we'd all be drenched to our skivvies.

I stormed through the front door of our newly rented office space and stepped out into the deluge. In the time it takes to tell about it, I was as soaked as Lenny.

"There!" I screamed. "I'm wet! You happy?"

"It's a start!" Lenny roared over the downpour. He had a hammer in one hand, and it looked like he was using considerable willpower not to bonk me on the head with it. "I need you to hold the ladder while I hang this shingle!"

A sizzling bolt of lightning shot across the sky above our heads, and we both ducked. Thunder followed about two seconds later. It was a fairly impressive celestial display, especially for San Diego, where it hardly ever rains.

"Are you nuts?" I yelled above the storm. "You're holding a metal hammer and you want to stand on a metal ladder to hang a metal sign in the middle of a lightning storm! What could possibly go wrong?"

"Shut up and do it!"

I squeegeed the rain off my face like one of the Three Stooges and traipsed through a puddle to do as he asked, mumbling to myself as I did it, "Fine. I'll be incinerated, but what do you care? No skin off your nose."

"Stop mumbling," Lenny snapped, ducking through my arms to climb the ladder in front of me. He climbed until his ass was in my face, natch, and there he stopped.

"Now hold the ladder!" he bellowed down at me.

No sooner had he said it than his foot slipped on the rung and he muttered, "Oh, crap," as the hammer fell from his hand and banged me on the head.

He looked down at me reeling around, stomping through puddles, holding my head. "Maybe you should stand on the other side of the ladder," he suggested.

So as soon as the last twirling star disappeared from before my eyes, I growled something unkind and quite possibly racist, fished around in a mud puddle to retrieve the fucking hammer, and handed it back to him.

"Just finish," I growled. "I'm drowning here."

Considerable hammering ensued, a few cuss words about the rain followed, and then a triumphant "Oho! It's done."

I stepped out to the curb as Lenny descended the ladder. He joined me, and together we gazed up through the downpour at the brand-new sign proclaiming a brand-new business in town. Two Dicks, the sign read. And that's all it read. We couldn't afford a sign big enough to add the words Private Investigators for Pets. Or even Pets. So the sign read simply Two Dicks.

Lenny and I stood in the gutter with what felt like the Mississippi River flowing over our shoe tops and stared proudly at the sign, the storefront, our very own door, and our very own shop window.

"Open for business," Lenny proudly proclaimed.

I turned to him and saw his dark face beaming back at mine. His coal-black eyes, framed in curly lashes, were wide and excited, the whites as white as white can get. "We did it," he said. "We finally did it!"

I felt a lump rise in my throat, and pressure behind my eyes started working its way toward my tear ducts. I figured it was either from the emotion of the moment, or the fact I was already coming down with pneumonia from standing in the rain like a fool. Lenny and I had been talking about this day, this joint venture, forever. And now it was a reality. Or at least it would be as soon as we snagged a few clients.

Lenny looked down at his hands. "I've lost the hammer again. Where'd it go?"

I patted my still-aching head and gazed skyward. "Beats me."

"Screw it," he said. "Let's get inside before we wash away."

"About time," I grumbled.

Draping his arm over my shoulder, he led me through the front door out of the rain, and as we stood in our very own brand-new office, dripping water all over the nice clean floor, which rented for ninety-three cents a square foot, he pulled me into his arms and gave me a hug so enthusiastic it might have killed a lesser man.

"Partner," he said and kissed me on the mouth. And he kept kissing me on the mouth until I was beginning to enjoy it.

"What are you doing?" I asked, licking his taste from my lips. "We're not on stakeout."

"What can I say, Mait? Grand openings make me horny. And we're both between boyfriends."

"Yes," I groused again, "because our two boyfriends ran off and eloped with *each other* after you introduced them in the bar that night."

"How was I supposed to know they were such sluts?"

"Well, they were with us. That should have been your first clue."

"True." He ground his crotch against mine. I have to admit it felt nice. Crotch grinding is always a pick-me-upper.

"There are no curtains on the window," I said around his tongue, which was burrowing its way down my throat. I tried to swallow a gasp of desire before it got away from me. I mean, our two snuggling peckers *really* felt nice bumping heads down below. And Lenny's strong brown hands on my ass felt pretty nice too.

Lenny smiled as if he knew exactly what I was thinking, which I'm sure he did. He ground his crotch against mine a little harder. "It's a monsoon out there, honeybuns. There's nobody on the street to look in."

"Don't call me honeybuns."

"Okay." Lenny's voice had ducked down an octave or two, like it always did when he was feeling amorous. We were both as hard now as the handle of the hammer we'd used to hang the sign, which, as far as I knew, was still lying in a puddle somewhere outside. The hammer, I mean, not the sign.

Lenny was already going for the zipper on my fly, and he had that sexy look on his face I knew all too well, so I figured there wasn't much point in trying to turn the course of future events. Licking my lips, I reached for his fly as well. What the hell. When in Rome....

And that's when the front door opened behind us, and Lenny and I practically jumped out of our skins. Thank God the door hadn't opened twenty seconds later or the Two Dicks sign hanging outside would have been right on the money.

While Lenny and I struggled to hunch inward to camouflage the erections tenting the front of our slacks, I threw myself into my desk chair and used the desk to hide my crotch while Lenny quickly plopped down on top of the desk amid a flurry of papers and hurriedly crossed his legs.

"May we help you?" we said in unison, as innocent as cherubs.

The woman in the doorway blinked back a wee bit of confusion, then proceeded to step in out of the rain, closing her umbrella as she came inside. She wore an expensive handmade Stutterheim raincoat with matching hat and a calfskin Gucci handbag on her arm. If the handbag wasn't a knock-off, it must have cost more than Lenny and I had in our two bank accounts together.

"Gucci," I said to Lenny under my breath.

"Money," he whispered back.

The woman was in her well-maintained forties and appeared to be the type who was used to getting her way. She had a no-nonsense glint in her eye that said she would emasculate any man without thinking twice if he did anything to piss her off. Being gay, as I mentioned before, women pretty much scare the bejesus out of me anyway. Our visitor was certainly no exception.

"Are you the two dicks?" the woman asked.

Lenny turned to me and frowned. "Maybe we should have rethought that sign."

The woman stood in the doorway and whipped her hat off, shaking out a long flowing mane of ash-blond hair like a *Sports Illustrated* swimsuit model crawling out of the surf. For an old broad, she was a knockout. I mean, if you're into that sort of thing.

The woman eyed first Lenny, then me, as if trying to gauge who was in charge. *Good luck with that.* The fact that we were sitting there soaking wet trying to hide our hard-ons didn't seem to impress her at all.

"My name is Lorraine Johns. I'd like you boys to help me find Frederick."

The way she said "you boys" made me think Lenny and my sexualities were not as well concealed as I might have hoped. Not that I cared much. What I cared about was acquiring a paying client, and by jingles, Lorraine Johns might be it.

"Who's Frederick?" I asked, trying to appear businesslike and competent. An uphill grind at the best of times.

"My lizard."

I dug a pound of imaginary earwax out of my ear. "I'm sorry, I thought you said your lizard."

"Yes. That's right. My husband stole him."

"Your husband stole your lizard." As an aside, I nudged Lenny in the butt and whispered, "Close your mouth, love, you're dribbling."

Lenny slapped his mouth shut like an oven door, and as soon as he did, I turned my attention back to our visitor.

"That wasn't a very nice thing to do," I commented because, well, come on. What are you supposed to say when some woman drops in out of the blue and tells you her husband stole her lizard?

Lorraine shook the raindrops from her coat and peeled it off. Underneath the coat she wore a skirt so short it barely covered her doodah. Once again, not that I cared. Doodahs are of very little interest to me. What goes *into* doodahs I find much more fascinating.

Lorraine looked around for a chair, and Lenny kicked one toward her with his foot. Always the gentleman. She sat, primly crossing her legs as if trying very hard not to show off what was pretty much already hanging in the wind anyway. If she was expecting a slavering response from either of the two men in the room to the fact that her legs climbed all the way up to her neck, I'm afraid she went away sorely disappointed.

"My husband hated Frederick," she said, pulling a Virginia Slim out of her Gucci bag and setting the tip of it on fire with a gold lighter I noticed was embossed with an onyx *L* and *J*. Lenny crawled off the desk and walked around her to open the front door and let the carcinogens out. Lenny wasn't totally stupid. She ignored him and went on, "Actually, he's my ex-husband, or he will be as soon as the divorce becomes final."

"Why did he steal the lizard?" Lenny asked as he climbed back on the desk, thinking maybe he should get in on the interrogation, I suppose. Why should he let me have all the fun?

"To get back at me."

"And why," I asked, "would your husband feel he had to get back at you?"

Lorraine blew a perfect smoke ring between peach-colored lips and almost smiled. "Because I set fire to his Camaro."

"Get out!" Lenny exclaimed, obviously impressed. I was less than impressed. In fact, I was beginning to wonder if the woman was perhaps no saner than we were, which would be a disturbing development.

"Why'd you set fire to his Camaro?" I asked.

She blew another smoke ring. The office was beginning to stink. "Because his Rottweiler ate Rosemary."

Lenny snatched the words right out of my mouth. "Who, might one ask, is Rosemary?"

"Rosemary is—was—Frederick's mate."

"Ah," I said, stroking my chin, squinting my eyes, and doing my best Charlie Chan impression. "Honorable lizard number two."

Lenny turned to me and asked, "Do we have any Tylenol?" Sometimes Lenny's needle skips a groove.

I ignored him. The woman had a Gucci bag. And there was probably a very nice calfskin checkbook holder inside that matched the Gucci bag. And she probably had a pen in there with which to write a check to retain the services of the two nice pet detectives. And if she didn't have a pen, I'd loan her one. We needed the money.

"What year?" I asked.

Lorraine blinked. "This year, of course."

I sighed. "I don't mean what year did he steal the stupid lizard. I mean what year was the Camaro."

"Oh. A '69 Z28 RS."

"No shit!" Lenny barked. "That's a classic!"

She appeared unimpressed with that observation. "Yeah, well, now it's a classic piece of toast."

"Wow," Lenny said. "You take your amphibians seriously. What kind of lizard are we talking about?"

"A Gila monster," she said, giving her long blonde locks another shake, a la Rita Hayworth. "A big one."

"Holy crap!" Again Lenny and I spoke in unison. Maybe we'd been together too long. "Those things are poisonous, you know," I added.

It was her turn to say no shit. "No shit. I have rattlesnakes too. And a small asp and several other species. I'm a herpetologist."

"You mean like a bleeder?" Lenny asked, and Lorraine and I stared at him as if he'd beamed himself into the room through the back wall.

I rolled my eyes. "That's hemophiliac, you twit. She means she's a reptile expert."

"Oh. Well, uh…." Lenny flailed around as if trying to find a way to redeem himself and not look so dumb. "I'm sure it's a very nice asp," he said. "Even if it is small."

Lenny is great in a fistfight or a fuckfest, but put him in any sort of *cerebral* situation, and he sinks like a rock.

Lorraine took three drags off her cigarette in quick succession, never taking her eyes off Lenny's face. I suppose during that time she made a few tactical decisions because from that point on, she stared at me and tried to pretend poor Lenny wasn't in the room at all.

I heaved a sigh. "So you want us to find your poisonous lizard. Just how poisonous are they exactly? Deadly, I presume."

She *pshawed*. I hate it when people *pshaw*. "Gila monsters aren't deadly at all. You might get sick from the venom, but that's about it. Basically, Frederick is harmless, although he is a little cranky and can inflict a reasonably nasty bite if you're dumb enough to stick your finger down his throat and leave it there long enough for him to chew on it. You'll never die from the bite of a *Heloderma suspectum*. Although you might wish you had."

"Good to know," Lenny commented. "Uh, what does this guy look like? Give us a description in case we run into a convention of the little fuckers and have to pick Frederick out of a lineup."

Again, Lorraine Johns turned her attention to me—after staring at Lenny for a minute as if wondering what subdivision of the human species he might have hailed from since his genus had apparently escaped her attention during her years of herpetology training. "He's twenty-three inches long, weighs approximately five pounds, and has orange-and-black spotted horizontal stripes from his head to the tip of his tail. He looked chubby the last time I saw him. He'd just eaten a rat and two eggs. He's twenty-one years old, and he likes show tunes."

"Really?" I asked. "He likes show tunes?"

"Yes."

"Wow," Lenny said. "Maybe he's gay."

Lorraine glanced skyward as if beseeching help from a higher power. "Jesus God, help me," her eyes seemed to say. She heaved a sigh and stifled a growl, but she didn't do a very good job of it. She was obviously getting upset. Not because of the frigging missing lizard, but because Lenny was really starting to get on her nerves. I knew because he was starting to get on mine too. I could only pray she wasn't packing heat.

"We'll take the case," I quickly said, heading off the approaching homicide I could see burning in her eyes. I handed her a business card. "Everything is on there. Home address, home phone, cell, every contingency you might need to get in touch with us in a hurry. We require a three-hundred-dollar retainer, which covers our expenses for a week. If we haven't found the little beaded handbag by then, we'll require another week's retainer to keep looking for him. If your check bounces, all bets are off."

"I'll pay cash."

"Even better. Cash *never* bounces."

We had her jot down all pertinent data concerning her lizard-stealing louse of a husband and her own personal contact information, and after that there was nothing to do but count the fifteen twenty-dollar bills she laid in my hand before sliding into her Stutterheim raincoat, plopping her Stutterheim hat on her head, popping her umbrella open with a snap, and heading out the door, determinedly ignoring Lenny while she did it.

Lenny still hadn't caught up to reality. The moment Lorraine Johns closed the shop door behind her and stepped out into the rain, he turned to me and said, "Golly. A gay lizard. Who'd a thunk?"

TO COMMEMORATE the acquisition of our first client, Lenny had his hand on my zipper tab and was about to drop to his knees and go to town in celebration when we were interrupted again.

The phone man stuck his head in the door that opened into the office from the back room. I'd forgotten about him. He'd been out in the alley trying to find the circuit board so he could hook up our first business phone. Heady stuff for a couple of guys who'd spent the last two years running their little pet-finding business out of Lenny's dad's basement. We'd finally vacated the premises at the old fart's insistence. Lenny's dad was tired of us parking our asses in his basement all the time because when we did he couldn't play with his electric trains. Lenny's dad was sixty-three.

The phone guy staring around the doorjamb was holding an umbrella over his head. The umbrella had pink roses on it and a pink fringe. That umbrella carved serious inroads into the phone guy's ability to look butch.

The phone guy was wetter than we were. He was also kind of cute. Even with the pink umbrella hovering over his head. Lenny's attention wavered from my zipper to the phone man's zipper in less than three seconds flat. Lenny was a slut.

"You're in business," the phone guy said to me, eyeing Lenny askance. Apparently he didn't like having his crotch stared at by customers. Go figure.

Also to me, he added, pointedly ignoring Lenny, "If your coffee-colored partner keeps staring at my balls like that, I'm going to pop him up the side of the head with a wrench. I'm straight. I've got six kids. This is my daughter's umbrella, for fuck's sake. It's not a personal fashion statement."

"Ooh," Lenny crooned. "Straight daddies are hot."

The phone man went for a wrench in his tool belt, and I rushed to steer him back the way he came before he could kill Lenny dead. I thanked him for his hard work, sympathized with him over his nellyass umbrella, and assured him my partner was on medication and didn't know what he was saying.

"Well, *harrumph*," the phone man grumped, still offended to the core. He ripped my invoice off his clipboard and shoved it in my face. With that, he hiked up his nuts in one last attempt to look masculine. Grunting like a camel, he huffed his way back out into the rain under his silly pink umbrella, mumbling something about fruit cups.

Lenny came up behind me and stuck his head out to watch the phone man's retreat. "You should be flattered, you fucking breeder!" he screamed into the rain. Then he turned to me. "He didn't check the phone to make sure it worked. I hate shoddy workmanship. He had a nice ass, though. Did you notice? Nice basket too."

At that precise moment, the brand-new nine-dollar Walmart telephone sitting on the desk in the other room began to jangle.

"Guess it works," I said and hustled off to answer it. Lenny trailed along behind me and pushed the button for speakerphone as I picked up so he could hear our first honest-to-God business call on our first honest-to-God business phone.

"Two Dicks," I sang out blithely. "How can we help you, kind sir or madam?"

A booming voice hailed, "This is Lester Fucking Boggs over on 13th Street! My motherfucking parrot just flew out the fucking window! I need your firm to set up a search party, with perimeters and the whole nine yards, and bring that shitheaded nitwit back! You hear me?"

"Everybody on this side of the twentieth parallel heard you," I answered. "So what kind of parrot was it?"

"It was a goddamn African grey! Still fucking is, for all I know."

"So he's gray, then," I said.

"Who are you?" the voice bellowed through the speaker. "Sherlock Fucking Holmes? Of course he's gray! With red tail feathers on his ass."

"Can he talk?" Lenny leaned in to ask.

Lester seemed to think that was a pretty dumb question. "Hell yes, he can talk! He never fucking shuts up! Shitfire, man, I've been teaching him to talk for thirty years."

I rolled my eyes. "He must have quite a vocabulary."

"Fuck yes! He talks as good as I do!"

Lenny gave me a look as if to say "Must be a real charmer, then."

"So when can you come?" Lester Boggs screamed. "He could be in fucking Tahiti by now!"

I peered through the shop window. The rain was easing up. "Okay, sir. We'll be right there. Give me your address."

"I'm at 2917 Fucking 13th Street! Bring a goddamn net with you. Toodles is a slippery little shit."

"His name is Toodles?"

"Yeah! You got a fucking problem with that? My wife named him. The bitch."

"Fuck you!" we heard the little woman yell from somewhere nearby. If anything, her voice was even more piercing than Lester's, but apparently they shared the same expletive coach. Clearly a match made in heaven.

"Cow!" Lester yelled.

"Turd!" Mrs. Boggs screamed back.

"Slut!"

"Dick!"

"That's us," Lenny interrupted. "We'll be there in ten minutes. We'll expect a three-hundred-dollar retainer when we get there."

"Three hundred dollars?" Lester railed. "I'm not made of fucking money! That's outrageous!"

Lenny did his best mobster growl. "If you want the bird back, you'll cough up the cash."

"Fine!" Lester snapped. "Just get here! And I mean fucking now!"

I pressed the disconnect button, hung up the phone, and grinned.

"Wow. Two clients in one day."

Lenny grinned right back. "Let's motherfucking roll."

"You sound like Lester," I said, as we hustled out the door.

Chapter Two

TWO DICKS already had a few irons in the fire, thanks to anxious pet owners citywide. We had a gerbil a drag queen in one of the apartment buildings downtown had sworn had been kidnapped, and she was freaking out because it wasn't her gerbil. She had merely been gerbilsitting for a friend. We also had a couple of lost cats we'd been keeping a watchful eye out for the past week or so, but hopes of recovery there were low. Cats are masters at the art of concealment. Sometimes you can't locate your own cat in your own house. Give them the whole world to explore, and forget it. Happily, Lenny and I were still riding high on the bliss of a recent success. We had located a missing ferret that was pregnant and had gone into labor under a front porch on Bancroft Street. We managed to save the babies and the mother, too, who bit a chunk out of my thumb in the takedown, the ungrateful bitch. Man, those tetanus shots hurt! However, there had been a five-hundred-dollar reward involved, and that lessened the sting considerably.

So our business was on the rise, modestly speaking. Of course, we always had a lost dog or two to return to heartbroken masters. Once in a while, we got lucky on those, but more often than not the poor animal slipped through a crack somewhere and was never seen again. Telling the anxious owner we had given up hope of *ever* bringing the poor thing home was the saddest part of the business for me.

The happiest part, of course, was working with Lenny.

Lenny and I had been friends since grade school. The first time we had sex was when we were thirteen years old. We pretty much porked each other all through high school after that, but when we hit adulthood, we branched out to other conquests. Now it seemed we were heading back to our roots. Literally. While before we might go months and months without salivating over each other, lately we'd been getting a little more distracted when we found ourselves bumping elbows (or crotches). I was even beginning to think of Lenny in terms other than best buddy now and then. And if his penchant for getting into my pants as much as he had been lately meant anything, I could only assume Lenny was entertaining the same feelings as I.

But being best buddies, we didn't talk about stuff like that. Ever.

Until now. Which really showed what a red-letter day this was turning out to be.

The deluge had turned to a drizzle, so we were cruising toward 13th Street in my Mini Cooper wagon with the wire kennel cage in the back, empty of errant rescuees at the moment. We had all the windows down as we tooled along, enjoying the fresh air. San Diego looked clean and scrubbed and sparkly after the downpour. Even the palm trees appeared perkier. But apparently Lenny wasn't thinking about palm trees.

"Um, Maitland, I was just wondering."

"Yeah, Lenny? What were you wondering?"

"Um, uh, well, I was just wondering if you'd like to come over to the apartment tonight for dinner. I'll cook."

"You can cook?"

"Okay, I lied. I'll order a pizza. I mean, you know, if you don't have any other plans."

I was behind the wheel. I glanced over at him and saw him nibbling on his lower lip like maybe he was freaking out about something. He looked cute freaking out. His frizzy hair was glistening like wet Velcro on top of his head, his profile clean and handsome and strong, his little brown ears adorable. I loved Lenny's ears.

"Pizza would be good," I said. "So you don't have a date?"

"Nah," he said. "No date."

"Well, then, yeah, Lenny. We'll have pizza at your place right after work."

He turned to gaze at me. "You don't even have to go home first. You can clean up at my house. We'll pick up Pudding Pop along the way."

Pudding Pop was my Chihuahua. Pudding Pop could poop thirty times a day. It was kind of incredible. I should have named him Manure Spreader.

"Don't you have a new couch?" I asked. "You know how Pudding Pop is. If he sees something new, *anything* new, he has to poop on it to bestow his blessing."

"I've got a drop cloth. I'll cover the couch and make it Pudding Pop poop proof."

"Well, if you're sure."

"And you don't have to go home after we eat. You and Pudding Pop can stay over. Like we did in high school."

I grinned. "You mean stay over *exactly* like we did in high school?"

He turned his soulful black eyes on me and didn't smile one little bit. "Yes," he said. And that was all he said.

I felt my heart give a lurch, and something tucked inside the crotch of my pants gave a lurch too. "We've fooled around now and then," I observed, "but we haven't spent a night together for ages. What's up?"

He shrugged. I could never tell through his gorgeous umber skin whether Lenny was blushing or not, but I had a feeling he might be blushing now. He stammered around for a minute, fiddling with his seat belt, fiddling with the glove box button, fiddling with his shirt front. Then he turned to me and said, "I just want to be with you tonight. I don't need a reason, do I?"

His earnest expression took me aback for a second. "No, Lenny," I said, reaching out to pat his knee. "You don't need a reason. I'd love us to spend the evening together."

He let out a rush of air, managed a weak smile, which gradually broadened, then finally stroked my hand where it still rested on his knee, giving me a tingle.

"Good," he said. "Then it's settled."

He immediately began whistling a tune and rolling his hand through the wind stream outside the passenger window, like kids do in a moving vehicle. The rain had stopped completely by now, so he wasn't getting wet doing it.

"A Gila monster," he said, chuckling.

I grunted. "Yeah, and a parrot. Usually we're chasing down puppy dogs and puddy tats. Our business has turned exotic."

"Maybe we should charge more."

"Hmm. Maybe we should."

It was funny. While we were talking about business, my mind was centered on our upcoming evening together, and I knew, I *knew*, Lenny's was too. It was kind of confusing, really. What did this sudden need for each other's presence mean? Were we just horny? Was that all it was?

Or was it more?

Unfortunately, I'd have to figure it out later, for suddenly we were at Lester Boggs's address on 13th Street, and why was I not surprised to find the place was a dump? The weeds in the lawn were ass high, the house needed painting, and the windows looked like they hadn't been washed since before the Battle of Waterloo. Whenever the hell that was.

"Cute," Lenny said. "Let's try to get our business with Mr. Boggs out of the way before the photographers get here to work on the photo spread for next month's *Architectural Digest*."

I was impressed. I didn't know Lenny knew what *Architectural Digest* was. I'd never seen him perusing anything more taxing than an *Archie* comic book or a Chinese takeout menu.

We didn't have to knock on Boggs's door. He was already standing on the porch waiting for us, and he didn't look happy, what with his arms folded across his chest and his toe tapping on the porch and all.

"What the hell took you so long?" he bellowed across the sea of ragweed that passed for a front yard.

"We'd have been here sooner," I bellowed back, "but they haven't invented time travel yet!"

"Great! A fucking comedian."

Lester Boggs was about the same age as Methuselah. His belly hung over his belt buckle like he'd swallowed a medicine ball, and the only hair he had on his head was poking out of his ears. Paul Newman he wasn't.

Grumbling incoherent insults, he stepped aside and ushered us into the house. I guess it was the butler's day off.

The little woman looked up when the old fart herded us through the front door.

Mrs. Boggs was built like a refrigerator. She was sitting on a threadbare sofa that had a couple of springs sticking out of it, sort of like the hair in her husband's ears. She was reading a paperback novel with two naked men embracing on the cover. I looked more closely and realized I'd read it. Small world, huh?

"Good book," I said. "The resolution is weak, the writing is passable, but the sex scenes are dynamite. It was the typos that really took me out of the story, don't you know. Needed a more comprehensive edit. Goodreads rated it a low three, which I thought was a bit unfair to the author, but then the people on Goodreads never like anything."

She grunted, which I assumed meant she would get back to me later and we'd have a nice chat about it over a cup of tea. Or maybe it meant "Shut the fuck up, I'm reading." I wasn't sure.

She flipped the page, never taking her eyes from the book, so I turned back to the lord of the manor.

I gave him my most winning smile. "So. A missing parrot, you say."

"And there's the cage," Lenny said, pointing across the room. "It's empty all right."

I followed where Lenny the Sleuth was pointing. Standing in the corner of the room was one of those bigass birdcages made of black cast iron. It stood seven feet tall and had about six inches of dried parrot shit coating the floor. Sort of the Abu Ghraib of the avian penal system. No wonder the parrot made a break for it.

Lester pulled a snapshot out of his shirt pocket and handed it to me. "Toodles," he said, dabbing a tear from his eye.

His wife turned another page. Speed reader. She mumbled something under her breath that sounded remarkably like "Dumbass."

The bird in the photo was an African grey, all right. And it did indeed have red tail feathers, just as Boggs had said it did. What tail feathers it had. For it must be said, the beast's plumage was a little sparse. It looked like it might have recently been sucked through a turbine engine on a Boeing 737 and spit out the other side.

Lenny was leaning over my shoulder, gazing at the picture too. "Ratty little guy," Lenny said.

Boggs took umbrage. "He has a fucking skin disorder. Jesus, what are you guys, mange bigots? You never had a rash? You never had dandruff? You never had the heartbreak of psoriasis?"

Lenny waved his hands in submission. "Sorry I spoke. It's a lovely parrot. Truly."

I started to steer the conversation to safer ground by asking, "Did you give the bird free rein to fly around the house?" But then I noticed a glob of dried parrot shit on the coffee table, another glob of dried parrot shit on the drapes, and a sprinkling of birdseed and feathers and more parrot shit fossilizing on the console TV parked in the corner.

Maybe the maid and the butler *both* had the day off.

"My stupid wife was shaking the dust mop out the front door like a fucking moron, and Toodles flew off."

"Fuck you," the refrigerator said, not mumbling this time. Her enunciation was crisp and concise. Professor Henry Higgins couldn't have delivered that "Fuck you" with better diction.

I opened my mouth to say our business might be best served if we all remained civil to one another, but it was Lenny who cut through the chaff and went directly to the crux of the matter. "You mean to tell me you people own a dust mop?"

I bit back a laugh while Boggs's wife scratched her left tit, never dragging her eyes from her book.

Boggs growled like a pit bull and pulled a folded check out of his pocket. "Here's your fucking fee. I'd appreciate it if you'd stop standing around shooting the shit and go find my bird. The house seems empty without him."

Mrs. Boggs mumbled, "Not empty enough," but Lester ignored her.

Lenny and I exchanged a glance, obviously touched and humbled by the love resonating through the room. I thoroughly proofread the check in case good old Lester saw fit to write a fuck or two in the payment line, as in "three hundred fucking dollars and no fucking cents." Wouldn't put it past him. The guy had the foulest mouth I'd ever run across.

"Which way was Toodles headed when he flew out the door?" Lenny asked.

"Up," Lester said and ushered us onto the porch. "Now go find his ass! I want my bird back. He's all alone in the cruel world for the very first time. What if a fucking cat gets him? What if he flies into a fucking power line or crashes into a picture window? He's led a sheltered life."

I gave Lester a sympathetic pat on the shoulder, and only after I did, did I notice the sprinkling of dried bird poop on his shirt. Ick. Where was the Lysol?

"We'll find him, sir," Lenny proudly proclaimed. "They don't call us the best in the business for nothing." And with that, we headed toward the car, hopefully making our escape without having contracted avian encephalitis, or bird flu, or some other horribly contagious featherborne frigging virus.

Once we were inside the car and Lester was no longer watching us from the porch, I said to Lenny as I doused my hands from a bottle of hand sanitizer I kept in the console, "They *who* says we're the best in the business, cupcake?"

"They us." Lenny grinned, scanning the skies for an errant parrot going by the name of Toodles on the off chance he might get lucky. "About tonight," he added. "Pepperoni okay?"

"Sure. Pepperoni's great."

"Say it again," Lenny said.

I turned to stare at him as I cranked up the engine. "Say *what* again?"

"Cupcake," he said around a smile.

I reached out and tweaked his nose. "Cupcake," I said.

And his smile grew even wider.

LENNY TIGHTENED his seat belt. "So where we headed?"

I checked the address Lorraine Johns had scribbled down. "Thought we oughta introduce ourselves to the lizard thief. See what he has to say for himself."

Lenny thought about that. "I don't like a man who'll steal a woman's lizard. Doesn't seem right somehow."

"Yeah, I'm pretty sure Dr. Phil said the same thing."

Lenny's eyes brightened. "Really?"

"No."

He chuckled, and while he was chuckling, he eyed me up and down. He didn't appear to be too disappointed in what he was seeing. "You look good in that shirt. You look *really* good."

"You should see me out of it," I said.

He smiled. "Maybe later?"

"Maybe later."

And from that suggestive little snippet of repartee alone, I got a boner. A good one too. I was beginning to look forward to tonight. Sneaking another glance in Lenny's direction, I could see his mouth was puckered up and he was whistling silently through a grin as he stared out the window. I guess he was looking forward to tonight as much as I was. Hell, it was his idea. He'd better be.

But back to the now.

After separating from his wife, Jason Johns had taken up residence in a double-wide trailer at the Mission Bay Mobilehome Park, not physically far from the Hilton Hotel. Economically speaking, however, it was a gazillion light years away. Truth was, the Mission Bay Mobilehome Park was looking a tad rundown these days. Or maybe it always had. I wasn't sure. I'd never been here before.

The lot number on Lorraine Johns's note read 1312. We found it on a cul-de-sac on the farthest edge of the trailer park beneath a row of dead palm trees. The front of the trailer overlooked a seaweed-splattered beach that smelled like rotting whale. Lovely.

Lenny and I stood on the makeshift concrete blocks that were supposed to pass as a front porch and knocked. Mr. Johns opened the door right off the bat. Well, he *sort* of opened the door. What he really did was creak it ajar a couple of inches, which apparently was as far as the security chain would allow. He studied us with one eyeball peering out through the crack he'd made.

"What do you guys want?" he asked.

"We're looking for a lizard named Frederick. Have you seen him?"

"My wife sent you," he said.

"Duh," Lenny answered.

I had no idea what Jason Johns looked like. He had one brown eye, and that eye was about five feet six inches off the floor, which would probably make him five nine or five ten. That's all I knew.

"Tell my wife she's wasting her time," he growled.

Then I realized it wasn't Mr. Johns growling at all. It was the dog that had just stuck its snout through the door down around our knees. A black snout. It must have been the Rottweiler that ate Rosemary. Am I quick, or what?

"Down, Stella," Johns said to the dog.

"If your dog bites us, we'll sue your ass," I said.

"That's funny," Johns giggled. "My wife took everything. What do you think you'll get by suing me?"

"Satisfaction," Lenny said.

"Probably not nearly as much satisfaction as I'll get by watching my dog rip your nuts off."

"You may have a point," Lenny said.

Mr. Johns opened the door an inch more, and the Rottweiler went crazy, trying to wedge his head through the crack and get at us, growling, snapping, straining, tossing dog slobber everywhere. He sounded like Lenny in the throes of an especially vigorous orgasm, only not as friendly. Below Mr. Johns's one brown eye, I saw a finger snake out through the crack in the door and wag itself in our direction. "Listen, you guys. I know it's not your fault. Lorraine is paying you to do this. But if I were you, I'd take a step back from that woman and not get too involved.

She's nuts. She's nuts and she's dangerous. And when I get through with her, she'll be chowing down on prison food and having sex with the lesbo brigade because that's all she'll have available to her."

"What the hell are you talking about?" I asked, keeping a wary eye on the damn dog, who looked like he was about to break through any second. "Are you saying your wife is doing something illegal?"

Mr. Johns's mouth appeared in the crack, and he dragged his fingers across it, making the gesture like he was zipping it shut. Then he made the gesture like he was locking it closed with a key. Then he made the gesture like he was flipping the key out past our heads through the crack in the door. What a nitwit.

"What the hell was that all about?" Lenny asked.

So Johns poked his *nose* through the crack and tapped the side of it with his finger like he knew something we didn't. "You'll see," he said like a sneaky five-year-old.

I was tempted to snap his finger off and feed it to the dog, but I restrained myself.

"Don't let that mutt eat Frederick like he ate Rosemary."

"If somebody ate Rosemary," Johns said, "you can rest assured it wasn't Stella. Lorraine's reptiles have a bad habit of going missing. Maybe you ought to ask her about that instead of pestering me."

"Yeah, right," I said. "We'll be back."

Johns grunted. "I'm trembling in my boots."

"Frederick had better be in good shape," Lenny said.

"He's never been healthier," Johns said. "In fact the three of us—me, Stella, and Frederick—will probably go jogging on the beach later if you'd care to join us."

Then he laughed and slammed the door in our faces.

Lenny studied me and said, "Well, that could have gone a little better."

We traipsed back to the car and headed for the freeway.

"What do you suppose he meant about his wife going to prison?" Lenny asked. "Think she's really doing something illegal?"

"I don't know and I don't care. All I know is she's paying us to get her lizard back, and that's what we're going to do. I want to come back later and stake out the guy's trailer. Maybe we'll get lucky."

Lenny narrowed his eyes. "You were supposed to come over to my place tonight so *I* could get lucky."

I chucked him under the chin. "We will. I promise. We just have to run an errand first."

"What errand?"

"The gerbil guy. I promised him I'd stop by and give him an update on how the gerbil hunt is going. The friend he was babysitting the little guy for gets back into town soon, and he's beginning to panic."

"Drag queens are always so emotional."

"No kidding. Everything's a Tony-winning production number. Chorus boys, a full orchestra, and lots and lots of sequins."

We laughed, and while we were laughing, we pulled up to the apartment building with the old rattletrap sign on the roof that said The Belladonna Arms in orange neon. Since the day was almost over and the sun was sinking over the San Diego city skyline, the sign was already lit.

Lenny and I knew the grounds and a few surrounding blocks of the Belladonna Arms as well as we knew each other's asses. We should. We had spent thirteen man-hours crawling all over the property, inside and out, looking for the missing gerbil. We had finally come to the conclusion that the little beast had either been beamed into outer space by aliens or somebody had made gerbil fondue out of the creature for dinner, but we didn't quite have the nerve to tell our client that.

"Wonder what he's wearing," Lenny commented with a *tsk*.

"Who?" I asked. "The gerbil?"

"No, silly. The fat guy who hired us to find him."

"God only knows," I said, locking up the car.

"What's his name again?" Lenny asked. "I forgot."

"Arthur," I said. "The drag queen's name is Arthur."

WE COULD hear the tippy-tap of stiletto heels before Arthur opened his apartment door. When the door swung open, all three hundred pounds of him stood there in a leopard-print gown of flowing silk that trailed ten feet behind him, billowing in the wind like the fifty-foot American flag flapping atop the statehouse. I wondered how he could traverse the apartment in the thing without raking every knickknack off every shelf he passed and sending it crashing to the floor. He wore a sequin-studded turban on his head, and from his ears dangled what I first took to be two hubcaps off a '59 Chevy, but later realized were merely really big earrings. Arthur was a large guy to begin with, but in five-inch heels, he was an alp.

He took one look at us and screamed with delight. "You found Ethel!"

Ethel was the missing gerbil. Ethel, or any others of her ilk, were also considered illegal contraband as far as the state of California went, but we wouldn't squeal on the little rat to the authorities if Arthur wouldn't. Besides, Ethel was just a tiny thing, and she was all alone in the world. I couldn't quite see how she could breed a line of descendants to wreak havoc on the state's indigenous ecosystem without a Mr. Gerbil to canoodle *with*.

I hated to burst Arthur's bubble, but I didn't have much choice.

"I'm sorry, no," I said. "She hasn't turned up yet. Just wanted to stop by and let you know we haven't given up the search. These things take time."

"Time!" Arthur wailed through bee-stung lips painted the reddest red I'd ever seen. "It's been two weeks, darling! My friend is going to be back in town soon, and when I tell him I've lost his gerbil, he'll hate me forever. Time, you say. Time!"

"Cue the chorus boys," Lenny whispered at my side.

Arthur had big fat tears trembling on the edges of his eyelashes. The lashes, by the way, were glitter encrusted and two inches long. When he blinked they fluttered like fans. I could feel the downdraft they produced from three feet away.

I have a few steadfast rules that help me navigate my way through life. One of them is this: When in doubt, lie. Prodigiously.

"Arthur, we have a lead. I'm sure it'll prove to be just what we've been waiting for. Don't give up hope. Stay strong. Remain stalwart. Stiff upper lip and all that. Or hell, I don't know, just pray," I finished up, for lack of a more constructive suggestion to offer since I was basing my whole premise on a big fat lie anyway.

Arthur pouted, but tried to stick out his three chins in a brave manner. "I suppose I owe you more money," he said stoically. He had paid us six hundred dollars already for two weeks' work in searching for an animal you could buy in any pet store in any state but California for maybe five bucks, tops. Even I was beginning to feel guilty about taking his money. Besides, I was sure he needed his ready cash for other things. Like fifty-gallon drums of beard concealer and truckloads of marabou feathers and size fourteen stiletto heels, which by all accounts don't come cheap.

"Not a penny," I said, stepping into Arthur's massive arms and giving him a hug. The moment I did, Lenny stepped forward and hugged him too. Still, Arthur's bosom would have been big enough for a couple of additional pet detectives to snuggle up to if we'd known any, which we didn't.

As he hugged us back, I saw Lenny give me a quizzical look as if to say "He's offering us more money. Are you nuts? Take it!"

I pulled my head from between Arthur's two gigantic breasts before I suffocated and tugged Lenny away with me with an almost audible *pop*.

I patted Arthur's cheek. "Never fear," I said. "Before your friend arrives, your little truant will be back home safe and sound. I swear."

Lenny looked doubtful, but Arthur seemed to take my bald-faced lie as the gospel truth. I couldn't imagine why.

While I had his attention, I asked, "Do you have a picture of the little sweetie? So we'll be sure to ID the right gerbil." (Like they're under every rock.)

"Certainly," Arthur said, still sniffing. He reached into his décolletage, pulled out a sheaf of gerbil photos, and handed them over.

I grasped them gingerly. They were warm to the touch. Ick.

"Maybe these will help," he said, giving Lenny and me a brave smile and dabbing at his tears with thirty or forty yards of leopard-print silk. He twiddled his fingers at us with a grateful moue on his face as we headed off down the hall shuffling through the photographs. Ethel was indeed cute. In fact, she looked like Stuart Little. Without the clothes and red tennies, of course. This was reality here, not a frigging cartoon.

Outside in the car, Lenny said, "You made some pretty astonishing promises back there. We haven't found his bloody gerbil during the last two weeks of searching. How can you promise Arthur we'll find it now?"

"Because I have a plan," I said, buckling my seat belt.

Lenny gawked at me.

"Don't worry," I said. "It's a perfectly good plan. It'll work like a charm."

What was I, nuts? It was the worst plan ever. It was so bad, in fact, I was embarrassed to tell Lenny what it was. Still, it *might* work.

Lenny certainly wasn't convinced. Neither was I, actually. But at the moment I was more concerned with the other question.

Why the hell was Arthur storing gerbil pictures in his bra?

Chapter Three

IT WAS almost dark when I swung by my place and picked up Pudding Pop so the three of us could head off to Lenny's apartment across town. Well, I couldn't actually rush off to Lenny's apartment immediately. I had to spot clean a few stains off my carpet first. While I worked with a jug of 409 and a rag, Pudding Pop spent the downtime washing Lenny's face with his little tongue.

Pudding Pop loved Lenny almost as much as he loved to squat.

Before we headed out the door, Lenny reminded me to grab the Domino's pizza menu from on top of the refrigerator. Then he reminded me to bag up the beer I had in my fridge because he was all out, and what good is pizza without beer? Then he reminded me to bring some work clothes for tomorrow since I was going to spend the night. Then he had me grab Pudding Pop's kibble and his toy elephant and his pooper-scooper, the 409, and maybe a couple of extra rags, some deodorant since Lenny was out, and the box of condoms he knew I always kept stashed in my nightstand drawer.

"I have some lube," he said when my arms were full and I was starting to look like maybe I was ready to wring his neck. "I think I do, anyway," he added, after mulling it over for a minute.

So I gave an exasperated sigh and grabbed my lubricant too.

Pudding Pop was wiggling in Lenny's arms and looking like he might want to poop again, so we hustled out the door and dropped him in the yard. He decided he wanted to leave a deposit on the neighbor's yard instead since he apparently didn't like the texture of our grass, so we didn't have much choice but to let him toddle over to the neighbor's to do his business. Then we had to leave the poop where it lay because I hadn't brought a plastic bag with me. Okay, so I'm not the best neighbor in the world.

We eased into my car as quietly as we could and rolled out of my neighborhood like sneak thieves vacating the scene of the crime. I had tangled with my neighbor before concerning the bathroom habits of Pudding Pop. All the neighbors knew my dog, in fact, and not because of his charm. While Lenny and I might be hunkered down behind the dashboard in shame, Pudding Pop, on the other hand, was all over the car, staring from one window to the next, hopping over our heads, licking our faces, barking at everything that struck his fancy, humping Lenny's arm (a pastime I thought I might try myself later), and being way too cheerful for a dog who, since the day he was born, had fought obedience training tooth and nail. No shame in Pudding Pop. No siree. Social anxiety disorder? Not an ounce.

Lenny reached through the shadowy car interior amid the flashes of passing streetlights and the occasional strobe of approaching headlights to stroke my arm as I drove.

"Thanks for this," he said quietly.

"No problem," I said. "This is what best buds do."

"You mean fuck?"

"Well. Yeah."

"It's not just the fucking I need tonight, Mait."

I turned to study him in the glow of the dash lights. "No?"

"Uh-uh. I want to talk about some things."

"So talk," I said. "What's wrong?"

"Nothing's wrong," he answered. "Not yet, anyway. I just need to get a few things out in the open."

"So hit me with it," I said. "What's on your mind?"

"Later," he said, turning away and staring out the passenger window.

So I clammed up and left him to his thoughts. Truthfully, I was starting to get a little worried. Lenny wasn't the sort to be mysterious. Usually Lenny was a fucking billboard. Whatever he was feeling could be immediately read on his face in fourteen-foot letters. Likewise, he didn't have a duplicitous bone in his body. I always knew exactly where Lenny stood on every issue simply by looking into his eyes. Except now. Now I couldn't see his eyes.

Pudding Pop didn't seem to like this new and confusing Lenny either. He crawled up onto Lenny's shoulder and began gnawing at Lenny's ear with his little tail flying back and forth like a metronome on meth until Lenny started giggling, and then Pudding Pop tried to stick his head down Lenny's throat to see where the giggles were coming from. Pretty soon we were all laughing.

At Lenny's apartment, Lenny did indeed hustle into the closet to get an old paint-spattered sheet to cover his new sofa because Pudding Pop wasn't in the apartment more than two seconds before he started looking at it like it was exactly the porta potty he'd been searching for.

Lenny phoned in the pizza order while I bustled off with a beer in hand to shower the day's grime away. I was still on the first soap down when Lenny stepped naked into the shower with me, as I had suspected he might.

He buried his face into the back of my neck and slid his arms around me to clasp them over my stomach, pulling me close against his chest.

"You're mine now," he said, his lips moving against my shoulder. His dick, soft and warm, lay against my ass all snuggly and friendly like. I figured that snuggly and friendly business would soon shift to shock and awe once we both set our minds to it, but there wasn't any hurry. We had all night.

I slipped around inside his arms, and soaping up the washcloth with the handy-dandy bar of Ivory soap lying in the soap dish, I went to work scrubbing down Lenny's chest, making time for a kiss or two on the mouth every now and then—just to be sociable.

By the time I dropped to my knees to run the washcloth over his lovely brown legs, he was already trembling. And not from the cold.

I peered up at him through the shower spray and watched him smile down at me when I laid my face against his now-stiff cock and nudged it out of the way so I could bury my nose in his balls, which you can rest assured didn't make him tremble any less.

He dug his strong fingers through my hair as he rubbed his dick back and forth over my nose.

"Turn around," I whispered into his ball sac, and when he turned, I washed the back of his legs, working my way slowly up to that beautiful ass of his. He bent forward a tad to allow me to lather up every silly centimeter of hidden territory, and when he was all sparkly clean and pristine, I hauled myself to my feet, and he turned back around to step into my arms.

We stood there like that and let the water wash over us while Pudding Pop scraped his toenails against the Plexiglas shower door and whined, trying to get in. We ignored him.

Lenny ran his hands over my arms. He cupped my chin between his fingertips and tasted my mouth. He lowered himself slowly to his knees in front of me, and along the way he slid his lips down my chest and stomach until my stiffy was pointed directly up his left nostril. Without putting in a work chit or asking permission or anything, Lenny angled my cock into his mouth and pulled it as far down his throat as he could get it.

Now it was my turn to tremble. I rose up on tippy-toe, with every muscle in my body flexed to full capacity, and let Lenny work me like he obviously needed to do. When he really got going and the proper motivation was there, nobody could suck dick like Lenny could. He loved his work, and it showed.

"You might want to slow down," I said.

Lenny didn't slow down one little bit.

"I mean it, Lenny. Slow down."

But of course he didn't.

"Uh-oh," I finally gasped, grabbing the sides of his head, trying to make him stop doing what he was doing. But I already knew it was too late.

With his eyes on me, squinting into the shower spray peppering down on his face, I watched as he smiled and grabbed my ass all the more tightly. With my cock buried all the way down to what felt like his spleen area, I let myself go and squirted a magnificent glob of hot steaming come right down his throat.

I watched his eyes open wide as the first splash of semen ricocheted off his uvula, and then his face took on this beatific expression of bliss as he proceeded to drain me of every further drop of come I could manufacture on the spot. And it was a considerable load, if I say so myself.

With his forehead against my stomach and his mouth still luring the last strings of semen from my softening cock, I collapsed against the shower wall and clutched the nozzle over my head with both hands before I fell flat on my face.

Lenny gazed up at me, his fingers cupping my balls as he let my dick slide free from his lips. "Sorry," he said. "I couldn't wait."

I grinned down at him and stroked the side of his face. "Obviously neither could I."

I cranked off the shower, and with both of us still dripping wet, I slid the shower door aside. I neatly scooped Pudding Pop off the floor with my wet foot and scooted him out into the hall before slamming the bathroom door in his face.

While Pudding Pop went into apoplectic seizures trying to get back in, I gripped Lenny by the shoulders, manhandled him across the bathroom floor still dripping wet, and pushed him down onto the commode. I dropped to my knees in that heavenly space between his two splayed legs. Slurping his erect cock into my mouth, I went to work.

Lenny laid his head back and stroked my hair as I sucked and sucked and jiggled his balls and stroked the hair on his thighs and breathed in the clean, clean scent of his mocha skin, and before I knew it, wonder of wonders, my exertions were rewarded.

Or they were about to be. Just as Lenny started to lift his ass off the commode, primed to pump a quart of jism down my throat, the doorbell rang.

"No!" Lenny wailed.

I slid his cock from between my lips and laid it gently on his stomach like a bomb about to explode, which indeed it was. It lay there throbbing like a snake with the hiccups.

"Don't touch yourself," I said. "I'll be right back."

Lenny shuddered and gazed down at his own dick in panic. "Oh God."

I wagged a finger in his face as I pulled a bathrobe off the back of the bathroom door and slipped it around me. "Wait," I commanded. "Don't beat off. Don't come. Don't do anything!"

Lenny, sweating bullets, could only nod. "Okay, okay. Hurry," he pleaded.

I ran from the bathroom, collected the pizza from the surprised delivery dude, and flung a twenty-dollar bill in his direction before slamming the door in his face.

I tossed the pizza box on the dining room table and took off running down the hall, stripping the bathrobe away as I ran.

From the bathroom up ahead I heard Lenny yell. He sounded like Mercedes McCambridge screaming for Father Merrin in *The Exorcist*, only deeper and with much more desperation.

"Maitland!"

I flung myself through the bathroom door and spotted Lenny going into nuclear orgasm without even touching himself. His cock bobbed up and down all by itself as a thick stream of snow-white Lenny juice erupted from the fat head of it and splashed across his stomach, chest, and chin. One particularly energetic squirt flew past his left ear and splattered the wall behind him. His knees were still splayed wide and trembling like crazy, his balls were absorbed all the way up to his rib cage, and his face was beet red. His eyes were so tightly closed they looked like they'd been welded shut.

I slid across the bathroom floor on my knees like Pete Rose sliding into home plate and gripped Lenny's still spurting cock just in time to allow the last jet of jism to shoot across my face. And what a lovely experience it was too.

"Couldn't… wait…," Lenny breathed as I tucked his spent cock between my lips and stroked my hand through the mess on his belly. His legs came together to clamp me in place. And when both our hearts stopped pounding like jackhammers, I pulled Lenny to his feet and steered him once again into the shower where we hosed ourselves down. Lenny's legs were still wobbly.

I laughed. "I love having sex with you. It's always a surprise."

"Thanks," he said, a gentle grin softening his face. He pressed me to the shower wall and laid his mouth over mine, his long hard body touching every inch of me at once. We kissed for the longest time.

Then we both stopped and froze. The apartment was too quiet.

"Where's Pudding Pop?" Lenny asked in a whisper, his mouth still on mine.

"Oh, shit," I whispered back. "He's all alone with the pizza."

We quickly exited the shower stall, dried off rather perfunctorily, and set off in search of the pooch. We found him atop the dining room table gnawing at one end of the pepperoni pizza. At least he hadn't pooped on it yet.

Lenny and I breathed a sigh of relief. We slid Pudding Pop's slice of pizza onto a plate and fed it to him on the floor like a proper dog. Still naked, Lenny and I scooped up the rest of the pizza, a few napkins, a couple of beers, and headed for the couch, where we dumped everything on the coffee table, and sitting side by side, bare knees touching, we had our dinner while watching the evening news on TV.

Just like an old naked married couple.

WE LAY in each other's arms. My wilting cock was still buried in Lenny's ass, tucked snugly inside a come-filled condom.

"That was great," Lenny sighed, as his breathing began to slow and our two heartbeats ratchetted down to a reasonable cadence. He reached around behind him to place his hand on my hip, holding me in place. "Stay in me as long as you can. Please, Mait. It feels so good."

My lips were buried in his spongy hair. I loved the way it tickled my face and smelled like strawberry shampoo. "Okay, Lenny. I will."

We lay like that in silence while Pudding Pop snored at our feet. This was our third coupling of the night, and our amorous antics were starting to bore the mutt. I gazed out through the bedroom window over Lenny's head and tried to count the stars in the sky, but I soon gave it up. There were way too many of them. California skies are endless.

"What are you thinking?" Lenny softly asked.

There was no sense lying. He would know if I did. So I told him the truth.

"I'm wondering why anybody in their right mind would want rattlesnakes, an asp, and a pair of Gila monsters for pets."

Lenny wiggled his ass back into me, trying to maintain our connection a little longer. "Yeah," he whispered. "That's a puzzler, all right. Even if she is a hermaphrodite."

"Herpetologist."

"Whatever."

His warm hand stroked my hip. His other hand twisted around behind him to twiddle my hair as I still lay there with my lips at the nape of his neck. We were in that after-sex glow of contentment that was the best feeling ever if you had the presence of mind to slow down and let it take over. Lenny and I were masters at slowing down. We'd been slowing down our whole lives. The fact that we were both in our midtwenties and barely solvent seemed to substantiate that statement. Still, we had fun. Maybe that's what really counts.

"What was it you wanted to talk about?" I asked, my voice lazy and mellow. After my third orgasm of the night, sleep was pawing at me like a loving cat. "Earlier. You sounded like something was on your mind."

Only silence greeted me for about ten seconds, and during that ten seconds, we both lost the battle and my limp cock slid free of Lenny's luscious grip. It was enough of a distraction to make me forget what I had asked him.

I slipped out of bed and padded into the bathroom to clean myself up. When I crawled back into bed, it was Lenny's turn to clean up. Soon we were both back in bed and back in each other's arms. We were facing each other now. He had his head on my chest and our four fuzzy legs were tangled together nice and comfy.

"Sleep, Maitland," he whispered against my breast. "Let's go to sleep."

I thought how his lips tickled my skin, how safe I felt in his arms, and those were the last two thoughts I remember.

The next thing I knew, it was morning.

DAWN CAME early. Funny how it always does. I squinted into a blast of golden sunshine that had been sent from on high to drag my lazy ass out of bed. Lenny's lazy ass was already gone. So was Pudding Pop, which was troublesome unless, of course, Lenny was out taking him for a walk. Please God, let it be so.

I creaked my way out of bed, slipped on a pair of Lenny's boxer shorts because I hadn't worn any, and headed off toward the kitchen and the smell of coffee.

Standing at Lenny's kitchen counter and pouring a cup of java into the biggest cup I could find, I saw my two best buds outside on the lawn. Pudding Pop was squatting and pooping, then moving forward a few feet to squat and poop again. He did this continually, from one end of the lawn to the other, like maybe he was planting a poop garden. Too much pizza last night, I presumed.

Lenny, looking mightily pissed off, followed along behind Pudding Pop, gathering up his deposits, one after the other, in a fistful of plastic grocery bags. At the last stop, while Lenny was cleaning up the mess, Pudding Pop hiked up his leg and peed on Lenny's foot.

I choked back a laugh when Lenny shot straight up in the air and came down ranting, waving his arms around, and sort of executing an insane version of *Swan Lake* in his fury. Pudding Pop watched him, yawned, then turned and sauntered back toward the apartment building's front door, jaunty tail flung high, a satisfied smirk on his little Chihuahua face.

Only then did Lenny stop jumping and stomping around and simply stand there on the lawn with three bags of poop in his hands, panting his way to calmness. Which was probably for the best. He looked like he was about to have a stroke. I wondered if maybe he should have his blood pressure checked.

I had my head in the fridge looking for something to eat when Lenny and Pudding Pop arrived back at the apartment. Lenny had calmed down by then. Pudding Pop, of course, looked as unfazed as he ever did.

"How'd it go?" I asked innocently enough.

Lenny gave me a surly glare, opened his mouth to rave, then thought better of it and slapped his mouth shut like a car trunk.

"No problem," he droned. "Pudding Pop's empty. I've drained the pooch."

Lenny stood at the kitchen sink and scrubbed his hands for about five full minutes with every sort of antibacterial concoction he could find, then joined me at the table with the bread and butter and jelly I'd found in Lenny's refrigerator.

We smeared ourselves a couple of sandwiches, slurped down an entire pot of coffee between us, and planned the day ahead.

"I want to check out the lizard guy again. I think if we give Johns a chance, maybe he'll cough up Frederick to get us off his ass."

Lenny didn't look convinced. "You have more faith in the guy's sense of reason than I do."

"After that we'll take a spin through Boggs's neighborhood. Maybe we'll catch a glimpse of his fucking parrot, Toodles."

Again Lenny didn't look convinced. "You have more faith in our skills of detection than I do."

"And finally we need to search through the grounds of the Belladonna Arms again on the off chance that the gerbil might be hungry and tired of hiding and will come out and wave a white flag at us and hitch a ride home."

I watched Lenny expectantly, waiting for him to say something snide about that. But all he said was "We need peanut butter" and gulped down another jelly sandwich.

"We also need to have some flyers printed up concerning a few of our lost clients. The parrot, the gerbil…"

"…my virginity," Lenny finished up, to which I gave him a wide-eyed gaze of disbelief.

"I think we both know where your virginity went, cupcake," I said.

And he grinned. "Oh, yeah. I remember now."

"Thanks for last night," I said, reaching out to finger a smear of jelly from the corner of his lip and popping it in my mouth just to get rid of it.

"It was fun," he said, his eyes melting like chocolate, all warm and squishy and sweet.

"It was," I agreed. More than fun, actually, but I didn't quite know how to tell him that. Sometimes it's odd carrying on an intermittent affair with someone for a decade and a half, from the beginning of puberty onward. On one hand, there aren't many secrets left. But on the other hand, new secrets seem to pop up anyway.

Pudding Pop was sitting on his little Chihuahua ass on the countertop by the sink watching us. I snagged a slice of bread from the package and tossed it over my shoulder to him. He made short work of it, scarfing it down in a matter of seconds, little tail flying at a blur, little ears flat to his head like they always were when he was either mad or having a really good time.

When Lenny slapped his hands down on the table and declared, "Time to go to work!" Pudding Pop and I both jumped. Two minutes later we were out the door.

Chapter Four

THUSLY OUR new business venture began in earnest. We'd been plying the pet detective trade for a while now out of Lenny's dad's basement, but with a storefront of our very own and the rent we would need to pay to keep it, we had to work with a renewed mindset and reestablished sense of purpose.

Maybe that's why when a shift began to occur in our private lives at the very same time, I hardly took note of the fact at all. At least I told myself I didn't.

Or maybe I did take note of the changes in the way Lenny and I began responding to each other, but I was so flabbergasted by what was happening, I simply couldn't sit down and face it head-on.

Lenny and I had been best friends forever. We'd seen each other fly from boyfriend to boyfriend through all the years of our adult lives, dipping into the friends-with-benefits pool every now and then as well, like I mentioned earlier. We enjoyed each other's company, and we enjoyed each other's bodies. Maybe we were now heading down a road we'd been shooting toward all along but were too dumb to see coming.

We couldn't be that stupid, could we? Let me answer that. Yes. Yes, we *could* be that stupid. What other two adults would try to make a living in this day and age as pet detectives? Yeah, I think "stupid" probably describes us pretty well.

But we loved doing what we were doing. Businesswise, I mean. So while we didn't have many book smarts between us, at least we had the sense not to chain ourselves to careers we hated like so many people do. Looking at it that way, I'd have to say Lenny and I were pretty clever, wouldn't you? Besides, what else were we qualified for? Flipping burgers? Forget it.

With Pudding Pop deposited back at home with a stern warning not to poop everywhere, which I knew he would gleefully ignore, Lenny and I set out to solve a few mysteries. After all, we were honest-to-God pet detectives now, with an honest-to-God brick-and-mortar pet detective storefront to prove it. With a shingle and everything. How cool was that?

"So where we headed?" Lenny asked. He preferred to let me be the brains of the outfit while he focused on the grunt work. Every successful business needs a well-planned division of labor. That was ours. I think. He grunts. At other times we both grunt and *nobody* thinks.

Today I was thinking.

"Let's check out Jason Johns's trailer again. Maybe he's at work. Maybe we won't be disturbed if we do a little snooping on the premises." I wagged a finger in Lenny's face. "And I'm not talking about breaking and entering, here. I simply want to look around. Got it?"

Lenny had a bad habit of doing the first thing that popped into his head. During sex, it was a trait of his I rather enjoyed. During business hours—not so much. Occasionally the first thing that popped into Lenny's head was to take a rock to a window he thought it might be advantageous to crawl through if he was of the opinion that seeing what was on the other side would further whatever investigation we were pursuing at the moment. The bad part of that was we were supposed to be the good guys. We weren't zoned for breaking and entering.

"Rules, rules, rules," he growled.

I gave him my sternest glower and wagged my finger even harder. "Promise me!"

He did his little Boy Scout triple finger thing, although Lenny had never been in the Boy Scouts in his life. Neither had I, of course. We were raised on the wrong side of the tracks for group activities, unless those group activities included the two of us naked and rolling around in every secluded spot we could find during our formative years.

"Spoilsport," Lenny groused, shuffling his feet and pouting like a recalcitrant four-year-old. "Oh, all right. Sheesh. What a nag. I promise."

I rolled through the gates of the Mission Bay Mobilehome Park and wound around the quiet streets until I found the cul-de-sac with lot number 1312 on it. Yep, Mr. Johns's rickety double-wide with the jury-rigged front porch and the deadass lawn was still there. Since we could see no signs of life about the place, and since there were no vehicles in the driveway, I decided to risk it and pulled right up to the front door like I owned the joint. Ballsy, huh?

Lenny and I knocked on the front door, but there was no answer, thank God. If Johns had come to the door, I would have fumbled around with a few more questions about the missing lizard, but since he wasn't home, I didn't have to tax myself with such deceptions. Lenny and I both appreciated it when we didn't have to tax ourselves with trying to be sneaky. You have to be smart to be sneaky. Lenny and I aren't that smart.

I tried to peek through the window beside the front door, but the drapes were drawn so I couldn't see anything. We wound our way around the side of the trailer to the back, and lo and behold, sitting there in the backyard was the burned-out hulk of a '69 Camaro. The poor guy must have loved his car so much that even after his ex-wife torched the thing, he still couldn't bear to part with it.

Lenny gazed at the charcoaled wreckage through sad, sad eyes, said "*Tsk*" a couple of times, then crossed himself like a proper Catholic. Lenny wasn't any more Catholic than I was. He just liked classic cars. I liked them too, but I wasn't going to tear myself up over the fact that this one had been transformed into a charcoal briquette by the woman who paid us three hundred dollars to recover her lizard. Lenny needed to keep his priorities straight. Jason Johns wasn't the one paying for our services. The little woman with the penchant for setting things on fire was. The fact that she was a vindictive bitch with questionable taste in hemlines shouldn't have anything to do with where we chose to place our loyalties. Besides, maybe the husband wasn't all that great either.

"Get a grip," I said, and while I was saying it, I jiggled the trailer's back door. It was locked.

This time when I pressed my forehead to a window and peered inside, I could make a few things out. For one, Jason Johns was a slob. There were clothes on the floor of the bedroom I was looking into. The bed hadn't been made. And there was a dead houseplant sitting on a table on the other side of the window that looked like it hadn't been watered in three or four years. It was as dead as my Uncle Herbert, who'd swelled up and dropped dead a few years back from a fatal colon blockage. Not a pretty picture. The houseplant was so dead and dried-up, in fact, it was beginning to resemble the poor charbroiled Camaro parked in the yard behind us.

Unfortunately, I didn't spot a Gila monster gallivanting around the joint holding up a Rescue Me sign. Frederick was a no-show.

I turned my head and saw Lenny staring straight up into the sky like he was watching an eclipse.

"What is it?" I asked.

"Lookit," he said, pointing skyward.

I heaved a sigh. Lenny never could keep his thoughts centered on one subject at a time. He was always easily distracted. Either by food or a nice male ass or my crotch. I reluctantly trailed my eyes up to where Lenny was pointing and saw a bird flapping its way across the heavens about fifty feet up.

"Get a grip, Lenny," I said. "It's a bird."

"No," Lenny said. "It's a parrot."

I craned my neck to extend my vision and squinted like Mr. Magoo to sharpen my focus.

"Good lord!" I exclaimed. "It *is* a parrot!"

"And it's gray!" Lenny said, gripping my arm.

"With red tail feathers," I added, getting excited now and gripping him back.

"And it looks kind of ratty," Lenny finished up.

Together we yelled, "It's Toodles!"

Holy shit. Holy shit. What were the odds?

Toodles was flapping his way toward a stand of pepper trees at the edge of the beach about three hundred yards away. Lenny and I hopped over the hurricane fence at the back of Jason Johns's property and took off running along the sandy beach, shielding our eyes from the sun and trying to not lose sight of Toodles along the way.

We both cried out in frustration when Toodles disappeared among the pepper trees. The trees were hunkered up against the back fence of another crappy double-wide trailer that wasn't in much better shape than Jason Johns's was. There was a rusty old hurricane fence behind this property too.

Lenny and I stood panting beneath the copse of trees and tried to spot Toodles in the branches above our heads. The pepper trees were lush with foliage, and that foliage was shifting and swaying in the breeze that rolled in off the bay, making it really hard to spot anything.

Lenny went berserk for a moment, jumping up and down and tugging at his hair like a maniac. "We lost him! We lost him!"

But then from somewhere in the branches overhead, we heard a scratchy avian voice mutter a single word. "Morons."

Lenny and I froze.

"Was that…?"

I gaped at Lenny. Lenny gaped at me. We laid our heads together and squinted up through the branches of the pepper trees one more time, trying to home in on the place where we'd heard the voice.

Then Lenny saw him. "Maitland!" he hissed. "Right there. Two o'clock. He's pecking at his ass."

"I see him," I whispered back. And I did. There he sat. Toodles was perched on a high branch, intermittently pecking at his mangy bunghole and gazing around like a tourist. He looked like he'd lost a few more feathers since that last photo of him was taken. It was surprising he could fly at all. Aerodynamically speaking, Toodles was a mess. Poor thing needed a dermatologist bad. Or a reupholstering job.

Lenny and I eased forward until we were standing directly under Toodles, which proved to be a mistake. The minute we stopped and studied him from below, Toodles let loose with a massive squirt of parrot poop. His aim was impeccable. He got Lenny on the forehead and me on the shoulder. A twofer.

Lenny jumped back and cried, "Yuk! Ick! Ack!" all the while frantically wiping the parrot poop off his forehead with the tail of his shirt. I was a little less emotional about it, but then I wasn't the one who got hit in the face.

I looked around for a way to scale the tree. Maybe if I snuck up real slow-like, cooing calming phrases and smiling in a friendly manner and maybe cheeping now and then, Toodles wouldn't see me as the enemy and continue to sit there on that limb, pooping and scratching his ass, until I could get close enough to grab him.

Since it was the only plan I had, I decided to run with it.

I awkwardly climbed to the top of the hurricane fence and did a little balancing act there for a second until I could grab a pepper-tree branch that stuck out over the fence into the people's yard behind me.

Lenny held my ankles, probably in the hope that I wouldn't fall off the fence and land on my head. I managed to wrap my fingers around the protruding tree limb above, and the moment I did, Lenny hissed for me to stop. I froze.

Three limbs up from the one I had grabbed, we watched as Toodles sidled along his current perch until he was once again sitting directly over our heads. "Bombs away," Toodles said as plainly as a politician addressing Congress.

I wondered what he meant by "Bombs away," but I figured it out when he once again let loose with a barrage of white sauce and dumped it directly onto the top of my head. *Splat!*

It was such a shock, I let go of the branch and spun my arms, trying to maintain my balance atop the fence. Lenny wasn't any help because now he was bending over with his hands on his knees and laughing so hard he had a rope of snot dangling out of his nose. He was gasping for air with fat, happy tears rolling down his cheeks while I continued to buck and rock atop that fucking fence until finally gravity took command of the situation.

With an "Aaiiyee!" such as I had never heard myself utter before in my life, I pinwheeled my arms until they revved up to about 300 useless revolutions per second, and still blinded by parrot poop—which had started to dribble down over my forehead and burn my eyes, not to mention reek to high heaven—I sailed off into midair while Lenny screamed for me to watch out for the rosebushes.

Yes. You heard me right. Rosebushes. The prickly kind. Since it's hard to change your trajectory when you're already airborne, especially when you're blinded by bird excrement and can't see where you're going anyway, no matter how insane you are, I landed smack in the middle of the rosebushes with a horrendous and extremely painful *crunch*.

I lay there—pricked by thorns in a thousand places and sprinkled with rose petals of varying hues—while Lenny leaned over from the other side of the fence (he still had a rope of mucous dangling merrily from his nose) and tried to stifle his gasps of laughter.

"You all right?" he asked, and I'll give him credit, he did his best to say it with a straight face, but in the end it was too much for him. He leaned on the fence and buried his face in his arms, laughing all the harder. His shoulders shook and snot and saliva streamed down his chin. He crossed his legs while he was standing there as if trying not to pee his pants. One happy guy.

Above our heads, we heard Toodles in the branches, snickering. Like Lenny, he was obviously having the time of his life.

"Fuckheads," Toodles squawked, and with a merry *chirrup* of glee, he spread his scrawny wings and lifted himself into the sky. Grunting with every wing flap, he headed out across the water toward the city skyline in the distance. Maybe he had a brunch date downtown.

"See ya," Lenny said, lifting his hand in a good-bye wave, still sputtering and laughing like a lunatic while I painfully peeled myself out of the rosebushes like a strip of Velcro stuck to a carpet.

"Toodles one, Pet Dicks nothing," Lenny wailed happily, slapping his knee like some old codger who'd just heard a really good farmer joke.

He ignored my scathing sneer, which I managed to cast in his direction between "Ooches" and "Ouches" and "Aaiiyees" as I plucked myself out of the thorns.

"Poor guy," Lenny commiserated, finally trying not to act quite so cheerful. "Let's go back to the office and get you cleaned up."

Lenny helped me groan my way over the fence after I gathered up my shoes (they had flown off during the fall). Somehow I had also torn the seat out of my pants and lost a sock (which I never did find), but neither that nor the six- or seven-hundred puncture wounds—nor the fact that I'd been outwitted by a parrot—was what really bothered me.

My chin trembled as I limped along the beach with Lenny holding my arm and still trying not to laugh. "There's parrot shit in my hair, isn't there?" I asked. Humbled. Bereft of all pride.

Lenny pouted in sympathy, but there was a little too much sparkle going on in his eyes to carry it off. "Just a touch," he said, patting me on the back. "It's hardly noticeable. Except for the smell."

"Thanks," I said as we climbed the fence again into Jason Johns's backyard and approached the car. "You drive," I said, walking straddle-legged, arms akimbo.

Lenny patted my ass and plucked a rose petal out of my ear. "Happy to, dear boy. Happy to."

The rose petal was yellow. My favorite color. Whoopee.

WE STOPPED at a drugstore on the way back to the office for a tube of Neosporin for the scratches and a box of Band-Aids for my puncture wounds and a bottle of Febreze for the smell, which Lenny liberally sprayed me with from head to toe before we left the drugstore parking lot. By the time he was finished, I was dripping with the stuff and could hardly breathe.

Back at the office, I stripped down to Lenny's boxer shorts, which I was still wearing, and proceeded to squirt Neosporin over each and every one of my injuries, and there were many. Then I covered a few of the more unsightly wounds with Band-Aids. While I did that, Lenny took the stapler off the desk and stapled the seat of my pants back together. We were bachelors, after all. A needle and thread were too much to hope for.

With all that out of the way, I held my head under the sink in the bathroom (it was either that or dunk it in the commode since we didn't have a shower in the office) and rinsed the avian fecal matter out of my hair. To this day I still shudder when anyone mentions "avian fecal matter." Happily, it doesn't pop up in conversations very often.

Having cleaned up as best I could, I shakily redonned my clothes and tried to make myself presentable.

"How do I look?" I asked Lenny.

Lenny eyed me up and down. "Well, you're still missing a sock, but with the ass of your pants mangled shut with a stapler and with all those grass stains and teeny tiny holes in your shirt from all the pricker bushes, not to mention all the blood-smeared Band-Aids you've got plastered all over yourself and your wet hair and the fact that you now smell like parrot-poop-scented Febreze, I don't think anybody'll notice."

That made me feel better.

At the sound of the front door squeaking open, Lenny and I turned.

To our surprise, it was a kid. A little Filipino kid, maybe seven years old. Cute as a button he was too. At the moment, leaning in from the street, looking around like he wasn't sure if he was in the right place or not, he looked a bit apprehensive. But he also looked determined, like he had a job to do, and by cracky, he was going to do it.

"Come on in, kid," Lenny said. "We won't bite."

The boy stepped over the threshold and closed the shop door behind him. He was wearing a brown uniform from the Catholic school up the street. Little brown shorts. Little brown shirt. Little brown hat. His knees were scuffed, and he had a name tag hanging on a lanyard around his neck. I stepped closer and saw that the name tag read Danilo Dalisay. Below the kid's name was a street address I recognized as being a couple of blocks over.

"Well, Master Dalisay." Lenny beamed, looking all paternal. "What can we do for you?"

The kid shifted from one foot to the other like he didn't know what to do with himself, so Lenny perched his ass on the desk again (it began to seem like that was where Lenny would be doing most of his client interviews), and as he had done with Lorraine Johns, he scooted a chair to the kid with his foot while I parked myself in the chair behind the desk like a proper human, hoping I wouldn't stick myself in the ass with one of the staples Lenny had patched my pants with. I'd been poked enough already for one day.

"Danny," the kid said. "You can call me Danny."

His eyes were as big as fried eggs. He seemed to be particularly interested in me.

I felt a blush creeping up the back of my neck when I heard him ask, "You fall in a wood chipper or something?"

I gave the kid a glare. "A little tussle with a client," I said. That elicited a chuckle from Lenny, which I tried my best to ignore. "Were you here for a reason, kid, or did you just pop in to bust my balls?"

Danny pulled his hat off and fiddled absentmindedly with it while he studied the two of us—first me, then Lenny. He didn't appear to be exactly infused with confidence by the appearance of either one of us. I couldn't imagine why.

"My daddy said you guys are pet detectives."

"That's right. We are," Lenny said, while I thought, *Ooh, word's getting around.*

The kid cleared his throat like he'd been rehearsing this moment all day. "I need you guys to find my dog for me."

Lenny's expression saddened. He clutched his chest like a grieving widow wailing over her husband's casket. "Aww," he moaned. "You lost your doggy?"

Danny nodded. His fried-egg eyes were bigger now. Now they looked like two white dinner plates with a black olive in the middle of each one.

"We don't work pro bono," I said, trying not to get sucked into those big sad eyes. "Who's gonna pay for the man-hours we put in?"

"I'll give you my allowance. And I didn't lose him in Preebono. I lost him right here in town."

Lenny turned big watery eyes on me like that was the cutest and most pitiful thing he'd ever heard. He thought it was funny when I almost killed myself tumbling off a fence into a rosebush, but this kid opens his mouth and mispronounces Latin, and Lenny turns into a softhearted sap.

"I've had him almost my whole life," the kid said. His little chin was trembling now. "I don't know what's happening to him out there. He's just a puppy."

"If he's just a puppy, how could you have had him your whole life?" I asked, although I have to admit I was starting to tear up a little myself. The kid was playing us like a couple of violins.

"Just have," the kid said, his little chin quivering.

"How much is your allowance?" Lenny asked.

"Thirty-five cents a week."

I watched in bewilderment as Lenny grabbed the calculator off the desk and started crunching numbers. He mumbled to himself while he did it. "Let's see now. Thirty-five cents a week—multiply by—uh, wait a minute. Let me start over." He began tapping keys all over again. Worry trenches had formed in his forehead. Math was never Lenny's strong suit, and I could see he was already in over his head.

I snatched the calculator out of his hands and tossed it in a desk drawer so he wouldn't be tempted to pick it up again.

"What you're saying, kid, is that you'll give us your allowance until you're old enough to vote. That about right?"

He thought about it for a minute. "Sounds fair."

Lenny was watching me closely. I did my best to ignore him when he said, "It'll be like steady income, Mait. Money we can count on, on a regular basis. Sort of like a salary."

"Thirty-five cents a week? Oh, do shut up, Lenny."

"*Harrumph.*"

Danilo Dalisay might have been sitting in front of a TV, mesmerized by Saturday morning cartoons, the way he was staring at us. Tears had formed in his eyes, and his chin wasn't simply trembling anymore, it was dimpling and undimpling like crazy. Watching it made my eyes start to burn. A lump the size of my lost sock formed in my throat. Jesus, the kid was good.

"What'd he look like?" Lenny asked on a sigh.

Danny had obviously rehearsed this part too. He rattled it off like he was in English class. "Brown with black ears. A white tail. About the size of a cat. And he's got a scar across his back from where he got hit with a Weedwacker. My daddy did it. He didn't mean to. It was a accident. My daddy's a mailman."

"Poor little guy," Lenny whined. I wasn't sure if he meant the dog or the kid or the mailman. Whichever it was, he seemed to have made up his mind.

He hopped off the desk and doubled over at the waist in front of the kid, sticking out his paw.

"We'll take your case," Lenny said. "Let's shake on it."

I rolled my eyes so far back into my head I almost fell off the chair. Our new client shook Lenny's hand, then started digging around in his pocket for loose change to make a down payment, but Lenny waved him off.

"This is a freebie, kid. Keep your money. If we find—hey, wait a minute! You never told us the doggy's name."

"Oh, yeah." Danny grinned. He was looking considerably less anxious now. I wasn't, but he was. "His name is Fido."

"Original," I said.

And the kid said, "Thanks."

"Okay," Lenny finished up, grabbing the kid's hand and pumping it a couple of times to seal the deal. "If we find Fido and return him to you, you can maybe buy us an ice cream cone or something as payment. How would that be?"

"One scoop or two?" the kid asked.

"One ought to do it," Lenny answered.

I supposed he was feeling generous. Every time *I* bought him an ice cream cone, he ordered a jumbo grande triple scoop with sprinkles and a cookie.

Danny's grin stretched out on both sides until it almost reached his ears. If he smiled any wider, the top of his head would slide off. "It's a deal," he said. "Thanks!"

Lenny plucked the lanyard from around Danny's neck and passed it over to me. "My assistant will copy down the pertinent contact information in case we need to get hold of you so you can reclaim your dog."

"Oh, brother," I mumbled. But I copied down the info on the name tag anyway. What else was I supposed to do, what with being Lenny's assistant and all?

When I was done, Lenny snaked the lanyard back around the kid's neck and said, "We've got your phone number and address. If we find out anything, we'll let you know. And don't worry. We're very good at what we do. We're professionals."

Yeah, right.

Wide-eyed and clearly impressed with Lenny's line of baloney, the kid worked his way toward the door. Just before stepping out into the street, he turned back and said, "It smells like doo-doo in here. Did you know?"

"Uh, yeah," Lenny said. "We know. It's my partner. He had, um, an accident."

The kid scrunched up his face and said, "Eww."

"Not *that* kind of accident!" I said.

But the kid didn't look convinced. He let it slide, though. Two seconds later he was skipping down the street headed for home.

"An accident?" I asked, one eyebrow so high on my forehead I could feel it nudging my hair.

Lenny blushed. "Well, you did."

Oddly enough, I was glad Lenny had taken the case. Poor little kid. I hoped we could find his dog for him. Hell, I already knew what flavor ice cream cone I'd ask for when he paid for our services.

Rocky Road. I love Rocky Road.

I sniffed my shirt. The kid was right. I did smell like doo-doo.

Chapter Five

"ARTHUR THE drag queen called three times this morning, Mait. He's got his Big Mama pantyhose in a bunch about us taking so long to locate his gerbil. I think maybe we shouldn't accept gerbils as clients anymore. It's a big world out there, and they are just too teeny to find. Drag queens either. They're too emotional, and they have a skewed sense of style."

I laughed. "Don't worry about Arthur. He's a sweetheart. I like Arthur. I even like his sense of style."

"Actually, so do I," Lenny admitted with a kindly chuckle.

"Don't worry about the gerbil either," I added, what with *Supercilious* being my middle name and all. "We'll work on that later."

Lenny shot me a skeptical glance. "More crawling around in the bushes? Great."

"Oh, hush. Let's move on to more important matters."

Lenny's face lit up. "Like the parrot?"

"No."

"The puppy?"

I lowered my eyelids to the surly setting and gave him a glare. "No! Today I thought we'd work on the Gila monster. I got a bad feeling about this one. Usually our cases are pretty cut and dried. We locate missing animals. Period. No mystery, no angst. Straightforward snoop jobs. But with Frederick I think we've got somebody actually lying to us. The ex-wife says the husband stole her lizard, the ex-husband says the wife is going to prison if he has anything to say about it. The ex-wife said the dog ate the lizard. The ex-husband said the lizard might have been eaten, all right, but not by his dog. Who in the hell else would eat a Gila monster, I ask you! Obviously somebody's twisting the truth, and I don't like being lied to. What was your impression of Mr. and Mrs. Johns?"

Lenny didn't stop to think about it. "I didn't like either one of them. But I really hated the wife. Hate to say it, but my sympathy lies with the venomous lizard."

"Yeah, me too. But if the wife is doing something illegal, why would she bring attention to herself by hiring us to find her frigging Gila monster?"

Lenny stopped to think about it for a minute, and what he finally came up with made me stop and reconsider a few things. For one, maybe Lenny wasn't so dumb after all.

"Mait," he said, "I'm assuming there's a pretty high-dollar mark on a Gila monster. I mean, you don't see them behind every tree, now, do you? If somebody stole *my* expensive poisonous lizard, I wouldn't fool around with a couple of two-bit pet detectives who on their best day don't know their asses from two holes in the ground. No offense. I'd go right to the cops and press charges. Why do you suppose Lorraine Johns didn't do that? Especially when she hates her ex so much."

I was parked behind the desk and Lenny was sitting on top of it, swinging his legs like a toddler and gazing down at me. I reached over and laid my hand on his knee. "Gads, Lenny. You're right. She's obviously desperate to get Frederick back, but still she avoids going to the cops. I wonder why."

Lenny gave it some more thought while I resisted the urge to let my hand slide a little farther along his thigh. He was just so damned tempting. For once, he didn't seem to be too concerned with the fact that my hand was on him at all. Usually his antennae would be waving around (not to mention his dick), and he'd be going for one or both of our zippers the minute I brushed up against him.

"Mait, listen. I know you don't like it when we break into places, but I think maybe we need to get inside that rattletrap trailer and see exactly what Jason Johns is hiding in there."

"For one thing," I said, "he's hiding a bigass Rottweiler. And from what I saw through the crack in the door yesterday, I'd rather not go head-to-head with the beast unless I'm wearing a suit of armor and packing a bazooka."

Lenny blinked. "Oh yeah. I forgot about the dog. Hmm." He scratched his head, and after he scratched his head, he absentmindedly lowered his hand to lay it over the hand I still had resting on his knee. His hand felt so warm and comforting over mine I actually had to squeeze my eyes shut for a nanosecond to savor the sensation.

"Look," I said, dragging my thoughts away from ripping Lenny's clothes off and ravaging him up one side and down the other, "he has to take that dog out sometime or other. It's a big animal. It needs exercise. He can't let it poop everywhere like Pudding Pop does, or he'd be up to his neck in dog shit. We're gonna have to stake the place out and wait for him to leave with the dog."

"And then what?" Lenny asked, one eyebrow high, as if he already knew what I was hinting at but he wanted to hear me say the words.

I didn't want to say the words, but I said them. I said them because Lenny was right. We had to get inside that trailer. I heaved a big sigh. "And then I'll let you work your magic and pop a lock so we can get inside. You're right. We have to see what Johns is hiding."

Lenny was scratching his head again. "What the hell could Lorraine Johns be doing that's illegal?"

"Who knows. And who cares. Our job is to find the stupid lizard. That's what she paid us three hundred dollars to do. That's our one and only goal."

I shuffled through the scraps of paper on the desk and came up with Lorraine Johns's phone number. I punched it in and hit the speakerphone button so Lenny could hear too. Mrs. Johns answered the call on the second ring.

"Hello."

"It's Maitland Carter, from the Two Pet Dicks Detective Agency."

"Jesus," Mrs. Johns said. "I can't believe I hired somebody from a company with a stupid name like that."

"No need to get snippy," I snapped back. *Lenny's right*, I thought. *I don't like the bitch either.*

She didn't seem too upset that her paid flunky had his feelings hurt. She heaved a sigh as if valiantly attempting not to be such an ungracious cow. Sort of. "What can I do for you, Mr. Carter? I can't think of anything we have to say to each other unless you're calling to tell me you've found Frederick. But I can't be that lucky, can I?"

"Uh, no," I said. "But we're working on it. How would you feel about my partner and I breaking into your ex's trailer and scoping the joint out?"

"I'd be all gooshy inside with glee, Detective. Or Dick. Or whatever you call yourself. I'll even give you guys a bonus if you'll get in there and snatch my lizard back. I'm running out of time. I need Frederick back *now*."

I almost chuckled at that. "What's the big hurry in getting the lizard back? He's not due for an insulin shot, I hope? He didn't sign up for a learning annex course at the city college that starts on Tuesday, did he? Oh good lord, don't tell me you two are taking a cruise to Aruba and the tickets are nonrefundable."

Lorraine Johns did not sound amused. In fact she sounded bored. "Funny. Please stop. Oh my, I'm laughing so hard my sides are starting to ache. Is there anything else?"

"So you have no objections."

"Of course not! Do what you have to do. Just return what belongs to me! And don't let the cops catch you. And if they do catch you, leave my name out of it."

"One question," I said.

I thought I heard a growl over the phone. "What?"

"When does he take the Rottweiler out? Does he have some sort of schedule he keeps? My partner and I don't want to be eaten by the same animal that gobbled up Rosemary."

"I don't blame you," she said. "That dog is dangerous. It should be put down." *Says the woman with a houseful of venomous reptiles.*

I could hear a clicking on the line, like maybe she was tapping her fingernail on a tabletop while considering the problem. "Jason takes the dog out in the evening for a run on the beach behind his trailer. He's usually gone for a while. Jason fancies himself some sort of marathoner or something. He'll never be able to run far enough to get away from the fact that he's an idiot, but he keeps trying. Annoying man. He always was. While he's on his run, you should have enough time to get inside the trailer and check the place out. I suggest you take some leather gloves with you in case Frederick's there. The dog isn't the only one who'll try to gobble you up if he gets the chance. And the dog doesn't dispense venom."

"You said Frederick wasn't poisonous," I said.

"I said a Gila monster bite won't kill you. I didn't say he wasn't venomous."

"Oh," I said and hung up.

Lenny was watching me, all big dark eyes and luscious lips. "Exactly *how* do we have the gerbil problem solved?" he asked, still pondering my previous statement from twenty minutes back. It always takes Lenny a while to catch up.

I ignored him. "We'll stake out the trailer, and we'll take your van. Johns has already seen my car. We'll sneak in, rekidnap Frederick from the kidnapper, and then we can concentrate on our other cases."

Lenny's eyes lit up. "Is this going to be one of those naked, fuck each other in the front seat, come all over the dashboard kind of stakeouts?" he asked hopefully. "Because frankly, Mait, I'd sort of like to concentrate on a couple of things besides lizards while we're at it. Like your balls maybe. Or your cute little titties."

"No," I said. "This is strictly work."

Lenny's face deflated like a collapsed lung. Then he snorted. "Well, *harrumph*! I guess we'll just see about that."

Uh-oh, I thought. *I'm in trouble now.* But I was smiling while I thought it.

WE HAD a couple of hours to kill before it was time for the stakeout to begin, so Lenny and I did a bit of multitasking to keep ourselves busy. Lenny produced a flyer he had spotted on a light pole offering a hundred-dollar reward for a missing cat named Fluffy, a glorious white Persian with blue eyes. Fluffy was sporting a rhinestone collar just this side of pissy. Judging by the picture, Fluffy was a spoiled prima donna who wouldn't last two minutes out in the cold cruel world. Somebody had probably already snatched her to decorate their couch. Still, you never know when you're going to get lucky, and a hundred bucks is a hundred bucks. Lenny and I aren't always hired for our services. Sometimes the services fall into our laps from on high. I mentally filed the Fluffy case under that category.

The South Park section of San Diego where Lenny and I hung out was a community of older homes cashing in on new money and slowly gentrifying to the point where Lenny and I probably wouldn't be able to afford the rent on a storefront there in a few years. Hell, we probably wouldn't be able to afford a cup of coffee. The corner laundromat had become a sushi restaurant; a mom-and-pop market I still remembered fondly from our childhood had morphed into a place that hawked incense and batik fabrics and offered yoga classes in the back. An ice cream shop that once served ten-cent cones to the hungry kids on the street now pedaled fancy chocolates at forty bucks a pound and somehow managed to look down their noses at you while doing it. A couple of blocks up from where the brand-new Two Dicks shingle hung was a print shop that used to be a place where an old guy with body odor sharpened scissors and scythes and lawn mower blades. Lenny and I popped into the joint and picked up the flyers we'd ordered printed the day before. The flyers were for Toodles the parrot, offering a fifty-dollar reward for anyone helping us catch the damn thing. The fact that we had been paid three hundred dollars was beside the point. Two hundred and fifty bucks in profit was better than nothing. We'd be more than happy to cough up fifty bucks of that money if it meant effecting a capture. Anyway, I figured it was a big broad sky overhead, and we'd need more than two pairs of eyes if we were to ever spot Toodles up there again. By sheer chance we'd seen him once, but that stroke of luck probably wouldn't be repeated anytime soon.

With the flyers in hand, and with Lenny toting our handy-dandy staple gun to attach the Toodles posters to the occasional telephone pole, we patrolled the neighborhood. We were on the lookout not only for Toodles in the treetops, but on the ground we kept a keen eye out for Danilo's puppy and Fluffy the Persian cat. It was too much to hope we'd run across Frederick the Gila monster slipping into yoga class or ordering a latte from the corner barista, so we would concentrate on him later. It was a long shot we'd see Toodles either. Still, if we could solve the other two cases, we would have earned two ice cream cones and a hundred smackers. Not a bad day's work.

While we walked, we talked.

Lenny. "I don't suppose you're seeing anybody now."

Me. "You know I'm not."

Lenny. "I enjoyed you staying over."

Me. "So did I."

Lenny. "I liked waking up with you there beside me."

I watched his face as he stapled a Toodles poster to the side of a wooden fence. He seemed to be avoiding my gaze, like he knew I was studying him but chose not to show it. Somewhere in the background, I heard a godawful caterwauling, like a couple of mountain lions were ripping each other's throats out. But Lenny was trying to make a point here, and I had a feeling I really wanted to hear what it was. So I ignored the caterwauling behind me.

I reached out and laid my hand to the back of his neck. "What are you getting at, Lenny?"

"Nothing."

"Doesn't feel like nothing."

Lenny stopped what he was doing and turned to face me. The sheaf of flyers in my hand were flapping in the wind, so I hugged them to my chest to shut them up.

Lenny fumbled around for a minute until he found his voice. "Mait, remember when we were kids and we discovered how much we liked having sex with each other?"

"Sure."

"Remember how once we discovered it, we never wanted to *stop* having sex with each other?"

"Fuckin' A."

"And remember how we had never been with anybody else sexually so all we knew back then was what we'd done together?"

"Yeah. We had nothing else to compare it to."

"Right." Lenny studied my face for a couple of heartbeats, then said, "Remember how that seemed to be enough?"

I stared back at him. "Of course it was enough. It was all we knew."

Lenny opened his mouth to say whatever it was he was about to say, but suddenly his mouth gaped open even wider and the unspoken words dribbled down his shirtfront like spilled soup. I noticed he wasn't looking at me anymore. He was looking over my shoulder. He was looking in the direction of the caterwauling.

I turned to see what he was staring at just as he whispered, "Holy moly. Will you look at that?"

So I looked. What I saw was Fluffy. The white Persian. The one on the wanted poster in the rhinestone collar, looking like the snootiest pussycat ever, like maybe she'd been hand-fed live sardines her whole life and whose anal glands smelled of lavender and primroses.

Poor Fluffy didn't appear quite so virginal and pristine at the moment. She was perched atop a filthy trash can in an alley behind a deli that reeked of last week's potato salad and spoiled mayonnaise, being humped by the ugliest, mangiest stray cat I'd ever seen in my life. Fluffy's paramour had a torn ear, one eye mangled shut with scar tissue, half his tail missing, and a large part of his fur looking like it had been sawed off at the root by industrious fleas with teeny-tiny buzz saws.

We're talking one ugly cat.

Fluffy was the caterwauler, of course. I realized that then. While her uglyass boyfriend pounded her from the back—grunting and slobbering and acting like a pig, as men so often do—Fluffy rolled her beautiful blue eyes in bliss and shuddered with ecstasy while screaming out her joy and urging her suitor to pound her harder.

"Jesus, what a slut," Lenny said, and we both laughed.

Then Lenny hissed, "Let's grab her!" So we slipped into the alley on tippy-toe and snuck up on the two creatures, who were so lost in the glee of fucking we could have driven up in a garbage truck and they wouldn't have noticed.

I took hold of the mangy alley cat and ripped him off Fluffy's back. I flung him away, but not before he removed several strips of skin from my forearms. Apparently coitus interruptus wasn't high on his list of favorite pastimes.

But if the mangy alley cat was upset, it was nothing compared to sweet little Fluffy. She went nuclear, climbing up and down Lenny like he was a tree trunk and hooking her claws into everything she could find. Shirt, pants, ears, elbow. She was still caterwauling, and now Lenny was caterwauling with her. One in fury, one in pain.

Finally, simply because I couldn't stand to listen to the racket anymore, I ripped my shirt off and flung it over Fluffy to keep her from burrowing right through Lenny's chest and removing his lungs with her claws. I tied the shirtsleeves together, wrapping the furious beast in a bundle from which she couldn't escape, and while Lenny held the wailing, heaving package at arm's length, I scrambled around for the Fluffy flyer, which I pulled from Lenny's shredded back pocket, and found the owner's address.

"Thank God," I said. "Fluffy lives a block away. Let's go!"

We ran up the street, me half-naked, and Lenny holding his bundle of screeching fury high in the air while passersby practically broke their necks trying to get out of our way.

Lenny was mumbling, "Ow, ow, ow, ow," as we ran because Fluffy was trying to gnaw his fingers off. The only part of Fluffy that was exposed was her tail and her teeth. While the teeth did a number on Lenny's digits, the tail thrashed around, six times its usual size, like a big fat fuzzy bullwhip, whapping him in the face.

In our panic we ran past the address on the flyer twice before we realized it. The house was a rambling old Victorian monstrosity painted a garish pink and mauve. We flew up the front steps to the porch and pounded on the door. Fluffy hadn't calmed down even one little iota. Talk about the cat from hell.

We heard footsteps on the other side of the door. They were the slowest footsteps I'd ever heard in my life. We were dancing around in our excitement, panic-stricken, battling a raging ball of wrath. Lenny was probably bleeding to death, and whoever was on the other side of that door seemed to think they were taking a leisurely constitutional across town to watch a slow, meandering sunset.

When the door opened, I had the good grace to alter my opinion. The woman who answered was probably three hundred years old, and thanks to shrinkage due to old age, she stood about four foot one. In heels. On the beatific face of an angel, she wore rimless spectacles, perched low on her nose like those of Mrs. Santa Claus. She had on a red-and-white sweater decorated with reindeer, and there was an artificial poinsettia pinned to the side of her head. It was currently August.

She saw us dancing on her doorstep, still trying to control the spitting ball of fury being strangled inside my shirt, and after looking properly astounded for a moment, she finally smoothed her features into a semblance of welcome and said in a meek little voice, as sweet as custard, "Yes?"

Lenny was beyond niceties at this point. His blood pressure had spiked five minutes back.

"Is this your fucking cat?" he screamed.

The old lady's hand fluttered at her chest like a dying bird. First she took in Lenny in all his insane panic, then she took me in, still dancing around like a moron on her front step without a shirt, my forearms raw and throbbing, and finally she rested her eyes on the screaming mass of rage clutched in Lenny's bleeding hands.

The old lady's face instantly melted into relief. "Fluffy?" she squeaked. Reaching out, she grabbed the bundle from Lenny's grasp and held it up to her face, peeking through the folds of fabric to see what was writhing around inside.

I expected to see her eyeglasses go flying one way and the bloody stump of her nose go flying the other, but instead the lashing tail went limp and shrank three sizes. The screaming voice stilled. From inside the ruined shirt we heard a tiny, plaintive "Meow?"

"Oh, my little love, you're home," the old lady cooed. She turned to set the cat on the foyer floor, and Fluffy, tail high, set off in search of sustenance, obviously relieved to be out of the grips of the two monsters who had treated her so cruelly. She stalked off, ignoring us completely. No thank-you, no fuck-you, nothing. As for her ugly boyfriend and their interrupted liaison, I had no doubt she would pleasure herself to climax later. Slutty, virginal females like that always do. Or so I've heard.

The old lady handed me back my shirt, which was a dust rag now.

"I suppose you'll be wanting the reward," she said, clearly suspicious, as if maybe we'd been the ones to kidnap the cat to begin with.

From her apron pocket, she pulled out a wad of cash that would have choked a rhinoceros. From that, she peeled off a hundred-dollar bill. And then, after a moment of reflection, her face softened and she pulled off another.

"I'm so grateful, boys. Thank you for rescuing Fluffy." She handed us the money. One bill to Lenny, one to me. "Wherever did you find him?"

Lenny wasn't in the mood to be sociable. "She was in the alley behind the deli porking the ugliest goddamn cat I've ever seen in my life. She seemed to be enjoying herself too. I think Fluffy's a nymphomaniac. You oughta have that looked into."

The old lady nervously fingered a brooch at her throat. "That's impossible, young man. Fluffy's a boy cat."

Lenny blinked twice, staring at her. Then he said, "Oh, okay. In that case Fluffy's a raging homo. And a power-bottom homo to boot. A power-bottom homo with questionable taste in tricks and a totally cavalier attitude toward the practice of discriminate sex."

The old lady appeared wounded by Lenny's answer, as well she might. She opened her mouth to answer Lenny, then apparently thought better of it. She turned her gaze on me, ducking her head to look over her spectacles.

"Your friend's distraught," she said.

"That's because he's bleeding."

"Oh." She considered that for a moment, then apparently decided the hell with it. "Well, thank you anyway," she muttered, slowly closing the door in our faces. She didn't look happy. Maybe Fluffy was about to have her ass chewed out. Or maybe the old lady just thought it best to get the hell away from the two of us as quickly and quietly as she possibly could.

But Lenny and I didn't care. We were too busy staring at the loot we were holding in our bleeding fists. Happily, we wouldn't have to buy medicine for Lenny's wounds. We still had everything we needed back at the office from my unfortunate encounter with the rosebushes.

LENNY'S RUSTED-OUT Econoline van, which had most certainly seen better days, was parked across the street and two trailers over from Jason

Johns's piece of crap, rust-bucket double-wide. The van and the trailer might have been cousins. The sun had set, but the night hadn't completely fallen yet. There were orange streaks in the sky on the western horizon that reminded me of orange-swirl ice cream. It was a gorgeous sunset, but we're used to gorgeous sunsets in San Diego. They come with the territory.

Lenny and I were wearing so many Band-Aids and had so many boo-boos on every square inch of exposed skin, we looked like we'd been tied to a car bumper and dragged down a gravel road for a couple of miles. Even laughing about it hurt. But we were laughing anyway.

"You should have seen your face!" I howled. I was laughing so hard tears were squirting out of my eyes, and I could hardly catch my breath.

Lenny wasn't any better off. He was stomping his feet on the floorboard and trying not to choke to death on the double quarter pounder with cheese he was consuming for dinner. Every one of his snow-white teeth was on proud display as he wailed and jerked around and finally sputtered, "We have to stop, or I'm gonna pee down my pant leg!"

I couldn't help myself. "Did you see Fluffy's face when you yanked that flea-bitten scuzball off her back, depriving her of an orgasm? If looks could kill!"

"Stop! Stop! My Band-Aids are popping off."

I twisted out from under the steering wheel and dropped my head on Lenny's chest while the two of us tried to stifle our giggling. His hand came up and cupped my cheek, holding me close as we shook with silent laughter. I felt him bend forward and brush his lips over my hair. Through his warm chest, I could feel his heartbeat against my skin. It was racing just like mine.

Gradually silence took over and other emotions surfaced. I lifted my head and stared into Lenny's eyes from a distance of two inches.

"Partner," he said softly, and planted a virginal kiss on the tip of my nose.

I swallowed. "I stayed with you last night," I said. "Why don't you stay with me tonight?"

"It's getting serious, isn't it?" he said.

It wasn't really a question. It was a statement of fact, and I knew if I tried to deny it, I'd be lying. So I didn't. "Seems that way," I said, blinking back a residue of happy tears and losing all urge to laugh anymore. There was a Band-Aid on Lenny's cheek that was coming loose. I gently patted it back into place.

"Ouch," he said, and I smiled.

Suddenly he tensed. "Look!"

I followed his eyes through the filthy windshield and saw the porch light on Johns's trailer go on. A second later Jason Johns stepped through his front door with the Rottweiler, Stella, on a leash beside him. He was wearing running shorts and a bright yellow tee. Johns, I mean, not the dog. Except for his collar, the dog was buck naked, as dogs usually are.

Lenny and I watched as Johns locked up after himself, then stuffed his key in his shorts pocket. Our faces were still side by side, and Lenny's hand was now pressed warmly to the side of my neck. His heat and smell were turning me inside out with a sudden rush of desire, but I tore my mind away from those rosy possibilities and concentrated on the problem at hand instead. Frederick. We had to find Frederick.

Johns took a moment to pet the mutt, who had set aside her usual homicidal tendencies to be all tail-waggy and happy, knowing she was going for a run. Then Johns did a couple of stretching exercises while leaning against the outside wall of the trailer, flexing his calf muscles, stretching his back. When he was sufficiently loosened up, the dog dragged him across the street directly in front of us, and together they pranced off toward the corner where they could access the beach without having to climb over the fence at the back of Johns's property. Lenny and I ducked out of sight as they passed.

We gave the guy three minutes before easing ourselves out of the van and approaching the trailer just as the streetlights blinked on over our heads, making our hearts go into hyperdrive.

Rather than try to jimmy the lock on the front door where a nosy neighbor might spot us, we hustled around to the back of the trailer where the shadows were deepest. The orange streaks in the sky were gone now; the sky had morphed to black. One by one the stars were popping into focus over our heads. A fingernail moon seemed to be in cahoots with our need to be clandestine, not casting much light on us as we moved through the darkness as silent as ninjas. Lenny and I were good at being stealthy. God knows we had spent enough time creeping up on unsuspecting animals to know how to move in silence.

Lenny plucked a credit card from one pocket and a tiny piece of heavy wire from another. Investigative implements. Or, in the common vernacular, burglary tools. Lenny and I hadn't always been pet detectives. There was a short period of our youth—when we weren't banging each other—spent breaking into neighborhood houses for spending money. We weren't particularly proud of it, and our criminal careers were short-lived, thanks to a reasonable amount of common sense, but we did learn a few things in the process. Popping a door lock was one of them. Lenny was better at it than I was. That's why he had the honors tonight. I was the lookout. Always play to your strengths.

"Cheap lock," Lenny commented, and fifteen seconds later we were in.

Jason Johns had left almost every light in the joint on and almost every window curtained, so at least we didn't have to fumble around with flashlights. That would expedite the search considerably.

Johns's trailer was probably bottom of the line when it was new about a hundred years ago. Now it was crap personified. The floor squeaked when we walked across it. There were water stains on the ceiling, the wood paneling was bowed and cracked, and the harvest-gold carpeting was torn and puckered, worn down to padding in the high traffic areas.

There was stuff strewn everywhere. The place was such a mess, Lenny and I stood there in the kitchen for a minute stunned by what we were seeing.

"How does anybody live like this?" Lenny asked.

Cabinet and closet doors were open, their contents scattered across the floor. A sofa cushion in the living room was ripped to shreds, probably by Stella the Rottweiler. The white stuffing from the cushion was strewn around the room like a cotton gin had exploded. In the bedroom we found the bed stripped down to bare mattress, and again Stella had pulled a hunk of wadding out of the mattress and left it dangling over the side of the bed.

"He should train his dog better," I said. *Like I should talk.*

Lenny was staring into the bedroom closet. "I don't think Johns is living here, Mait. All his clothes are gone."

I peered over Lenny's shoulder and stared into the closet. The floor was covered with old shoes and stacks of *Zoonooz*, the in-house magazine of the San Diego Zoo. The hangers on the rod were empty. I tiptoed through the flotsam on the floor to a dresser in the corner and pulled out one drawer after another to check them all. No socks or underwear in any of them.

"You may be right," I said.

Lenny had wandered back into the living room. After peeking from around the edge of the blinds on the front door to make sure there was no one climbing the steps outside, he started rummaging through the mismatched end tables and bookcases scattered here and there.

I did the same in the second bedroom. In that room the closet contained several wire cages and terrariums. All empty. If Frederick had been here, he was gone now.

On the wall above the bed, I noticed a framed diploma certifying that Jason Johns had graduated from SDSU with honors and was now a certified herpetologist.

"Hey, Lenny! The husband's a herpetologist!"

"You mean like he has two sex organs?" Lenny called back.

I groaned. "That's a hermaphrodite, you moron. How many times do I have to tell you? He's a reptile guy, just like his wife!"

"His wife's a guy?"

"Oh, shut up!"

Back in the living room, I gravitated toward an old rolltop desk standing in the corner and started pulling out drawers and checking cubbyholes to see what I could find.

A stack of photographs in a secret compartment (which wasn't that secret) in the back of the upper right-hand drawer caught my attention.

I plucked the photos out and shuffled through them. They were pictures of Lorraine Johns. In a few of them, she was naked and obviously posing. A few photos deeper in the pile, I found some shots of Jason Johns posing naked too. Wow. The guy was hung like a horse. I felt a blush rise up the back of my neck. These were obviously snapshots from a time when husband and wife were doing what husbands and wives often do. Enjoying each other's bodies. Playing at sex. Lenny and I had been known to do the same thing now and then, although I didn't have any photos yet. I wondered if maybe it was time to rectify that situation.

I poked the sexy photos back where I found them, and only then did I notice a small manila envelope stuffed all the way in the back of the hidden compartment.

I tugged it out and undid the little metal clasp to see what was inside. Lenny had come up and was gazing over my shoulder while I did.

"Whatcha got?" he asked, his breath warm and titillating on the side of my neck. Jesus, even in the middle of tossing this poor guy's crappy trailer, I couldn't keep my mind off sex with Lenny.

I gritted my teeth and tried.

From the envelope, I pulled out another small stack of photos. Three of them this time. More porn shots, I thought. But then I quickly realized they weren't porn at all. They were all of Lorraine Johns, but she was fully dressed and outside in broad daylight, standing on a street corner. I didn't recognize the storefronts behind her, so I couldn't place what part of town she was in. She wore a form-fitting business suit. Her hair was done up in a rather austere bun, and once again her hemline came almost up to her belly button. She was wearing the highest high heels I'd ever seen. I couldn't help wondering how she walked in them without breaking her neck. There was a teeny gold chain around one ankle. Very sexy. For a broad. Personally I preferred the dick shots of her husband, but hey, that's just me.

In the photo an arrow had been drawn with a red marker. The arrow pointed to a door in one of the buildings on the street where Mrs. Johns was standing. In one of the other photos, Mrs. Johns was walking through that door. And the third picture was of the door itself and an empty street.

Weird.

Lenny's hands gently gripped my hips from behind. His chin was digging a hole in my shoulder. "Let's take those pictures with us," he said.

I turned to study his face. "Why?"

He looked a little uncomfortable at the question. "I'm not sure. I think maybe they're important."

"Okay." I stuffed the three pictures back into the manila envelope and folded the whole thing up to where it fit in my back pocket.

I grinned. "Wanna see some naked pictures of Jason Johns sporting a boner?"

"No," Lenny said. "I want to get out of here. We've been here too long already. The lizard's not here. That's what we came to find. Let's split while the splitting's good."

He was right, of course. We'd been here far too long. "Okay. Let's go."

I closed the desk drawer with the secret compartment in the back, and at that precise moment, we heard footsteps on the front porch. Oh no!

Lenny and I flew through the trailer on silent feet and were about to slip out the back door when the front door opened.

We heard a growl and a bark and Jason Johns screaming, "Sic 'em, girl!" and the next thing we knew, Stella the Rottweiler was chasing us through the back door and down the steps outside. We hurled our asses over the fence onto the beach and took off running. Penned behind the fence, the mutt wailed and roared, furious that her prey had escaped.

We were all the way down the beach to where I'd tumbled into the rosebushes when we heard Jason Johns screaming at us from his backyard. "You goddamn kids! Stay out of my trailer!"

Lenny and I ducked under the shadow of the copse of pepper trees where Toodles had landed earlier. We lay there in the sand catching our breath, our hearts going a mile a minute.

"That was close," Lenny finally gasped.

I was smiling. "He didn't know it was us," I said. "He thought it was some kids. Maybe he's had trouble with his trailer being broken into before. Maybe that's why he left all the lights on."

"Maybe," Lenny conceded, dropping his head to my shoulder and letting out a nervous giggle. "That was so close," he said again, still panting heavily.

I thought about the trailer. About the mess it was in and the empty closets. About the metal cages and the glass terrariums stacked in the bedroom closet unused.

"He's not staying here, Lenny. He's staying somewhere else. Wherever it is, that's where he's stashed Frederick."

"Yeah," Lenny said. "Which begs the question—why? Why is Jason Johns going to so much trouble to hide a stupid lizard? What the hell is the point?"

I touched the manila envelope stuffed in my back pocket, reassuring myself it was still there.

"Let's get home," I said, peering out from the shadows along the beach to make sure Jason hadn't dropped the damn dog over the fence so he could tear us into kibble-sized pieces. All was quiet. The only sound on the night air was the humming of insects overhead and the faint clanging of a channel buoy somewhere out on the water.

"I don't want to go home," Lenny said quietly.

I smiled at that. "You're not going to. You're staying with me tonight. Remember?"

In the shadows, I caught the flash of snow-white teeth. Lenny was smiling too.

"Oh, goody," he said.

We took the long way around and approached the van from the rear.

A few minutes later we were back at my apartment, and Pudding Pop was hopping around welcoming us home. He had only pooped in the apartment once while we'd been gone. And that was in the cat litter box I'd been trying forever to train him to use when I had to go to work.

I was so astounded by the fact that he'd used it, I wondered if he was sick.

Lenny stood behind me. He was just as amazed by what Pudding Pop had done as I was.

"It's the beginning of a new era," Lenny muttered, his arms snaking around me, his crotch pressing seductively to my more-than-receptive ass.

"Please, God, let it be so," I said. "But then the Popster has always been better behaved when you're around."

"Really?"

"Yeah."

"How about you?" Lenny asked. "Are you better behaved when I'm around?"

"You bet," I answered, and suddenly we weren't joking anymore. Lenny and I turned to face each other and melted together. His mouth tasted delicious as he laid it over mine. His lips were alive—probing, eager, hungry.

The kiss went on forever, but the moment I trembled against him, he eased me to arm's length and studied my face. I could feel the blood surging to my cheeks as his warm breath spilled over me. I wasn't blushing because I was embarrassed. I was blushing because I was so turned on I was about to pass out. I'm pretty sure Lenny knew that.

His mouth twisted into a gentle pout as he applied pressure with a fingertip to one of the Band-Aids on my forehead, probably trying to make it stick a little better.

"You look like you rolled down a cliff."

"So do you."

"You move like you're sore."

"I am sore. You?"

"Yeah. Everything hurts. Almost."

"Which part *doesn't* hurt?" I asked.

"Come with me," he whispered, "and I'll show you."

He took my hand and tugged me toward the bedroom.

I swallowed hard and followed.

Chapter Six

LENNY WAS sneezing every five seconds, and I was cussing rather creatively under my breath. We were crawling around on our hands and knees in Arthur's basement in a last-ditch effort to unearth the missing gerbil. I wasn't happy because the basement at the Belladonna Arms obviously hadn't been cleaned since along about the time Abraham Lincoln sprouted his first beard.

Something ran across the floor in front of us. I jumped.

"What the hell was that?"

Lenny sniffed. "Dust bunny."

"Oh. It was pretty big. You sure it wasn't a dust water buffalo?"

Lenny sniffed again, sneezed, then spit up a chuckle. For some reason his hand was on my ass. "Maybe."

"If you think we're having sex in this dump, you've got another think coming," I snapped.

"*Harrumph*," Lenny snapped back, but his hand remained on my ass. It was still on my ass when Arthur strolled into the room humming. "Yoo-hoo, boys!"

Arthur was wearing what looked like a replica of Beaver Cleaver's mom's best housedress straight out of the fifties, petticoat and all, only about ten times bigger. He had squeezed his fat feet into high heels, and his chubby ankles sort of melted over the sides like candle wax. The hair on his legs (Arthur appeared to be hairy all over) was smashed beneath nylon stockings, but the hair was still abhorrently noticeable. He wore an ankle bracelet like the one Lorraine Johns had sported in the photograph, but somehow Arthur's ankle bracelet didn't look quite as sexy. Maybe it was the furry shins that ruined the effect.

Screwed into his ear lobes, he wore chandelier earrings comprised of fifty or sixty rhinestones each. They shot out sparkles of light and tinkled like tiny bells every time he moved. He had a short blonde wig with finger waves across the top and a flip on one side that pointed due north, defying gravity. His face was made up for opening night at the

Old Vic—everything done to extreme so as to capture the attention of the myopic theater attendee in the back row of the upper balcony three miles away. Arthur's rouged cheeks resembled two stoplights.

If you looked up *subtle* in *Merriam-Webster's*, I was pretty sure you wouldn't see a picture of Arthur alongside it.

He was carting a tray with glasses and a pitcher of iced tea. There was a sugar bowl and a little plate of lemon wedges on the tray too. Alongside all this sat a plate of sugar cookies. When Arthur did June Cleaver, he did her to perfection. I half expected Eddie Haskell or Lumpy to pop in and join us for tea.

Arthur stopped just inside the door with a dainty "Oh! Am I interrupting something?"

I assumed Arthur was referring to the fact that Lenny's hand was still resting on my ass, so I slapped it away. Lenny chuckled again. He seemed to be chuckling a lot. Maybe the dust was getting to him.

"Come cool off," Arthur sang out, placing the tea tray on an old table in the corner. He dragged three chairs up to the table from different parts of the basement, pulled a rag from a box in the corner to dust off the chairs, and with a merry titter, announced, "Ooh, tea parties are always such fun. I haven't had one of these in ages!"

Lenny and I were dying of thirst and as dusty on the inside as we were on the out, so iced tea sounded pretty good. We plopped down in the chairs, while Arthur dropped lacy napkins in our laps and proceeded to pour tea over the ice in the glasses. After he had ascertained how Lenny and I wanted our tea—sweetened, unsweetened, with or without lemon— the three of us each grabbed a cookie and settled back to study one another.

Arthur was doing most of the studying.

"You boys are in love," he said out of the blue, almost making me drop my cookie.

"Don't be silly," Lenny and I said in unison, but unless it was my imagination, I thought we sounded a bit uncomfortable when we said it.

Arthur threw his head back and laughed, jarring his earrings and making them tinkle and shoot out sparks. "Nobody knows love like I know love, and you boys are in love. Maybe you don't know it yet, but it's true. So there. Have another cookie."

We did. And while we consumed our second cookie, Arthur bent down and ran his fingertips along the dusty floor. Sitting up again, he leaned toward us and sprinkled the dust over our heads.

Lenny sneezed while I exclaimed, "What the hell are you doing?"

"Love pollen," Arthur smugly stated, dusting his fingers on the rag before snatching up another cookie for himself. "This building is famous for its love pollen. People move in here all alone in the world, and after they've been here awhile, they suddenly find themselves head over heels in love. I call it the Belladonna Arms love pollen. You've been pollenized."

"Uh, thanks," I said, wondering if Arthur had skipped his antipsychotic drugs that morning.

Lenny said, "Thanks," too, but he said it with more sincerity. In fact, he said it with *such* sincerity, I turned to stare at him.

He looked back at me, all innocence and light. "What?" he asked.

I shrugged. "Nothing."

Arthur was still eyeing us—and still laughing while he did it. "Love," he said. "Definitely. Head over heels. I'd know the symptoms anywhere."

A comfortable enough silence settled over the three of us as we sipped our tea and crunched our cookies. Finally, Arthur set his glass of tea aside as if he had an unpleasant duty to perform.

"I'm afraid you boys are wasting your time. Ethel is gone for good."

"Who the hell is Ethel?" I asked.

Lenny nudged me with his elbow. "The gerbil," he whispered.

"Oh, yeah."

Since I still had a last-ditch trick up my sleeve concerning the elusive Ethel, I decided to set Arthur's fears to rest. After all, he had already paid us six hundred dollars. How much longer could we torture the man? Or woman? Or whatever the hell he was?

"Give us three more days," I said. "If we don't have your gerbil in hand by then, I'll refund your money."

Lenny almost fell off his chair, but Arthur didn't notice. His attention was centered solely on me. As he stared at me, I saw fat tears well up in his eyes. The tears shimmered on the tips of his false eyelashes for a heartbeat or two, then spilled out over Arthur's cheeks, trailing downward until they fell with a last gasp into Arthur's fuzzy cleavage, never to be seen again.

Lenny's eyes opened wide, as I suspected mine did, when Arthur leaped out of his chair and pounced on us. He dragged us into a crushing embrace, slopping tea everywhere and annihilating my third cookie.

"What a sweet thing to do!" Arthur cried, squeezing us even tighter. I thought I heard Lenny fart, that's how hard we were being hugged. "But oh my goodness gracious, I can't let you do that, boys. You've worked too hard. Too hard. Look at you, crawling around this filthy basement. I'll tell you what, I'll give you the three more days, but after that you keep the six hundred dollars. Use it on your honeymoon. You've got one coming up whether you know it or not. I'm never wrong about these things. You guys are about to make a commitment. Trust me. I don't know much, but I know love. It's kind of a gift."

Before Lenny or I could say anything, we received one more bone-crushing hug, and then in a swirl of taffeta or chintz or whatever the heck it was he was wearing, Arthur fled the room, wailing in happy tears. Thank God he left the rest of the cookies.

"He's nuts," I said, watching him go.

"He's brilliant," Lenny said, watching him go.

Then the two of us turned to gape at each other. A few minutes later, the tea was gone, the cookie plate empty, and Lenny's hand was back on my ass as we crawled around the baseboards whistling for Ethel to come out and play.

Ethel wasn't having any part of it. I wasn't surprised. I pretty much figured Ethel was in Tijuana by now. Or maybe in the belly of a cat.

I didn't doubt how smart Arthur was, though. I didn't doubt it for a minute.

I felt my ass tingle. Lenny's hand must have hit a nerve. Oh, wait a minute. It was the cell phone in my back pocket, set to vibrate. I had a call coming in.

I reached around, hauled the phone out, and pressed it to my ear. "'Lo?"

The voice on the other end of the line was female. She sounded old and feisty. "Are you the man looking for the parrot?"

"Uh, yeah."

"Well, I just saw it sitting on my windowsill. I live at 1326 Windham Street."

Windham Street wasn't far from our neck of the woods in South Park. "Is it still there?"

"Let me look." I heard a clunk as she set the phone down. Then I heard footsteps interspersed with the slo-o-ow *tap tap tap* of a cane on a hardwood floor fading away into the distance. About three days later, she came back on the line. "Now he's sitting in the birdbath, soaking his feet."

"We'll be right there!"

I reached over and brushed the dust bunnies out of Lenny's hair. "We gotta roll. Lady spotted Toodles sitting in her birdbath."

Lenny groaned his way to his feet. "Good. I'm tired of looking for this fucking rodent."

"Now, now," I said. "It's a living."

"Barely."

"Plus we got free cookies."

He almost smiled. "Oh, hush."

We hustled through the front doors of the Belladonna Arms, passing a group of six gorgeous gay guys coming in as we were going out. My kind of apartment building. Apparently Lenny's too. He stood there slack-jawed, watching the six hunks stroll away. I finally had to hook my arm through his and drag him toward the car.

I heard a strange noise. It sounded like growling. Then I realized the strange noise was coming out of me.

Lenny was watching me with a broad grin smeared across his face. Every snow-white tooth in his head was on full display. He still had a dust bunny dangling over one ear.

"You're growling," he said.

"No, I'm not."

"You're jealous."

"Oh, please."

"You are. You're jealous that I was staring at those guys."

"Don't be stupid. Why would I be jealous?"

He was right, of course. I was jealous. What did that mean exactly? I pondered the problem all the while we bounced our way to Windham Street in Lenny's rattletrap van, which only had one shock absorber. The other three had fallen off ages ago.

By the time we arrived at our destination, I still hadn't figured out the jealousy question, so I shoved it into an empty cupboard way in the back of my mind. That particular cupboard was labeled "Stuff I Don't Understand or Maybe I Do but Just Won't Admit It."

I grabbed the bigass net we used to catch critters, and together Lenny and I rapped on the old lady's door. Lenny was still looking smug, but I chose to climb on my high horse and ignore him. All the time I was ignoring him, I wanted to fling the net aside, jump his ass, rip his clothes off, and have my way with him right there on the old lady's porch.

Happily, the old lady answered her door before I became a slave to my urges.

The woman of the house appeared to be in her upper eighties. She was dressed in a sunny floral-print dress and had a little porkpie hat pinned to the top of her head. The hat had a rose poking off the top, swaying on its stem. The cane she leaned on had a mass of artificial flowers taped to it from the ground up, and an artificial corsage of lilies encircled one wrist. A blossom of posies graced the toes of her shoes, and the hemline of her dress consisted of a line of yellow daisies. If she told me her name was Flora, I was going to shoot myself in the head.

She eyed us up and down and didn't appear too impressed by what she saw.

I looked down at us as well and immediately saw the problem. We were still plastered with Band-Aids. And we were filthy. Our knees were dusty, we had smears of dirt on our shirts, and Lenny's nose was black. I mean, blacker than it usually was. I reached over and plucked that last dust bunny off Lenny's ear. Like that was going to help.

"I'm not letting you boys in my house," the old lady said. She leaned forward and whispered, "Rape. It's in all the papers. Rape here, rape there, rape somewhere else. I'm a virgin, and I intend to stay that way. So you boys can't come in. Plus you look like you've been crawling around a dirty basement."

Not only a virgin, but prescient too.

I doffed an imaginary hat and said, "I don't blame you, ma'am. I wouldn't let us into your house either. We don't want to impose anyway. We're just here for the bird. If it's all right, we'll simply toddle around the property and try to find the birdbath."

She appeared doubtful that was really what we intended to do, but she finally nodded and said, "It's in the back. And don't be trying no doors and windows while you're at it. I've got a gun."

"You do?" Lenny asked, as wide-eyed as I had ever seen him. Crazy old white women seemed to be unfamiliar territory to him. I had a spinster aunt who lived with twelve cats. Crazy old white women were right up my alley.

She gave Lenny a conspiratorial wink. "You're darn tootin' I've got a gun. It's an eight-shot Luger that'll put a hole in a Buick the size of a potato. I don't even want to think about what it would do to you. My husband brought it back from the war."

"I thought you said you were a virgin."

"Just because we were married doesn't mean I let him do the nasty on me."

"Poor bastard," Lenny said.

She gave a lackadaisical shrug. "Yeah, well...."

Plucking the Toodles flyer out of her dress pocket, she waved it in our faces. "Says right here there's a fifty-dollar reward."

"On the successful capture of the creature, yes."

"Then you'd best get at it," she said, eyeing us with a wily squint. "And don't try to sneak off without paying. I'll be watching."

I snagged Lenny's arm and dragged him off the porch before the old lady decided to fetch her Luger and give us a demonstration of its prowess. As we ambled around the house, we had to go through two gates. At each gate we could see her peering out through a window, suspiciously following our progress.

At the back of the house, we found one final gate. Beyond the gate, alongside a well-tended truck garden with cabbages and tomatoes and beets sprouting proudly from their well-hoed rows, stood a concrete birdbath.

In the birdbath sat Toodles. He was soaking his feet and sound asleep.

At the base of the birdbath lay the biggest dog I'd ever seen in my life. It looked like a cross between a Great Dane and a palomino. The dog was snoring like a steam engine, and his big feet were trembling and jerking around like he was chasing rabbits in his dreams.

"She didn't mention the dog," Lenny whispered as we cowered behind that last gate, afraid to go through.

We jumped when we heard the old lady hiss at us from a window above our heads. "That's Munch. He won't hurt you. He's older than I am. All he does is sleep. Go catch the parrot before it flies away. I want to get me a new perm with that fifty bucks."

"Munch isn't mean?" I whispered, trying to spot the old lady through the screen.

"He's a pussycat," she said. "As long as you don't wake him up. Go get the parrot."

"Why?" Lenny asked. "What happens when you wake him up?"

"You don't want to know."

"He's awfully big," Lenny said on a trembly sigh.

"Go get the parrot!" the old lady snarled. "I need me that perm, dammit." This time after she spoke, we heard a gun cock.

Lenny and I stared at each other. We both swallowed. Lenny's eyes were as big as Hostess Sno Balls. I had no reason to think mine weren't.

"Guess it's time to go get the parrot," he said.

"Guess so."

"You first."

"No, no. After you."

The gate gave out a mournful creak as we slowly swung it open, but the dog didn't wake. Neither did Toodles. Lenny and I crept into the backyard on tiptoe, holding our breath, net held high. My legs felt like rubber as we approached the birdbath, getting closer and closer.

Suddenly I felt Lenny's hand squeezing my shoulder. I gazed over at him and saw tears streaming down his face. His mouth hung open, and he was trying not to sneeze. Oh, crap.

We froze in place as Lenny covered his face with his hands. His body heaved, his eyes squeezed shut, and he went *Aaahshphltt*! Then he did it again—*Aaahshphltt*!

I peered through squinted eyes to see what the animals were doing. The dog was still sound asleep, but Toodles had one eye open, and that one eye was staring right at us.

"Nice birdie," I cooed as Lenny and I crept closer still.

The dog yawned but didn't open its eyes. Its tail wagged as it slept. What the hell did that mean?

Lenny had the net, so he took another step forward and raised it high. Just as he did, Toodles spread his scrawny wings wide and lifted himself into the air.

Splashing birdbath water and shedding a flurry of feathers, Toodles hovered six feet off the ground and squawked, "Twatwaffles!" Then he let loose with a barrage of parrot poop that landed directly on Munch's snoring head.

Two seconds later, Munch was on his feet, every hair perpendicular to his body, vibrating like a tuning fork, growling, snarling, snapping. Then his beady little killer's eyes homed in on Lenny and me, and he came at us like he was shot out of a cannon. He chased us through the first two gates before we had the common sense to slam the last gate shut and block his murderous path. Clutching our hearts and staring back the way we'd come, we watched Munch leap up and down behind the gate, insanely slinging dog spit and howling like a rabid wolf while the parrot crap dribbled off his head.

Been there, done that, I thought.

Somewhere in the sky above, we heard Toodles giggling as he sailed off into the ether.

It was the blast of a gunshot that got us moving again. The old lady must have taken a potshot with the Luger at *somebody*, and we seriously doubted she'd be aiming for her dog. We hightailed it to the van, threw ourselves inside, and roared off down the street in a cloud of exhaust fumes.

Gasping for air, we didn't take a decent breath until we were two miles away. When Lenny realized he was going sixty in a thirty-mile-an-hour zone, he eased his foot off the gas pedal.

"I don't like that bird," he said.

I didn't answer. I was too busy checking to see if I'd wet myself.

OUR MEAGER collection of animal-capturing tools were stored in the back room of our new office. Cages, nets, ropes, long-reach pincers that old people use to grab cans off high shelves but we use to snag trespassing snakes or any other creepy crawly creature we didn't want to lay our delicate pinkies on. Besides all that we had a set of walkie-talkies, a stun gun (in case we ever had to capture a hippopotamus), and a cattle prod or two. I almost blush to mention we also possessed a 50,000-volt Taser (found at a yard sale for thirty bucks) that Lenny and I were afraid to touch, although we told ourselves it might come in handy if Godzilla ever showed up on our doorstep. Happily, we weren't expecting him anytime soon. Also in the back room was the battered foldaway couch we had absconded from Lenny's dad's basement with when we moved out.

After a depressing morning spent being ignored by a gerbil, humiliated by a parrot, and chased by a slavering hound, we stood in the teeny-tiny office bathroom and washed Arthur's basement grit off ourselves by standing at the basin and taking Marine showers, compliments of a bar of soap and a couple of washcloths we found in a box of bathroom stuff I'd lugged here from my apartment when we moved in.

With the street door locked so we wouldn't be interrupted, we decided a nap was in order. After collapsing naked and exhausted on the sofa bed, freshly bathed, and suddenly maybe feeling not quite as drained as we thought we were, we rolled into each other's arms and heaved a joint sigh of relief.

Lenny felt wonderful—his hard body against mine, the two of us smelling of Ivory soap, his heated velvet skin a dream to touch. He scooped me into an embrace with his long, strong arms and buried his face in my chest. His cock lay like iron against my own, but we ignored them for the moment. That's the great thing about a lifelong sexual liaison. Sometimes being patient doesn't seem such a trial. Sometimes, in fact, it feels just right. Likewise cuddling naked in the daylight. New lovers might be sucking in their stomachs and worrying they had a booger in their nose, while seasoned veterans merely appreciated the clarity and freedom of it all. From my own vast experience on the subject, I had come to the conclusion long ago that there were few things in this world more enticing to behold than a naked Lenny Fritz lying sprawled in a golden ray of sunshine with me in his arms.

His lips moved against my chest when he talked. His hand moved, too, as he gently massaged my hip.

"We're making pretty good money so far, Mait. With the new business, I mean."

I slid my hand along his back, finding each and every vertebra with my fingertips. I discovered that by pressing firmly here and there into his spinal column, I could induce him to arch his body closer into mine, although he was already about as close as he could get without crawling into an orifice and disappearing completely. "If we didn't have two apartment rents to pay every month, life would be a little easier," I said.

He rose up onto one elbow and propped his head on his hand as he gazed down at me. "What are you saying?"

I eyed him back with all the innocence I could muster. "Nothing."

"Yes, you are. You're suggesting we move into one apartment instead of two."

"I didn't say that."

"Yes, you did." Lenny heaved a long, shuddering sigh. He stroked my cheek with his fingertips. He had that melted-chocolate look in his eyes that only came in moments of closeness like this one. "It would be awkward living together if we had dates, don't you think?"

We were getting into dangerous territory here, but I couldn't seem to shut myself up. "Maybe we shouldn't have dates, then. It wouldn't be fair to the other person—hogging the apartment with a date. And if we both had dates, the place would be Grand Central Station."

"Exceedingly awkward," Lenny stated. He casually checked his fingernails. "Especially if we, say, moved into your apartment and we only had one bedroom. That would *really* be a problem."

I closed my eyes because Lenny's hand, the one previously massaging my hip, had slid around to the front when he propped himself up on his elbow to gaze down at me. At that moment, he was absentmindedly twiddling my pubic hair between his fingers and periodically bumping my erect dick, merely by accident of course, making it jump every time he did.

He scooted down on the bed and laid his mouth to my rib cage. At the same time, he tucked my cock gently inside his fist and held it there, throbbing in his grip. It took every ounce of willpower I possessed not to lift my ass off the bed and arch my back like a footbridge.

"Think of the money we'd save," I said. There was a tremble in my voice that hadn't been there ten seconds earlier.

"The sun's in my eyes, Mait. Mind if I turn around on the sofa bed and aim myself in the other direction?"

"Not at all," I answered, gentlemanly as hell. "Do make yourself comfortable."

We both knew comfort had nothing to do with it, but why make a point of the obvious. I merely waited for Lenny to do a U-ey, then scrunch himself a little farther down in the bed until each of our crotches was in the other one's face. When Lenny squeezed over a bit more and pressed his stiff cock to the side of my head, by accident of course, I smiled. He looked a tad uncomfortable, so I adjusted his balls for him, which he seemed to enjoy immensely.

His own mouth had found the underside of my glans. I could feel his hot breath on it as he slid down my foreskin and kissed me there. I bent my leg up out of the way, and he rested his free hand over my balls, cupping their warmth in the palm of his hand.

With his lips still gently nudging the head of my cock, I let myself enjoy the sensation of his erection, veined and heated, pressing against my cheek. When a drop of moisture arose from his slit, sparkling in the light, I lapped it away with my tongue, causing Lenny to lurch toward me.

When he did, I let him slide that delicious cock between my lips. He groaned, and in the same moment, I did the same for him.

Once again, we found a use for patience. Slowly, oh so slowly, we pleasured each other as the sun lay warm across our skin. Every touch of Lenny's hands was a caress. The heat of his mouth a wonder. The taste of his precome lay like sweet nectar on my tongue.

As we made love, I lost all sense of place and time and memory. Every lazy moment was enough to keep me where I was, buried in pleasure, thrilled at the feel of Lenny's body against mine. The strength of his long legs. The smooth expanse of his perfect chest. The heat of his stomach. The taste of his cock. And the way he seemed to enjoy me the same way I enjoyed him.

When we came, simultaneously, each drinking the juices of the other, we lay trembling in each other's arms until every drop was shared, every unspoken gasp of pleasure given and received.

As I lay replete in Lenny's arms, his mouth still on me, his heavenly arms still clutching me tightly, holding me close, I found myself wanting to speak words we'd never spoken before. To say things I'd never said. To anyone. But I knew if I spoke those words, I would set us on a path from which there could be no return. It would be either the smartest thing I'd ever done, or the dumbest.

Since I didn't have the guts to find out which way it would end up going, I said nothing.

But Lenny knew. I'm sure he did. He knew exactly what I was thinking. And I was pretty sure Lenny's thoughts on the subject were the same as mine.

We were both afraid to say what we wanted to say.

And when the office phone rang in the other room, it gave us the opportunity to avoid speaking our minds for a little while longer. I wasn't sure if that was a good thing or a bad thing, but I did know it was the most comfortable.

I reluctantly stuffed myself into my pants and headed for the outer office to answer the call. Lenny still lay sprawled on the bed, his lips moist with my come. He was so beautiful it made my heart ache. He silently watched me as I went. When I edged around the sofa bed toward the door, his hand came out and brushed my leg—a lingering, gentle touch. I looked down at him and smiled, and he gave me a wink.

He understood the patience of our relationship as well as I did. Sometimes I think he understood it better.

In the other room, I picked up the phone, and Lorraine Johns barked into my ear, "Well?"

I was still in a sexy, mellow mood and didn't appreciate being barked at two seconds after getting my rocks off and almost declaring my everlasting love to my best friend, which had been the last thing I'd intended to do when I crawled out of bed that morning, but it had kind of sneaked up on me, dammit.

Whoa! I screamed at myself. *Did I just think that rambling-ass sentence, and what the hell does it mean?*

Then reality encroached.

"Well *what*?" I barked back at the bitch on the phone.

For Lorraine Johns, it was apparently that time of the month. Amazingly she was even testier than I was. "*Where's my goddam lizard?*" she screamed.

I forced myself to calm down. It wouldn't do any good to antagonize the woman any more than I already had. If I kept my cool, I might be able to string her along for another three hundred bucks in a few days when our first week was up and Lenny and I hadn't yet found her stupid lizard.

Letting myself deflate like an old basketball, I collapsed into the office chair and propped my bare feet up on the desk. I found my best business voice and dragged it out for show. "Frederick wasn't in the trailer, ma'am. We searched the place from one end to the other." Not exactly true, but close enough.

Lorraine Johns seemed to be forcing herself to calm down too. Good. She was scary enough when she *wasn't* screaming at me. I imagined her chewing on her lower lip, trying to bring down her blood pressure. "Then I guess Jason has stashed the animal somewhere else."

"Guess so."

"But you'll keep looking?"

"Yes. We'll keep looking. And by the way," I said, "you didn't tell me your husband was a herpetologist too."

She sighed, still obviously trying to hold her temper. "I didn't tell you he has three testicles either. So what?"

Three testicles? I wished I'd looked at those hard-on pictures a little closer.

She didn't give me time to make a salacious comment. What a pity. I'm sure it would have been a doozy.

"Just find Frederick," she said, sounding suddenly weary. And with that, she ended the call.

I felt Lenny approach from behind. He'd slipped into trousers too. His chest had a sheen of sweat from our little romp on the Hide-A-Bed. It broke my heart to see he was partially dressed again. I preferred Lenny naked. Boy, did I.

He stood behind the desk chair, laid his hands on my bare shoulders, and bent down to kiss the top of my head. "Thanks for the nooner," he whispered.

I leaned my head back against his firm stomach and smiled up at him. "We need to talk," I said.

He nodded. "I know."

Apparently it would have to wait. For at that moment, we heard a tapping at the door. We saw Danilo peeking through the glass. All three feet six of him. He was dressed in his Catholic school uniform again, and he had his book bag strapped to his back. The book bag was fat, with hard, pointy edges, and looked like it weighed about four hundred pounds.

Lenny rushed to grab a shirt before opening the door to let the kid in.

The lad studied Lenny and me with huge, hopeful eyes. "Any luck finding Fido?" he asked.

I didn't have the heart to tell him, but we hadn't actually looked for his dog yet. Not really. What kind of subhuman beings were we to leave a poor kid heartbroken and alone and not put in a modicum of effort to rescue his beloved puppy from starvation on the streets? I wondered if we'd have been that remiss if the kid had paid us our usual retainer. No, most certainly not. Jesus, I felt like scooping my guts out with a melon baller.

Since I didn't have a melon baller handy, I twiddled my fingers at the kid in greeting. "We're about to go scour the streets for him right now, Danny. We were on our way out the door."

While Lenny looked surprised by that statement, Danilo merely looked skeptical. "Yeah, right. You guys ain't even dressed."

I leaped to my feet and rushed across the room to give the kid a bracing pat on the head while I ushered him back through the door onto the sidewalk. "Trust us, son. We'll do everything we can to find Fido and return him to you. Now you run along home from school and have a peanut butter and jelly sandwich. Kiss your mama, do your homework, and leave the puppy detection to us."

Danilo let himself be shuttled out onto the sidewalk. I was afraid to look at his little face. There might be tears there, and I wasn't sure I could handle that. I gave him a nudge forward in the direction we always saw him heading when he was going home, then turned back to close the office door behind him. I looked up to see Lenny standing behind the desk with tears streaming down his cheeks.

"Poor little guy," he sniffed.

I nodded, one old softy to another. I gave Lenny my best Walter Brennan impersonation, limping around and sucking my gums. "Okay, then, durn it. Let's go find his dadgum puppy."

Chapter Seven

UNEARTHING LOST pets is a tenuous proposition at the best of times. It's a big wide world out there with a gazillion places to hide. For all Lenny and I knew, Fido and Ethel might have joined up with Toodles and the frigging lizard, and they were all touring the Baja coast on a Mexican lobster boat.

Odds were, however, they were still close at hand. You just had to be lucky enough to spot them.

"We need to talk to Jason Johns. Something's not right with the little woman," I said.

Lenny was down on his hands and knees, gazing under an oleander bush. We were exploring the neighborhood, trolling for a brown-and-black doggy with a Weedwacker scar on its back for a little kid with big sad eyes who couldn't reward us with anything more than two ice cream cones in repayment for our services even if we found his poor mutt. We had been scouring the surrounding blocks for the past hour, and the only thing we had unearthed was my sex drive. Again. Obviously, our nooner on the sofa bed had only been a temporary stopgap.

"Which woman?" Lenny asked. "You mean our actual paying client? The snooty bitch who floated us three hundred bucks to find her Gila monster?" Lenny hauled himself to his feet with a grunt. Apparently the oleander bush was a bust. No brown-and-black puppy under there.

I was beginning to think Lenny didn't like Lorraine Johns any more than I did.

"That's the one," I said.

"Her husband isn't exactly a peach either," Lenny noted. "He sicced his dog on us."

"We broke into his house!"

"Well, yeah."

"And there are extenuating circumstances about why we should or should not like the husband."

"What extenuating circumstances are those?" Lenny asked.

"Well, for one thing, he has a big dick."

"How big?"

"Never mind."

Lenny was wearing khaki pants that snugged his ass perfectly and a white T-shirt that was tight and small and didn't quite cover his belly. I had seen both men and women stop what they were doing and stare hungrily at him as we passed. I understood their attraction completely. Jesus God, Lenny was gorgeous. The fact that he continually reached out to touch my arm, my shoulder, the back of my neck, as we strolled along, pretty much swelled my heart to about three times its normal size. I was beginning to wonder how long I would be able to maintain this illusion that we were merely friends with benefits, when even the shoes on my feet were starting to realize I wanted more out of our relationship.

Lenny was never one to keep his thoughts corralled into one pen at a time. Lenny's brain was like that one little dogie that was always meandering down the wrong path, disappearing over the wrong hill, and leaving the herd behind. He'd been like that since he was a kid.

Case in point.

He turned to me and asked out of the blue, "Do you think Arthur is *always* in drag?"

"Uh, gee, Len, I don't know."

"Do you think he knew what he was talking about with that love pollen stuff?" That was a deeper subject. Way deeper.

I diligently gathered my thoughts together like a spray of daisies before I ran the risk of opening my mouth on that one. But when I did answer, no one was more surprised by what came out than I was.

"I think if there's any love pollenizing going on, then the only ones doing the pollenizing are us. It isn't up to Arthur and his magical Belladonna Arms schtick to decide who's being pollenized. He's a romantic is all. He *wants* everyone to be in love. How you and I feel about each other is a complicated matter. Even I can't figure it out sometimes."

Lenny stopped in the middle of the sidewalk to stare at me. He laid his hand over his heart. His eyes were so burrowed into mine I felt pinpricks inside my skull. When he spoke his voice was a little breathless.

"Sometimes, Mait, I can't figure it out either. I just know…."

"You just know what?" I asked. My pulse suddenly thudded inside my head. My palms were clammy. I was hanging on to whatever Lenny was about to say like a cat dangling from a windowsill by its claws. Was the moment of truth at hand at last?

Lenny opened his mouth to speak, but instead his eyes went wide, and he stared over my shoulder up the street. We were half a block away from the Two Dicks Detective Agency corporate offices, ha-ha, and it seemed to me Lenny was now staring right at it.

I turned to see what was important enough to interrupt maybe the most crucial conversation of our young lives. And when I did see, all I could bring myself to utter was two tiny words.

"Oh no."

Strapped to the office doorknob, directly under our brand-new shingle, was a capuchin monkey. It was Lenny's brother's monkey, Ed. I'd recognize him anywhere. Lenny's actual brother was nowhere in sight.

This could not be good.

"This cannot be good," Lenny said.

Lenny's brother's name is Leroy. Nobody in Lenny's family likes Leroy. Not even his own parents. The only creature Lenny hated more than his brother, Leroy, was his brother's monkey, Ed. On the annoy-o-meter, Leroy and Ed might have been identical twins.

Not only did Leroy and Ed share a cross-species annoyance gene, they were also both illegal, in one sense or another. Leroy was forever running from his most recent scrape with the law, and since it is illegal to possess a capuchin monkey in the state of California, Ed was considered by the authorities to be an illegal immigrant. Or maybe smuggled contraband. I wasn't sure which. All I knew was it was a no-no to own him.

A small crowd had already gathered on the sidewalk. They were bunched together, watching the little monkey tied to the doorknob. They were going "Ooh," and "Aah," and "Isn't he cute?" and all the while tearing their eyes away long enough to gaze up and down the street as if wondering where the organ grinder had gone.

Lenny and I joined the crowd. We were damned interested in knowing where the organ grinder had gone too.

Ed was a cutie. You had to admit that. He knew how to work a crowd too. He was sitting on his little monkey butt in front of our office door, making faces, jumping up to do a little dance now and then, and then humorously scratching the top of his head like he couldn't quite make out why the humans were all staring at him.

Unfortunately, Ed had a short attention span. This was made quickly apparent when he stopped scratching his head and started playing with his balls. He leaned back against the door with his little fuzzy legs splayed wide and worked his teeny monkey pecker into an erection. Once he had achieved lift-off, he really went to town, pumping that little guy for all he was worth. All the while, he did his own *oohing* and *aahing*. What a perv.

Suddenly the crowd decided they had better things to do. Whistling nonchalantly, or shaking their heads in disgust, the audience quickly moved away, dragging their kids behind them, realizing, one supposes, that they were at risk of being labeled perverts themselves if they didn't immediately stop watching the monkey play with himself.

Ten seconds later Lenny and I were the only ones remaining. Ed was still beating off and Lenny was so mad he had a little rope of steam issuing from each ear. Well, no, he didn't really. But it didn't take much imagination to see it there anyway.

"Stop that!" Lenny snapped at Ed.

"*Urp?*" Ed said, and dropped his teeny erection like a hot potato.

Beside Ed sat a wire cage with a folded towel in the bottom. Inside the cage was a bunch of bananas and a note.

"Oh crap," Lenny said, retrieving the note.

While Lenny perused the note, eating one of the bananas as he did (we hadn't had lunch), I untied Ed's leash from the doorknob, unlocked the office door, and snatched up the empty cage to carry it inside. Ed immediately leaped to my shoulder and stayed there as I plopped myself down at my desk and watched Lenny, still standing outside reading the note. The delicate umber of Lenny's face had already gone to brick-red, which I took to be a bad sign. Even Ed seemed to be eyeing Lenny warily.

"That moron!" Lenny sputtered, dramatically shaking his fists to the heavens.

"Uh-oh," I said to Ed while he leaped into my lap and buried his head in my armpit, looking for a place to hide.

Lenny stormed through the door, slamming it closed behind him. "Leroy is hiding from the law again! He's leaving the monkey with us until he gets back. Sometime around Christmas, he said. That's half a year away!"

"I hate to break it to you," I said, "but this monkey is illegal. We could lose our business license and maybe even go to jail if Fish and Wildlife catch us with him."

But Lenny wasn't listening. He was still ranting inside his head. And out. "I'll kill him! This time I'll kill him! I got more important things to be doing than babysitting his stupid monkey."

"Like what?" I asked. I was starting to feel sorry for Ed. He was trembling in my lap with his head still buried in my armpit.

"*Oop?*" Ed said plaintively, then started shivering again.

"*Oop* your ass!" Lenny barked at the monkey's back. He opened his eyes wide and stared at me as if I'd just peed on his french toast. "You're starting to feel sorry for him! Admit it, Mait. Geez, how can you be such an easy mark? Leroy *knows* you're an easy mark too. That's why he left the monkey with us."

I gave a shrug. I hated to admit it, but Lenny was right. I *was* an easy mark. Especially where animals were concerned. I patted the desk in front of me and motioned Lenny to have a seat. "Park your ass. Lower your blood pressure. Try to chill. And above all, stop screaming."

"Fuck you!"

I laughed. "That's mature."

Part of the blood suffusing Lenny's face dribbled down through his neck and rejoined its brethren. He began to appear a little less insane. His eyes softened momentarily as he gazed down at me. Then they shifted to Ed, who still had his head stuck in my armpit.

I could see Lenny expending a great deal of energy trying to regain his cool. He heaved a massive sigh. "Until we figure out what to do with him, we'll have to keep Ed with us. The last time I left him alone in my apartment, he found a screwdriver and took the guts out of the microwave."

I barked out a laugh.

While Lenny didn't return my laugh, he didn't appear to be mad anymore either. Now he just looked—*pensive*.

He reached out and laid a warm hand to the side of my face.

"Something's happening," he said, his voice at such a low register I could barely hear the words.

I leaned my cheek into his hand. "What do you mean? Something's happening where? You mean with the monkey?"

Lenny tapped his chest in the general vicinity of his heart. "No. Here. In the ticker."

I studied his face. The gentle heat in his eyes. I felt the faintest tremble in the touch of his fingertips on my cheek. I remembered the taste of his seed on my lips. The explosive moment in the other room when he'd offered it to me for what was probably the thousandth time in our lives. So why did it always feel like the first? I recalled his hands on my body. Felt again my hands on his. The velvet softness of his skin.

Both of us lost in each other's arms. When we were alone like that, the world always seemed to be a silent shadow on the outskirts of awareness. The only reality, the only thing that was really real, was us.

The phone rang, and it startled me so I almost fell off my chair.

Ed said, "*Erp?*"

I snatched the phone off the cradle. "Two Dicks Detective Agency."

A moment later I added, "We'll be right there."

"What now?" Lenny asked as his eyes rolled to the top of his head.

"I FEEL like we're canoodling with the enemy," Lenny said. We were tooling along the freeway, headed for the Mission Bay Mobilehome Park yet again. I had informed Lenny that Jason Johns had insisted on seeing us immediately.

"He's not the enemy," I said. "He's just not our client. There's a difference."

"If you say so."

I was driving, and Ed was standing on the console between us, his little legs bowed, his teeny head peering over the dashboard. I saw his hand gliding toward his crotch, so I thumped him gently on the noggin like I was testing a watermelon to distract him from pleasuring himself yet again. Jesus, the monkey was worse than I was.

"No beating off in the car," I said.

Lenny gave an operatic groan. "Well, darn."

I grinned. "I wasn't talking to you."

"Oh. Thank God."

"What do you suppose he wants?" I asked.

"Who?" Lenny asked. "Ed? He probably wants mad monkey sex. Don't we all?"

"No, dummy. Jason Johns."

Lenny thought about that. "Maybe he figured out we're the ones who broke into his trailer."

"I'm pretty sure if that's what it was, he would have simply called the cops, and we'd be in lockup by now. It must be something else."

To my surprise Ed turned and sprang to Lenny's shoulder. Wrapping his clever arms and prehensile tail around Lenny's neck, he curled up and immediately went to sleep, issuing little monkey snores while Lenny sat there looking uncomfortable.

"See? He likes you," I said, causing Lenny to snort. But I noticed when he spoke, he kept his voice down so as not to wake the little guy up.

"He's stressed out," Lenny said. "It can't be easy living with my brother."

"Still, we can't keep him," I said. "You know that, don't you?"

Lenny didn't look happy about it, but he nodded anyway. "I know. We need to find him a home where he'll not only be safe from the authorities, but safe from Leroy too. A place where Leroy can't get him back. We'll have to figure something out."

I patted Lenny's thigh. "Don't worry," I said. "We will. I kind of like Ed. Our sex drives are so similar, his and mine."

Lenny laughed. "Yeah, but your pecker's bigger."

At the sound of Lenny's laughter, Ed's eyes opened briefly, but then they drifted closed again. He pressed his forehead closer to Lenny's neck and went back to sleep. As we drove along, Lenny idly stroked Ed's tail. Ed's snores deepened.

I tried not to smile too overtly. I didn't want to tip Lenny off to the fact that maybe he didn't hate the monkey as much as he thought he did. I preferred to keep that revelation my little secret.

Just as I was keeping the other revelation secret. The revelation of how I really felt about Lenny. Sometimes I kept that one from myself.

Jason Johns was sitting on his rinky-dink front porch waiting for us. The man-eating Rottweiler and Frederick the Gila monster were nowhere in sight. Johns looked forlorn sitting there, and I wondered what had happened to make him decide to contact us. If anyone was canoodling with the enemy, it was him, not us.

He didn't rise when we approached.

"What's with the monkey?" he asked. Ed was staring at us through the car window, unhappily *hoo-hooing* the fact that he'd been left behind.

"New business partner," I said.

Johns grunted, which I took to mean he didn't savor my sense of humor. Instead, he eyed us one after the other. I noticed there were dark circles under his eyes. Maybe swiping venomous reptiles from his vindictive ex-wife was encroaching on his sleep time. Or maybe he couldn't rest with a poisonous animal residing on the premises. God knows I couldn't have.

To my surprise, he let his weary face soften into a semblance of a smile. "I guess you boys are an item," he said.

Lenny and I both blinked in surprise. *Why does everybody keep saying that?* While I was floundering around for the proper response, Lenny went ahead and beat me to it. Back at the car, Ed was being silent. He was probably humping the stick shift and getting ready to shoot monkey jism on the steering wheel.

"The only thing you need to know about Maitland and me is that we're detectives paid to recover the property you stole from our client," Lenny said, sounding so professional I almost burst out laughing.

Johns's smile widened too. He was a handsome guy, in a world-weary, bedraggled sort of way. I would have thought so even if I hadn't seen a snapshot of his erect wanger, which was a doozy.

"You don't like her any more than I do," Johns said, just short of a chuckle. "She must be a joy to work for."

It was my turn to get a few words in. "She isn't paying us to like her. She's paying us to get a job done."

Johns patted the front step beside him. "Park yourselves," he said. "We need to talk."

Lenny and I remained standing. For the first time, I heard a low rumbling growl coming from the other side of the trailer's front door, directly behind where Johns was sitting. It was Stella, obviously, the canine from hell, hungry for a couple of detective shins to gnaw on for lunch. Or maybe a brainpan to lick clean.

When Johns realized we weren't going to sit, he let out a resigned sigh and said, "I'm assuming since you boys are in the business you're in, you harbor a certain affinity for animals."

"So?" Lenny asked.

Johns eyed us sadly, as if it truly pained him to think he wasn't one of our favorite acquaintances. "I don't know what my ex told you about me, but I want you to understand something. Reptiles are my life. I work at the San Diego Zoo in the reptile division. They are fascinating creatures, reptiles. Some are loving and make wonderful pets. Others are, through no fault of their own, dangerous. Even deadly."

"Why are you telling us this?" I asked.

He ran a hand through his hair. "I figure you guys are going to be a pain in the ass, and since I can't figure out a way to get rid of you, I've decided that maybe we should work together."

"To what end?" I asked.

Johns sighed. "I want you to understand that whatever I've done concerning my ex-wife's collection of exotic reptiles, I've done for the sake of the animals. They aren't safe in her hands. They need to be protected from her at all costs."

"Does your wife work at the zoo too?" Lenny asked.

"She did," Johns said, "until she was fired."

"Why did they fire her?"

"Too many animals were disappearing on her watch."

"What the hell is that supposed to mean?" I asked. "Are you saying she stole them? Why the hell would anybody steal a bunch of venomous lizards?"

"They weren't all lizards, Mr. Carter. There were snakes, young crocodiles and caimans, newts, frogs, you name it."

Lenny wasn't buying it. "If they suspected her of stealing animals, why didn't they press charges?"

"Not enough evidence," Johns said. "My ex-wife might be a vicious, thieving cow, but she is also very smart."

"If what you're saying is true," I interrupted, "explain to me what it is she thinks she's going to do with these animals she stole. I mean, there can't be much of a profit in the trafficking of poisonous reptiles. How many people are nuts enough to want one?"

Johns appeared pained by my question. It didn't take me long to realize my words upset him because he didn't understand the woman's motives either. And it obviously bothered him even more to have to admit it.

"I don't know what she does with the animals. She must be selling them. But to who? How are deliveries made? Where is she keeping them while they're waiting to be shipped? How does she find buyers?"

He scooped a teeny gecko out of his shirt pocket. The gecko was bright green and maybe six inches long. Johns laid it on its back in the palm of his hand and gently stroked the lizard's pale belly with a fingertip. Immediately, the little guy closed his eyes. Johns smiled, gazing down at it.

"I'm assuming that thing isn't poisonous," Lenny said.

"No. Just a friend," Johns answered. "Just a teeny-tiny friend."

It was at that moment I realized I liked the guy. And I believed him too. I believed what he had told us about his ex-wife. Her motives were still a mystery, but I didn't doubt she had done everything Jason Johns said she'd done. What I couldn't understand was why?

"Where's Frederick?" Lenny asked. "What have you done with the Gila monster?"

"He's safe," Johns answered. "So are the other reptiles I stole from the bitch."

"You stole others? She didn't tell us that."

"No," he said. "I don't suppose she did. If she told you they were stolen, she'd have to tell you where she got them and what it was she was intending to do with them."

I considered that. "So you're saying it's something illegal."

"Yes, gentlemen. Illegal and profitable. I just don't know what it is."

Apparently this was the juncture in the conversation where Lenny decided it was time to get down to brass tacks. "What are you asking us to do, Mr. Johns? Do you want us to go all Benedict Arnold and betray our client and work for you?"

"Would you consider it?" Johns asked.

I laid my hand on Lenny's arm, letting him know I would appreciate the chance to answer that question myself. Lenny was smart enough to give me the floor.

"If we thought your ex-wife was harming these animals and that what she was doing was illegal, yes, our sympathies would immediately shift to you. We aren't in this business to break laws or hurt animals. We're in it to help them find their way home to the people who love them. Answer me truthfully. Does your ex-wife love these animals at all? Or does this unknown black market scam you say she's operating only serve the purpose of turning an illegal profit?"

"Profit," Johns stated flatly. "Money is all Lorraine has ever cared about. She has no love in her heart for anything but herself."

"She must have loved you at one time," Lenny said. "She married you, didn't she?"

Johns carefully slipped the gecko back into his shirt pocket. "She married me to gain access to the inner workings of the zoo. I know that now."

"To steal animals," I said.

"Yes, Mr. Carter. To steal animals."

"And you have no idea what she's doing with them?" Lenny asked.

"No. But while we were together, I knew there were other animals coming in as well. Reptiles from private collections. She had a couple of reptile wranglers who captured wild creatures for her. In both the desert here in this country and in South Africa. I saw a green mamba she had crated to be shipped to some unknown destination. When I asked her about it, she told me to mind my own business. Shortly after that she filed for divorce and threw me out of the house. *My* house, I might add."

"Couldn't you have fought it? What right did she have to throw you out of your own house?"

"I let her throw me out as a matter of self-preservation. She would have killed me if I hadn't left. One of her animals would have got to me. I know it. She would have arranged it somehow. She's a frightening woman, gentlemen. If you have any brains at all, you'll come to the conclusion that it's safer to work for me."

"What exactly are you asking us to do?" Lenny wanted to know. "What exactly do you think we *can* do?"

"Those pictures you stole from my trailer—"

Lenny and I both jumped. I found my voice first. "I don't know what you're talking about."

Johns merely shot us an incredulous smile. "There's no point denying it. I saw you that night. I saw you both sail across the back fence trying to get away from Stella. Later I noticed the snapshots were missing."

"Okay, fine," Lenny said. "We stole a few pictures. But we left the dirty ones behind."

Johns gave an impatient grunt. "I don't care about the dirty ones. I care about the three pictures with Lorraine entering the building. You know which pictures I'm talking about?"

"Y-yes," Lenny and I both readily admitted, which was sort of disappointing. I had always imagined us the brave sorts who would stand up to torture and never spill our guts no matter what horrors were inflicted on us. Guess not. Here we were admitting to breaking and entering and burglary without so much as one ripped-out fingernail or one 300-watt light bulb shining into our eyeballs.

And since we'd admitted it, I could see no reason not to ask my next question. "What was the importance of those photos? They seemed innocuous enough."

Johns laid his hand gently to his shirt pocket as if reassuring himself the gecko was still safe. "It was the place where Lorraine was conducting her illegal business. But somehow she knew I followed her there. Since then she's moved her center of operations to another location. I want you boys to find out where that location is."

"What's in it for us?" Lenny asked, trying to look clever and cool-hearted.

"You'll have saved a bunch of innocent creatures' lives. That's what's in it for you. I can't pay you, if that's what you're asking. Lorraine wiped me out."

I grumped, "I was afraid you'd say that."

"Fine," Lenny grumped as well. "We've heard your proposal. We'll think about it."

"Just be careful, you two," Johns said, reaching out to lay one hand on my arm and one on Lenny's. "And remember one thing. The reptiles might be venomous, but the only one who is truly conniving is Lorraine. Don't let her know what you're doing, or you're liable to wake up with a boomslang crawling around under your blankets." He gave us a wink. "And I don't mean that in a good way."

Lenny gulped, which was fortuitous because his gulp camouflaged the sound of my own gulp. I was so unnerved by the boomslang comment, I didn't pick up on the gay innuendo until two hours later. And I call myself a detective.

Suddenly I found myself wondering what Lenny and I were getting ourselves into? It was Jason Johns's boomslang crack that brought it home.

I immediately realized Lorraine Johns scared the crap out of me. Jason Johns, on the other hand, I trusted implicitly. Even I had to admit the fact that he had a big dick probably influenced my thinking. I have a blind spot. So sue me.

Chapter Eight

"I BELIEVE him," I said. "Johns. I believe everything he said."

The day was ending, and it was almost dark. In preparation for the night ahead, I had flicked on the headlights. We were lumbering down the freeway in the van with Ed in the back, screaming like a banshee, going "*Hoo-hoo-hoo!*" and ricocheting from wall to floor to ceiling like a gas molecule. Lenny and I had to yell to hear each other over the damn monkey.

"I believe him too," Lenny said. "Although I'm still not exactly sure what it is we think we're believing. What I can't figure out is what his bitch ex-wife is doing with all the reptiles. If marketing venomous animals is such a gold mine, how come Walmart doesn't have a spitting cobra aisle? How come there isn't a Lizards"R"Us on every street corner like Starbucks? How come Amazon doesn't have a special on poisonous tree frogs right next to their page for blowgun darts? You know, like 'people who buy this product also purchase this' kind of shit."

I turned to stare at Lenny. It was all I could think to do. Even Ed stopped *hoo-hooing* for a minute.

"What?" Lenny asked, his eyes grown all big and round and innocent. "Something I said?"

Speechless, I tore my own eyes back to the road in time to see our exit ramp coming up.

The house Lorraine Johns appropriated from her well-hung sap of a husband was a midcentury modern located on a corner lot in one of the more staid parts of town. It was obvious the lawn had been well cared for once upon a time, but now it appeared a bit down on its luck, as if the person who truly loved it had flown the coop. Or been replaced by a salamander. Sawgrass poked out of the hedges, and weeds grew through the cracks in the sidewalk. Dandelions were everywhere. An overturned bucket lay in the side yard, looking like it had been there for months. The gutters were filled with dead leaves, giving the house an unkempt look. Junk mail had dribbled onto the porch from the mail slot by the front door, and the wind had scattered half of it across the yard. The house was pale yellow with white trim, and even in the waning light of dusk, I could see the windows needed cleaning.

Were the property fixed up, I could imagine Jason Johns living there. Lorraine Johns was more of a stretch. It seemed to me her tastes ran in snootier circles.

There was a Saab hatchback parked in the driveway in front of a closed garage door. The bitch was home.

I eased the van into the cool shade of a magnolia tree across the street so Lenny and I and the monkey wouldn't all die of a heatstroke while we cased the joint. It was a warm evening. Lenny had his binoculars out, trying to see what he could see through Lorraine Johns's windows, which wasn't much, and Ed was playing with himself in the back of the van. He had curled into a corner and was energetically jacking off. I could hear his elbow thumping against the van's back door and his little lungs panting up a storm. I didn't have any monkey porn on me, so I tossed him a banana and a box of Kleenex.

"For when you're done," I said, eyeing him in the rearview mirror.

Ed said, "*Orp*," then went back to pounding his pud. One almost had to commend him for his singleness of purpose. I mean, for a pervert he had commitment. Goals. And quite possibly even a quota. That's a good thing, right?

We settled in for a long wait. I never knew how our stakeouts would go. Would we chat? Would we have sex? Would we sit around bored out of our minds, scarfing down candy bars and wishing we had a place to pee? This time Lenny made the decision for us.

"We have unfinished business," he said. I noticed right off he was talking to me, not the monkey. "At least I think we do."

I squinted through the shadows and studied Lenny in the darkness, or what I could see of him. At the moment it was eyeballs only. If he'd smile it would be eyeballs and teeth.

I didn't have to ask what Lenny meant. The unfinished business he referred to hadn't been out of my mind for more than thirty seconds at a stretch throughout the course of the entire afternoon. Nor had the fond recollection of everything we'd done the night before in my apartment, as well as in the back room during lunch hour. I'd been sporting a hard-on most of the day because of those memories. If I'd been alone, I'd have probably crawled into the back of the van and joined Ed in a whack-off marathon.

Draping my arm across the back of the seat, I let my hand rest on Lenny's shoulder. He looked away when I did.

"What if we moved in together and then you didn't like living with me?" I asked. "There's Pudding Pop to consider. He isn't an ideal roommate, you know. I buy spot remover by the gallon. I purchase new sheets on sale for the sole purpose of chopping them up into rags. Every one of my neighbors hates my guts because of Pudding Pop's bathroom habits. Do you want to get involved in that?"

"I want to get involved in *you*," Lenny said. "That's all I care about."

"What are you saying?"

He turned to study me with an amazed expression. Amazed and hurt. "You don't know what I'm saying? *You don't know what I'm saying?*"

I hemmed and hawed while a few beads of sweat popped out on my forehead. "Well, gee, Lenny, you haven't exactly spelled it out for me to—"

"I love you, Mait! I don't think we should be just friends anymore. I think we should be lovers. *Live-in* lovers. Until we die even, or maybe longer. I haven't figured that part out yet."

He swallowed hard. Then he shook his head and muttered to himself in the darkness, "I don't believe I actually said it at last."

"I love you too," I heard myself say. "That still doesn't mean we should live together." *The hell it doesn't. Why am I being so stubborn?*

The one remaining shock absorber in the van squeaked beneath our asses as Lenny pivoted in his seat to stare at me. In the back I could hear Ed's elbow pounding out a faster rhythm on the door. He seemed to have advanced from a polka to a tarantella. I wondered if he was getting close to shooting his little monkey rocks all over the van carpeting. Not that I really cared. Well, yes, I did. I'd probably think about it every time I crawled into the back of the van for the next twenty years. Sometimes spot remover doesn't cut it, you know?

Lenny appeared to be on the verge of going apoplectic. "It's *every* reason for us to live together, Maitland Carter, you twit! Well. I mean, you know, if you really love me too." I could feel Lenny's shoulder vibrating beneath my hand. It felt like he was shaking all over.

"I do love you too," I whispered, tracing his ear with my fingertip. "I just said I love you too. Didn't you hear me say I love you too?"

There it was. Lenny and I had finally said the words. In fact, I'd said them about five times. After banging each other since we were thirteen years old, we'd finally voiced the way we actually felt. The realization left me stunned for the space of a heartbeat or two. Then I felt an incredulous smile creeping across my face.

"But you don't want to live with me?" he asked. There was a timbre of heartbreak in his voice that I didn't like hearing at all. It pretty much knocked the smile off my face as quickly as it had come.

"Actually I *do* want to live with you, Len. If you remember, I'm the one who brought it up first."

"I brought it up first."

"No, you didn't. I did."

"Nope. That was me."

"Jesus, you want to fight over it?"

"No. And don't call me Jesus." Then he grinned, and a little row of Chiclets glimmered in the shadows.

I grinned back.

"This is a big step," I said, my voice all hushed and reverent.

"It's a big step we've been leading up to our whole lives."

"I think you're right."

"We'll even save some money. One less rent to pay."

"There's that too. Plus steady sex."

"Now you're talking."

Lenny awkwardly straddled the floor shift and slid across to join me in the driver's seat, cramming me against the door while scooping me into his arms. "I love saving money and having steady sex," he purred, laying his mouth over mine.

I lost myself in his kiss. Coherent thoughts went the way of the dinosaur. I was a bundle of nerve endings and nothing else. They were the good nerve endings too. When he was motivated, nobody could kiss like Lenny could.

In the back, Ed's elbow started bumping the wall like crazy. The tarantella had morphed into a two-step. "*Uhh, uhh, uhh,*" Ed grunted. Now his head was banging against the back door too. The echo of it reverberated through the van and sounded like some circus clown bonking coconuts together. I imagined hearing Ed's little monkey heart go into hyperdrive with an audible *whoosh*, like a Hemi supercharger sucking gas.

"I feel like we're in a three-way," Lenny murmured around my tongue.

"Yeah," I said, "and the short guy is getting all the action."

"*Urp, oop, eep!*" Ed gasped, and suddenly the van fell ominously silent. Ed's panting stopped. Did he masturbate himself to death? A moment later I heard the rustle of tissue paper being plucked from a box. After a beat or two of silence, during which I didn't want to know what the hell Ed was doing, I heard the unmistakable sound of monkey teeth chomping away at a banana. Then a sigh, which I chose to interpret as a by-product of sexual afterglow in a simian. Yuk. What next? Would he light a cigarette?

During all this, Lenny and I were still kissing. We were quickly arriving at the point where clothes would need to be shed and the action taken to a whole new level when we heard the scrape of a garage door sliding up.

We scrunched down in the seat and peered over the dash. Lorraine Johns was all decked out in one of her damn-near-doodah-exposing dresses, this one black and flouncy and sexy. She wore high heels that showed off her long, gorgeous legs, and she had a red silk shawl draped around her shoulders for a splash of color. Her long blonde hair had been gathered up into a clumpy mass of curls at the back of her head. She looked chic. Going by appearances alone, you'd never know she was such a bitch. She ducked outside through the open garage door, toting a metal cage in each hand about the size of two breadboxes, which she dumped in the back of the Saab.

"Cages," Lenny whispered. Sherlock Holmes was on the case. I half expected him to pull out a pipe and say, "The game's afoot."

With a click of the remote in her hand, Lorraine Johns lowered the garage door, then hopped in the Saab and drove away, sliding right past us on the street without once glancing in our direction. Phew.

"What do we do?" I asked, spinning around to look through the back windows to watch her taillights recede in the darkness. "Do we follow the cow or do we check out the house?"

"Uh, uh, uh," Lenny said, never adept at making rush decisions and sounding a little like Ed in the throes of a monkey orgasm. By the time I decided I'd better make the decision myself, it was too late. The Saab's taillights were gone.

We turned our attention back to the house.

"Got your investigative paraphernalia?" I asked.

"My what?"

"Your credit card and that little piece of wire."

"Oh, yeah," Lenny said, patting his pocket. "I never leave home without them."

"Good, baby. Let's go to work."

Lenny didn't budge. He merely continued to sit there staring at me.

"What?" I finally asked.

"You called me baby."

I smiled. "That's because we're lovers now."

Lenny's eyes lit up in the darkness, catching all the moonlight they could grab. "Are we?"

"You bet."

"Till death us do part?"

"Yeah," I said. "Let's just hope it doesn't part us tonight."

It was totally dark outside now, and the only light burning around the house was on the front porch. "When we get inside," I said, "watch where you step."

"You mean don't make a mess so she won't know we broke in?"

"No, Lenny, I mean watch where you step so you don't stomp on a reptile with bigass fangs and a venom pouch stuck in each jaw. Surely to Christ they're caged, but you never know. Maybe she left her pet rattlesnake roaming free as a night watchman."

Lenny laughed at that, then he seemed to think about it a little more, and soon his laughter quietly petered out. "She has a pet rattlesnake?"

"Merely a whimsical jest," I said, hoping it was true.

"*Oop*?" Ed asked, resting his chin on the backseat and staring at each of us in turn.

"No," I said. "You stay here and guard the van. And stop beating off. You'll go blind."

That was a lie, of course. If it wasn't a lie, my own vision would have been seriously compromised by now. In fact, it would have been seriously compromised by the time I was fourteen. But Ed was a monkey. He didn't need to know all that.

LENNY AND I slunk through the shadows at the side of the house, avoiding the porch light out front at all costs. There seemed to be no interior lights on at all. Peeking through the windows was like staring into a series of black holes. I had a penlight in my hand, but I was afraid to use it until we got inside. You never knew when a nosyass neighbor might call the cops on a prowler casing the house next door. Lenny and I wanted the police to get involved about as much as we wanted to come face-to-face with Lorraine's pet rattlesnake. If she had one. After all, we weren't exactly on the moral high ground here, even if we did call ourselves detectives. In this case, in fact, what with us about to commit a B&E and all, it was probably much more fitting to simply call us dicks and leave it at that.

There was a toolshed in the backyard. I quietly jiggled the door, and lo and behold, it wasn't locked. I peeked inside with my trusty penlight and saw about what I expected to see. A lawn mower, rakes and shovels, bags of mulch, and a stack of dusty old flower pots standing in the corner. No poisonous reptiles anywhere.

"Nada," Lenny muttered, peering over my shoulder. He sounded relieved.

We gazed back at the house.

Slipping through the shadows like a couple of vaudeville comics, with Lenny pressed up against my back, matching me step for step, we snuck up on what looked like some sort of ramp abutting the house. Sort of like a wheelchair ramp. But that was odd because it didn't lead to a door but to a solid outside wall.

Stepping closer and squinting in the darkness, I realized it was one of those slanted doors that opened upward and afforded access to a series of steps leading down to a basement. Briefly flashing my penlight, I saw the trapdoors were held closed with a simple hook-and-eye latch secured with an old Yale lock.

"Can you open that?" I hissed to Lenny.

"Does a chicken have a pecker?" he hissed back. And bending down while I rolled my eyes, it took him all of twenty seconds to pick the Yale lock and remove it from the hasp.

Together we lifted one side of the basement door, cringing at the squeaks it made. Ducking onto the concrete steps leading down into the shadows beneath the house, we quietly laid the basement door all the way over onto the grass, in case we needed to make a fast escape. We crouched there at the bottom of the steps for a minute, listening.

The basement was as still as a tomb, as was the house above our heads.

I flicked on the penlight and pointed the beam around the room. As far as basements go, this one was fairly typical. Furnace in the corner, washer and dryer up against a sidewall. Built-in shelves on two walls holding everything from cleaning supplies to canned goods to crap the owner was probably too lazy to haul out to the trash. Two expensive bicycles lay tangled in the middle of the floor like they were having sex. What did the bitch do—take Jason Johns's Cannondale in the divorce too? On the final wall, a wooden staircase led up toward the house proper. There was a door standing open at the head of the stairs, with no artificial light shining through it. What did shine through was moonlight from an outside window that spilled into the room above, outlining the door and beckoning us forward.

The wooden stairs creaked beneath our feet.

Lenny climbed behind me, again matching me step for step. "Ack!" he said.

I stopped, and he plowed into me. "What is it?"

"Cobwebs," he growled. "I hate cobwebs."

"Oh, hush. Come on."

We stuck our heads through the door at the top of the basement stairs and looked around. It was the kitchen. The floor appeared to be white tile, which greatly enhanced our ability to see without switching on any lights. Still, I used the penlight sparingly.

The kitchen was neat enough. A couple of dirty dishes and a milk-stained glass lay in the sink. There was not a lot of homey-looking stuff sitting around. No homemade cupcakes cooling on the counter. No mums stuck in vases. No *Joy of Cooking* cookbook splayed open to a favorite recipe.

In fact, Lorraine Johns's kitchen looked like my kitchen. Boring and unused.

I stepped through a side door into another room, and suddenly the house wasn't boring anymore.

We heard a rustle of sound, sort of like dried chickpeas being shaken in a plastic cup. Lenny grabbed my arm and we froze.

"My God," he hissed, "she *does* have a rattlesnake."

I flashed my penlight around the room. The beam of light was trembling like crazy. No surprise there since my knees were knocking too.

Lenny dug his chin into my shoulder and pointed at something up ahead. "What's that?"

It was a cage. A big one. About the size of one of those tiny refrigerators. We stepped closer and peered through the wire mesh at what lay inside.

"Oh crap," Lenny muttered.

It was a rattlesnake, all right. A big long fat one. And it was about to get even fatter because poking out of its mouth was what appeared to be the ass end of a rat. At the ass end of the *snake*, rattles were going a mile a minute, sort of like the way I jiggle my foot when I'm scarfing down a really scrumptious piece of pie. Only my pie doesn't have a tail.

"Eww," Lenny said. "Poor little guy."

I assumed he meant the rat. I trailed the penlight around to take in the rest of the room. There were cages everywhere. Big ones, small ones, some made of wire mesh, some made of glass, like terrariums. Peering into each one, I spotted some form of reptile or other, and none of them looked friendly.

There were Post-it notes stuck to every cage. I spotted names I recognized and names I didn't recognize. What did strike me as absolutely fundamental to know about what we were looking at here was that each and every one of these creatures was venomous. The name tags were neatly typed. Coastal Taipan. Venomous. Many-banded Krait. Venomous. Tiger Snake. Diamondback Rattler (that was our boy with the rat hanging out of its mouth). There was a spitting cobra that was five feet long if it was an inch (we steered well clear of that cage, although it was glass). A rough-skinned newt. Also venomous. A beautiful blue poison dart frog (one of the ones quite possibly from Lenny's Walmart collection). A black mamba and a green mamba, both looking sleek and elegant and meaner than shit. A pair of coral snakes. An uglyass water moccasin. A salamandrid salamander (with a side note beneath its name that read Beware of Venom-tipped Ribs, whatever the hell that meant).

Last but not least, on the floor in the corner sat the biggest cage of all. Inside the box lay the biggest *snake* of all—a king cobra, sleek and black and twelve feet long. It said so on the label. The king cobra was staring right at us.

Holy shit.

I flicked off the penlight and turned to Lenny. "These animals are all illegal."

"But Lorraine Johns is a herbivore."

I sighed. "*Herpetologist*. And it doesn't matter. It's illegal to have venomous animals in a civilian setting. This house is a civilian setting."

Lenny considered that. "So what do you think she's doing with them?"

"Don't know. Black market, like we figured earlier?"

"Maybe." Lenny plucked the penlight from my hand and played it across a tabletop beside him. There was nothing on the table but a single index card. Lenny picked it up and read it.

"What the heck does that mean?" he asked himself.

It was my turn to look over Lenny's shoulder. On the index card, again neatly typed, were five words, all capitalized: Nevada Tenderloin with Rosemary Sauce.

Maybe she does cook after all, I thought. How nice.

"Look at this," Lenny said.

"What?"

"It's a bigass box of rats."

"Say what?" I hustled over to where Lenny was standing by a sideboard. There was a candelabra on either end of the sideboard and a large aluminum box sitting between them. Lenny had lifted the lid on the box and was training the penlight inside. I peered over his shoulder to take a gander myself. He was right. It was a box of rats. They were all staring up at the light shining down on them like a herd of tiny reindeer frozen in the beams of approaching headlights.

"Snake food," I said. "The family pack."

"Let's see what this is," Lenny said, pushing the box of rats aside and opening another box.

I peered over his shoulder into that box and saw about a gazillion crickets. Unlike the rats, they didn't freeze in place when the light hit them. Instead they scattered like cockroaches, swarming over the sides of the box in waves, like gravy slopping over the side of a gravy boat. Five seconds later there were crickets everywhere.

"Oops," Lenny said. "I hope she has a bug man." He was hopping around tap-dancing, trying to jar the crickets off his shoes to keep them from running up his pant legs.

At that moment the cell phone in my back pocket started whistling *Dixie*. I'd been meaning to change that annoying ringtone but was too lazy to do it. With the first wailing note of *Dixie* screeching through the house, Lenny and I jumped four feet straight up into the air. Crickets flew everywhere. Apparently they didn't like my ringtone either. The spitting cobra in the glass terrarium off to our left raised his ugly head and stuck his tongue out, probably trying to decide which way to spit. The diamondback rattler with the rat poking out of its mouth ratchetted up the rattling until it sounded like a maraca player on speed.

Trying not to think about whether I'd made lumpies in my underpants, what with all the excitement going on, I frantically fumbled around with the phone while Lenny clutched his heart. His mouth hung open, and he looked like maybe he was experiencing some sort of coronary infarction. I hit Receive and stuck the phone to my ear.

"What?" I hissed like a snake, which seemed fitting under the circumstances.

At the other end of the call, I heard a voice that irked me even before I figured out what it was saying. The voice belonged to Lester Boggs. I could tell by his vocabulary.

"Where the hell is my goddamn parrot?" he screamed.

I calmly disconnected and took a painful moment to carefully set the ringer to Shut the Fuck Up.

"Who was that?" Lenny asked.

"Wrong number," I said.

"*Orp?*" said a voice in the corner.

Lenny and I jumped again. After we came back down, we whirled to see Ed standing in the middle of the room. In his hands he held a metal terrarium lid. Lenny and I both stared at the lid as if it was the most fascinating thing we'd ever seen in our lives.

"Uh, gee, Mait," Lenny said in a hush. "Where do you suppose Ed got that lid?"

I switched on the penlight and swung its radiant beam toward the glass cage in the corner with the spitting cobra inside. Or should I say, the glass cage in the corner that *used* to have a spitting cobra inside.

The cage was now empty!

"Time to go," I said.

"Yep," Lenny answered. "Ciao."

We took off running like the opening gun at the Boston Marathon had just gone off. Scooping up Ed as we passed, and surprising the bejesus out of him, we hurled ourselves through the kitchen, down the basement steps, and up the other steps into the backyard, where we took five precious seconds to slip the Yale lock back into the hook and eye and relock the basement door. From there we tore around the house and across the street. There we threw ourselves into the van and slammed the doors behind us.

Shuddering and wincing and flapping at our clothes, hoping to dislodge any hitchhiking reptiles or crickets, we finally calmed down enough to stare down at Ed sitting between us. He was still holding the terrarium lid.

Lenny pointed to the half-open window beside my head. "Lookit," he said. "Ed got out by rolling down the window. We can't lock him in the van anymore. He's too smart."

"No way," I said. "Nuh-uh. He's not smart. If he was smart, he would have left the damn lid on the cobra cage." I didn't mention the fact that we weren't so smart, either, or we would have left the damn lid on the cricket box.

"You may have a point," Lenny said. "Shall we go home, then?"

"Yes, let's," I said, still wondering if I needed to shake out my shorts. "We've done all the damage we can do here." I figured no truer words were ever spoken.

"What about the snake?" Lenny asked.

"Let the herbivore worry about it," I said, cranking up the engine.

"What about the crickets?"

"They'll die off in a few weeks."

"What about the rats?" Lenny asked.

"What *about* the rats?"

"I knocked the rat box off the sideboard when we started running. Rats scurried off in every direction. Now the woman has fifty million crickets, a shitload of rats, and one pissed off spitting cobra loose in her house. She's not going to be happy."

"That's okay," I said. "We won't tell her it was us that did it."

"Oh," Lenny said. "Cool. But what if she tells the cops?"

"She's not going to tell the cops. Those animals are illegal!"

"Oh, yeah."

Two minutes later (after tossing the terrarium lid into Lorraine Johns's front yard) we were headed to my apartment, which was no longer *my* apartment but *ours*. Joint residency. What a concept.

We were less than three blocks down the street when we realized we couldn't just walk away. We had to warn the woman.

We stopped at a pay phone outside a 7-Eleven (so she couldn't trace the call) and left a message on Lorraine Johns's answering machine informing her she had a snake loose in the house and not to peek under any furniture looking for it without first donning sunglasses to deflect the snake spit. Speaking through a handkerchief so she wouldn't recognize my voice, I told her she might also find an abundance of crickets and rats running free on the premises and that Truly Nolen, the exterminating company that put mouse ears and mouse tails on their Volkswagens, were rated rather highly on Yelp if she needed a little assistance gathering up the free-range vermin. As for the spitting cobra, she was pretty much on her own with that one.

After that, our guilt appeased, Lenny and I smiled all the way home in the van while Ed happily played with himself in the back.

Chapter Nine

IT'S FUNNY how near-death experiences can rev up the sex drive. Especially when there is a commitment of undying love tossed on top of it like a sprinkling of parmesan cheese over a slab of lasagna.

Lenny and I were all over each other the minute we walked in the apartment door.

While Pudding Pop and Ed squared off for the first time in the living room, both with their pelts sticking straight up like blowfish, Lenny and I pawed at each other all the way into the bedroom, then slammed the door closed behind us when we got there. We were out of our clothes in approximately the same amount of time it takes Ed to peel a banana. After a quick but thorough joint shower, which is always good for aerating a few hormones, Lenny and I tumbled into bed, all smiles and smooches and hard-ons.

"Lover," Lenny said, kissing my throat and molding himself over my body like a seaweed wrap on a ball of sushi.

In the other room we heard squeals and barks and growls and *hoo-hoo*s. I suspected the *hoo-hoo*s could be translated from monkey to human to mean "Why is this yappy-looking rat snarling at me?"

While Pudding Pop was less than gracious with his new houseguest, I was all over myself trying to make Lenny feel at home. I started by flipping around in the bed and cramming his dick down my throat. He was kind enough to reciprocate, and we were off and running. None of this was new, of course. Like I said earlier, we'd been exploring each other's bodies since we were thirteen. There were few surprises left. That didn't mean there wasn't a whole lot of enjoyment still to be had.

Just as my back was beginning to arch and it looked like this particular round of sex was going to be a short one, Lenny flipped me onto my stomach and straddled me with his long legs.

Bending over me, he found the back of my neck with his lips. His hands in my hair and his iron cock resting snugly in the small of my back, he whispered words in my ear I had never heard him say before.

Words that made me tremble, not merely with hunger for the man, but for the sincerity with which he uttered them. His voice was somber and calm, yet they resonated not only with passion, but with longing. This was Lenny at his most beautiful, his most giving. This was a Lenny I had rarely, if ever, seen before.

"I'll do everything in my power to make you happy, Maitland. I think I've known I loved you since the very first time you held me in your arms back in your little bedroom on 33rd Street, with your Batman bedspread on the bed and your folks snoring softly in the other room. Remember? We were in the seventh grade, and it was the first time I slept over. The first time we shared a bed. We were so young your folks probably couldn't have dreamed we were doing what we were doing. But, oh man, Mait, I can still remember the way you tasted that night. Your young come on my lips. The way you cried out when you splattered me with it. The way we held each other afterward. That most of all, I think. The holding. The cuddling that lasted all night long. Your body in my arms, the smoothness of your skin, the way you arched into every touch of my fingers. The way you gave me everything I asked for, and the way you accepted everything I offered you back."

As he spoke, Lenny's lean body sprawled across mine with such all-consuming intimacy I could feel every breath he took, every thud of his heart, every rasp of his leg hair over mine. I smiled at the way his cock strained against my ass, pleading to be let in. The soft pillow of his pubic hair was cotton against my hip. There was the faintest tremble of need in his thighs as they pressed against the back of my legs.

I reached behind me and cupped his head in my hand, twisting around to find his mouth with mine. From inside the kiss, I whispered the words he needed to hear—the words I ached to utter.

"I remember every minute of that night. I remember how amazed I was to realize you wanted the same thing I did. That you wanted me as much as I wanted you. In all the years since, Lenny, I've never stopped wanting you. I think about you all the time. Lately more than I used to. You've grown to be a part of me, I think. A part I know now I can't live without. And wouldn't want to."

I had to stop speaking because his moistened fingertip had lightly come to rest on my opening. I spread my legs wider as he gently stroked me there. His long cock strained against the back of my leg, his hips thrusting gently. With excruciating slowness, he eased himself down farther in the bed, his lips traveling the skin of my back as he moved ever closer to the place I knew he was going. When he pleadingly spread my legs even wider and his mouth found me there at the very center of my hunger, I let out a cry. My utterance made him smile. I could feel it as he tasted me, as his tongue slowly drew itself across the hidden place I so needed it to reach.

When his finger gently entered me and I cried out again, all the while shuddering with desire, he gave a little laugh and reached for the nightstand drawer. He found the oil there and tenderly anointed me with lotion, his finger entering me now so smoothly, so delicately, and with such exquisite care that I gasped and bucked beneath him.

While he pleasured me with his lightly prodding fingertip, I freed a condom from its wrapper and reached around to drop it on my shoulder, where he scooped it up with a kiss of thanks on the back of my neck.

For a long moment, I felt him draw away from me—long enough to roll the condom over his lengthy cock—and the moment it was in place, Lenny rested the head of his dick against the opening he had so lovingly prepared. With his arms pulling me close and my mouth once again twisted around to find his in a kiss, he slowly eased his cock deep inside me.

I experienced his slow entrance into me like I might have experienced a time warp. I remember every heart-stopping centimeter of it. I can still feel his dick pulsing inside me, growing fatter with need, growing ever harder, burying itself ever deeper. His strong hands clutched my hips, his fingertips reaching beneath me to press against my belly as he held me in place—his thumbs on my ass, spreading me wider, exposing me completely. The heat of his breath on my neck was a dream. The way I shuddered and lunged beneath him—wanting him to hurry, wanting him to wait, wanting him to never ever stop doing what he was doing. It was all a confusing mix of pleasure and pain and longing. I squeezed my eyes shut, basking in the tactile sensations of his unrelenting cock sliding effortlessly through me. All I could think about was laying claim to him, wanting him to bury himself inside me where I could forever hold him as my own.

When I was impaled by Lenny completely, he held me unmoving beneath him as I adjusted to his length and thickness. I lay trembling in his arms while I molded my opening around him, accepting his size, getting comfortable, getting even more turned on than I already was.

Only then, only when I was fully relaxed, only when we were truly one, did he begin to rock and move inside me, launching into that slow, easy slide in and out that had me shuddering with need and gasping for air.

Pulling my ass high, he rose up on his knees behind me. Still clutching my hips in his strong gentle hands, he eased my head down onto the bed, positioning me at just the right angle, and only then did he begin to pummel me in earnest.

I buried my face in a pillow and tried not to scream from the sheer joy of feeling Lenny buried to the hilt inside me. Reaching beneath me, I grabbed my cock and began to stroke myself in rhythm to Lenny's long lunges. He was a good fuck, Lenny. He knew all the right moves to make and the right buttons to push. With me, he not only knew them, he had them memorized. Every single one of them.

He continued to slide his cock into me with ever-increasing passion, and when I truly cried out beneath him, no longer even attempting to remain silent, he leaned down over me and whispered in my ear, "Are you ready?"

I could only nod. There was no voice left in me.

While I stroked my cock and Lenny burrowed his own cock deep inside me over and over again, he reached beneath me and cupped my balls in his broad hand. Oh so gently he caressed me there. And that was the touch that led me to orgasm.

My heart bucked inside me, and I cried out as my hand filled with spurting come. And as my own come emptied out of me, Lenny's come shot forth to fill the condom he wore. Our gushing releases were so explosive, we both gave out a gasping laugh of joy.

Ass still high in the air, my face still buried in the pillow, I trembled and shuddered beneath Lenny as he continued to slowly drag his fat cock in and out of me, ever more tenderly, and as his erection slowly dwindled, he at last softly slipped from me completely. Finally we collapsed onto the bed, Lenny's arms still wrapped around me tight.

When I found my voice, I muttered the only words inside my head. "I love you, Lenny."

Once again I felt his smile on the back of my neck and his thudding heart beating against me as he pulled me ever tighter into his arms. I laid my lips to his muscled bicep and savored the soft heat of his skin, the rolling muscle beneath his satin flesh, the silky smoothness. The heavenly scent of him poured through me.

He whispered into my ear on a ragged breath, "I love you too, Mait. I always have."

It was the response I most needed to hear. And the response I knew to be the absolute truth. I didn't doubt Lenny's words for a second.

Those words thundered through me, swelling my heart, even as I slipped into sleep in his arms.

LENNY AND I sat goo-goo eyed at breakfast, slurping down coffee, annihilating a box of donuts, and playing toesies under the kitchen table. We constantly reached out to each other, touching a hand, brushing fingers over a warm arm, tweaking an earlobe. We sighed over our coffee cups, batted eyelashes, and made swoony faces like a couple of heartsick schoolgirls. For two guys who had been bonking each other since middle school, it was pretty funny. Even we saw the humor in it.

But it was also a testament to how we truly felt about each other that we could come this far over such a long expanse of time and only now, at this late date, have the good sense to step back and admit to our feelings. No love at first sight for us. We needed long years of buildup to make it happen. Or did we? Maybe our "love at first sight" epiphany had simply been lost in the mind-numbing flurry of puberty, camouflaged in the thrill of sexual discovery in each other's arms when we were little more than kids. Maybe there was love between Lenny and me then, but we were too immature and horny and rambunctious to see it.

Well, we saw it now. But love wasn't the only emotion raging through the Carter/Fritz household that morning. There was considerable crankiness on display as well.

The crankiness came from the two lesser species perched at the table. Pudding Pop sat trembling in fury over a bowl of kibble at one end of the table, trying to chew and growl at the same time. He constantly cast murderous glances at the other end of the table where Ed sat, starting his day with the breakfast of champions—a banana and a bowl of Froot Loops. Ed's eyelids were squeezed into two hate-filled slits as he glared back at Pudding Pop. Every once in a while, his little hand came up, his middle digit rose up out of his furry fist, and he gave my dog the finger. When he did, Pudding Pop's snarling and trembling intensified until the kibble was dribbling out of his jaws and every tooth in his little head came out to play. A six-pound Cujo, insulted to the core, rabid and cruel and ready to kill.

We supposed Ed and Pudding Pop would either grow accustomed to each other or kill each other in their own good time. The decision was up to them. Lenny and I had other things to worry about.

"What's on the agenda for today?" Lenny asked. His eyes warmed as, underneath the table, his toes slid through the hair on my shin. "Maybe we should stay in bed all day, Mait. I can think of a few moves I'd like to try out now that we're a committed couple and all."

I laughed. "Your moves will have to wait. We have bigger fish to fry."

"*Harrumph*," Lenny said.

I tried to hide a grin. "And what happened to the poet of last night? You were so eloquent and romantic and sweet. Now all you want to do is shag."

"*Harrumph*," Lenny said again. "You didn't seem to mind the shagging last night."

"Yes, and today I can barely walk."

The phone gave a jangle. I reached out and plucked it off the counter.

"'Lo," I said, while Lenny reached under the table and slid his hand inside my boxer shorts, tugging Mait Junior out into the open air and cradling him in his fist. He stroked his thumb across my slit, and my eyes crossed. I tried to find my voice while my dick began to lengthen in his hand.

"Maitland, here," I gasped into the mouthpiece. It took every ounce of concentration I could muster to focus on the voice in my ear instead of the hand on my crotch. I finally had to slap Lenny's hand away completely. He gave a malicious chuckle and went back to his donut, leaving my brand-new hard-on to fend for itself.

The call was one I had been expecting. It was Lorraine Johns, and she didn't sound happy. At least she was alive. She hadn't died from snakebite. I have to admit I was relieved about that, even if I did hate the bitch. I reached over and hit Speaker so Lenny could eavesdrop.

"Someone broke into my house last night, *Mr.* Carter, and I think we both know who it was."

"My partner and I were nowhere near your house last night," I said, lying through my teeth. Lenny stifled a merry gurgle.

"Not you, you moron!" she snapped. "Jason! He broke into my house and made a mess."

"What do you mean?" I asked, trying to be sly. "Define mess."

If I had thought she would admit to the truth about her little break-in, I quickly realized I was mistaken. She stammered over her answer for a moment, then grudgingly said, "He made a mess is all."

"Is anything missing?" I asked, trying to be even slyer. *A spitting cobra perhaps? Two hundred rats? A gazillion fucking crickets?*

"No," she all but snarled. "Nothing is missing."

"And you have everything back where it's supposed to be?" *In other words, did you catch the snake before it spit in your eye, bit your foot, and sent your cranky ass to herpetology heaven?*

"Yes," she said with teeth-grinding patience. "Everything is back where it's supposed to be."

Lenny clapped his hand over his mouth, trying not to laugh out loud. He silently mouthed the C-word, then stuffed more donut into his mouth. He was smiling from ear to ear.

"Then, all's well that ends well," I crooned. "Was there anything else you wanted this fine morning?"

I could picture her sitting at the other end of the line, vibrating in fury. But all she said was, "Find my lizard, Mr. Carter. I'm tired of putzing around with all this. I have a business to run."

My ears perked up at that. Even Lenny stopped chewing to listen. "What sort of business?" I asked. "And how could your business rely on the return of a lizard?"

"Never you mind," she snapped. "Just find him."

I thought I'd get a little dig in, for the chuckle factor of pissing her off a bit more. "The next time you're broken into, perhaps you should call the police. You hired us to find your missing property. Burglary is a totally different matter. We don't investigate burglaries." *Unless we were the ones who did the burglarizing.*

We heard a clattering crash on the speakerphone. It sounded like someone tossing a plate into a kitchen sink. Lorraine Johns *really* wasn't happy.

"I'll remember that," she snarled. The next thing we heard was a dial tone. She'd hung up.

"She's afraid to call the cops," Lenny said. "You were right. She's up to something that isn't kosher, and frankly, Mait, I'm starting to get a little worried about the safety of all those animals caged up in her house. I know there isn't one decent pet in the whole lot, nothing that wouldn't kill you as soon as look at you, but it still doesn't make it right that she's treating them like merchandise. I've got a bad feeling about this."

Then he turned toward the window and, in a dreamy, pondering voice, muttered the words, "Nevada tenderloin with rosemary sauce."

"What?"

"Nothing," he said. "Forget it."

I turned my attention back to Pudding Pop and Ed. "Are you two going to slaughter each other if we leave you on your own?"

Pudding Pop growled. Ed said, "*Hoo-hee*," then yawned. I reckoned that was as good a response as I was ever likely to get.

"Well, good, then," I said. "And see that you don't."

I snapped open the morning paper, and with Lenny leaning over my shoulder, we checked the want ads for lost pets. A morning ritual for us. Nothing caught our attention, so twenty minutes later, we were fully dressed and headed out the door. We walked both beasts through the neighborhood on leashes so they could tinkle and stuff (and there was a gargantuan amount of stuff—from both of them). Once they were empty, we locked them in the apartment, still snarling at each other, and headed out the door to begin our day.

The two pet dicks were back on the job. The only difference being that now we were most definitely an item. And I couldn't have been happier.

Fancy Arthur spotting it first. I couldn't wait to tell him he'd been right all along.

WE HAD no more than unlocked the office door and stepped inside when the phone rang.

"Your parrot's in my mom's backyard," a young voice said. The voice was cracked and raw and sounded to be in the throes of puberty. I remembered that condition well from living through it myself, words creaking and croaking and jumping from one octave to another in the middle of every sentence. It was embarrassing. Not to mention the hormones driving you nuts. Oy, the hormones. *Poor kid.*

"Where are you located?" I asked.

"On Felton," the kid said. "Just beyond the overpass. At 7312. You can't miss it. It's the house with the stupid ugly yellow mailbox out front. My mom painted it."

I remembered that too, being embarrassed by everything your parents did.

"Okay, son, we'll find it. That's only a few blocks away. What's your name?"

He cleared his throat, trying to settle on a register. "Jamie. Are you bringing your partner?"

"Sure. We work together. Why wouldn't I bring my partner?"

"Are you the white one?"

"Uh, yeah, why? Do you know us?"

"Seen you around is all. I'll be waiting for you out front. Thanks, Maitland."

The kid threw my name out there like he'd known me since he graduated from Pampers to Underoos. What the hell was that all about?

Before I could ask, he'd hung up. I turned to Lenny, who was already eyeing me like he thought a tumble on the Hide-A-Bed in the back room would be a great way to start the day. Hormones indeed.

"It's Toodles," I said. "There's been another sighting. Let's roll."

Lenny executed a judicious crotch adjustment on the front of his blue jeans (stiffies are such an annoyance in the workplace), then swung open the office door and salami-salami-baloneyed me out into the street. We took the van.

We found the stupid ugly yellow mailbox on Felton right off the bat. Our jaws dropped into our laps when we saw the kid leaning against it, waiting for us.

Little Master Jamie was a dish. He looked about fifteen or sixteen and wore cutoffs that were cropped so short they barely hid anything at all. One good shake and the kid's semen dispenser would have flopped out into the morning light like a python tumbling out of a tree. I say python because, judging by the bulge in said cutoffs, Little Master Jamie, unless he had his schoolbooks tucked in there, was hung like no schoolkid should ever be hung. He also wore a chopped off T-shirt that barely covered his nicely delineated pecs. He had actual honest-to-God abs, a teeny-tiny belly button that looked like it was made to be licked, and nice golden legs that were well-muscled and tempting as hell. Imagining them splayed wide was enough to make my vision blur and my heart race.

Sweet Jesus.

Just looking at the kid would probably warrant eight to ten in a California penal system maximum-security lockup.

I turned to Lenny and said, "Stop slobbering."

Lenny merely nodded and wiped a dribble of drool off his chin.

The kid's face lit up when we climbed out of the van. I was astounded to see that little Jamie eyed us up and down the same way we'd eyed him. And I mean exactly the same way.

Lenny gave a low whistle beside me and muttered, "We're in over our heads."

"Just be professional," I whispered back. "And try not to stare at his crotch."

"Yeah, right," Lenny said, but then he planted a phony smile on his face and stuck his hand out as we approached the lad. "You must be Jamie," Lenny said, not sounding like a lech at all. Who knew he had such acting skills?

Jamie beamed into a heart-stopping smile. One handsome kid. He rested his hand on his bare stomach, and I found myself envying the hell out of that hand. With his other hand, he brushed the front of his cutoffs, as if checking to make sure the goods were still there. I envied that hand most of all.

Handshakes ensued, and all the while we were shaking hands, Jamie's eyes roamed over our bodies like the lad was starving and we were a couple of Hungry-Man dinners. While his hand was still in mine and I was molding my face into that face you always try to make when you're being businesslike and attempting to act mature, I felt the kid's fingertip drag itself across my palm in a way that can only be described as lingeringly.

If this young man wasn't gay, then I was not carbon-based and Lenny wasn't a walking sex machine. Speaking of which, Lenny seemed to have arrived at the same conclusion I had. And unlike me, Lenny appeared to have pulled himself together well enough to realize he wasn't liking it much.

"Kid, what's this all about? Is Toodles really here, or did you just drag us here to check out our packages?"

Jamie's cocksureness faltered. He gulped and his eyes shifted from Lenny, to me, then back to Lenny.

"The bird is in the back. We've got chickens back there. He's in with the chickens eating the chicken feed."

"No kidding?"

"No kidding."

"So why are you cruising us?"

"Was it that obvious?"

"Hell yes, it was that obvious. My balls are still blushing."

The kid looked hopeful. "Can I see?"

It was my turn to jump in. "Kid, what is it, exactly, you want? And don't say sex, because it ain't going to happen."

"I want to work with you. Both of you."

"What do you mean you want to work with us?"

"I want to be a gay pet detective like you guys are. I saw you moving into your new office. I—I liked the way you looked. I think we could—" Here the kid had so much blood rush into his face I thought his ears were going to ignite, but he straightened his shoulders and blurted out what he wanted to say anyway. "—I think we could have a lot of fun working together. If—if you know what I mean."

Lenny and I both knew what he meant. If the staff from the San Diego District Attorney's Office had been present, they would have known what the kid meant too, but I'm afraid they would have been a wee bit less amused by the circumstances than we were.

"What makes you think we're gay?" Lenny asked.

It was obviously the wrong question. The kid bit back a chuckle of incredulity as if to say "Who the hell *wouldn't* know you're gay?"

"Your ass," Lenny growled.

"Look, kid," I said, "we're flattered. But have you ever heard the term 'jailbait'?"

Lenny popped in to help me out. "Or chicken hawk?"

"Or diaper dabbler?"

"Or pedophile?"

"Or 'life in prison without the possibility of parole'?" Lenny and I both threw in as a last resort.

Jamie's face fell, and all the while it was falling, it got even redder. "You think I'm too young."

"You *are* too young!" Lenny railed.

"I'm sixteen and a half!"

"That's *still* too young!"

I stepped up and gave the lad a gentle slap on the cheek, half-playful, half-serious. "Snap out of it, kid. We understand how you're feeling. We don't quite understand why you're feeling that way about *us*, but that's beside the point. We were your age once. In fact we were younger than you are now when we started having the feelings you're having. What you need to do is find somebody your own age. Somebody who feels the same way you do. Somebody who it isn't illegal for you to couple with. But even if you do find somebody your own age, don't rush it, kid. You've got your whole life ahead of you. And don't throw it away on a couple of old farts like me and Lenny."

"You could have left *that* part out," Lenny grumbled.

"And don't waste your time being a pet detective either," I lectured like the father I was thankful I knew I'd never ever be. "I think you've probably got better accomplishments than that waiting for you. Don't sell yourself short. And speaking of shorts, don't speak to any other gay men wearing that outfit you've got on, or they might not have the willpower Lenny and I have."

"One more thing," Lenny said. "Mait and I are in love. You wouldn't want to come between two guys in love, would you? Trust me. You don't want to be the other woman. It never works out the way you think it will."

Jamie took umbrage at that. "I'm not a woman. I'm a man."

Lenny took umbrage at *that*. "Not yet, you're not. Although you're damn close to it."

We saw tears rise in the boy's eyes. His chin made a sad little dimple. "You think I'm an idiot."

"No," I said. "We think you're like we were at your age. Oversexed and riddled with testosterone. You're a walking hard-on, to put it bluntly." I chucked him on the arm, hoping to bring him out of his funk. "Maybe we'll call for your help now and then when we have a real important case come up. How would that be?"

His eyes brightened. "Really? You'd do that?"

"Sure. Why not? But if you work for us, you have to wear real clothes. I'll already have to bonk Lenny three days straight to calm him down after he's been standing here looking at you half-dressed in front of us."

"Really?" the kid said again. If he'd won the lottery, he'd have the same expression on his face.

"Yup," Lenny said, his face serious and pained. "'Fraid so."

Then we all laughed.

"Now let's go snag Toodles. And keep your ears closed, kid. This bird's got a mouth on him like you wouldn't believe."

"So do I," the kid said with a wink, causing me to blush.

"Jesus, son," Lenny groaned. "You're killing us here. If you were five years older, you'd be in big, big trouble."

"Then I wish I was five years older," Jamie lamented, and he lamented it like he meant it.

I pointed to the corner of the house. "The bird, Teaser Boy. Let's go get the frigging bird."

The kid had been telling the truth. Toodles was standing in a fenced-off part of the backyard, mingling with a pack of chickens. The makeshift citified chicken coop held ten or twelve hens. They were all pecking at a bowl of chicken feed, chattering about the weather, and being sociable, and while the chickens were clucking and cock-a-doodling like chickens always do, Toodles was doing what Toodles always did. He was cussing like a sailor. It sounded like a meet and greet for spinster aunts and Tourette syndrome sufferers.

"*Cluck, pcawk, cluck.*"

"Fuck a duck, fuckface."

"*Cluck, cluck, cluck!*"

"Blow me! Suck a wet one!"

"*Cluck, cluck, cluck, pcawk, cluck.*"

"Butthole sniffers unite!"

"Jesus," Jamie said. "Glad my mom's not listening to this. Whoever taught this parrot to talk must have a few issues to work around."

"No kidding," I said. "We've met the guy. His name is Lester Boggs, and he's quite the orator."

Lenny laughed and stepped over the low fence as quietly as he could so as not to scare the parrot. Toodles seemed to be entranced by a Rhode Island Red who was making feather-fluffing motions of intrigue as she stared at the parrot, like maybe she was in the mood for some funky interspecies sexcapades with the mangy runt who'd popped in from God knows where for breakfast. What a slut.

"We forgot the bird net," Lenny groaned. "I'll have to wing it."

"So wing it, then," I grinned, figuring this was going to be good.

Lenny crouched forward like a sneak thief and delicately tiptoed over and around and through the herd of chickens, approaching Toodles from the rear. Toodles was too busy eyeballing the slutty red hen to take notice of the pet detective creeping up on his ass from behind.

"Hey, Lenny," Jamie whispered. "Watch out for Harold."

Lenny ignored the kid, but I didn't. "Who's Harold?" I asked, as Lenny stepped ever closer to Toodles, who was now bobbing his head and bristling his feathers, what feathers he had left, and puffing out his skinny chest in an attempt to look manly for the horny hen's benefit.

"Harold is the rooster over there in the corner. The big one." Jamie's mouth turned up into a grin. "He's a character all right. And he hates people."

"Oh, don't be silly. Why would a rooster hate people?" I guffawed.

But my guffaw died in my throat when Harold the rooster let out a cock-a-doodling roar and leapt skyward like a Samurai warrior, his three-foot wingspan flapping like crazy. A cloud of dust billowed around him like a helicopter taking off. He brought his spurs up to attack position, clicked them in place like a couple of air-to-surface missiles and, launching himself through the air, descended with a scream of fury on Lenny's unsuspecting head.

Lenny screamed like a little girl and blindly took off running. He tried to sail over the mob of chickens in his path, but tripped over his own feet and landed splat in their midst. Feathers flew everywhere. While the startled biddies flapped around, squawking and clucking and cackling in panic, Harold continued flapping and gouging and digging at Lenny's head with his spurs while both Lenny and the rooster rolled around in the chicken shit and birdseed, mowing pullets down left and right and causing even more pandemonium than had already been unleashed. Lenny was sounding considerably like Toodles by this time, cussing and swearing and frantically trying to pry the rooster's claws out of his scalp.

During the melee Jamie and I were doubled over with laughter by the fence, and Toodles was sitting on the roof of the henhouse staring down at the unholy fracas unfolding below like a pissyass schoolmarm overseeing a pack of juvenile delinquents.

"Fucktoads!" Toodles squawked, dumping a load of parrot poop to lighten his ballast. Then lifting off with a grunt, he sailed over Jamie and me heading east, as if to say "Well, I'm never coming *here* for breakfast again! These chickens are *nuts*."

Lenny was screaming to high heaven with a furious Harold now clamped in his hands. Lenny wrestled with the rooster while the rooster pecked, flapped, and flashed its spurs at anything he could reach, which was pretty much every appendage Lenny possessed.

Lenny finally gave a great heave and threw the rooster twenty feet through the air like a football. The moment he was free from the insane Harold, who was hauling himself to his feet and looked like he was gathering up strength and rearming his missiles for round two, Lenny took off running again, sailed over the fence like an Olympian hurdle jumper and didn't stop until he plowed head-on into a tree on the south end of the lawn. The instant he hit the tree, his body went rigid like a two-by-four, and he keeled over backward in a dead faint. He'd knocked himself out.

Jamie and I rushed to Lenny's side and stared down at him lying there on the grass covered in feathers and chicken droppings. There was a perfect indentation of tree bark on his forehead, and he was softly snoring. Still out like a light, Lenny gave a dainty cough, and a feather flew out of his mouth.

"That's disconcerting," Jamie said.

"No kidding," I said. "Those feathers are nasty with mites and stuff. Think we should pick him up?"

Jamie frowned. "I ain't touching him."

"Me either. He stinks."

"That's because he's covered with chicken poop."

"I know."

Jamie sighed. "Nobody ever listens to me. I told him to watch out for Harold."

Chapter Ten

LENNY WAS sitting slumped over in the office chair with his forehead on the desk, arms splayed wide. He had Band-Aids on his cheeks and one on each ear. There was a wet hand towel plastered to the back of his noggin, and it was stained pink with blood. I noticed a couple of bald patches on the top of his head where the rooster had plucked him bare. For self-preservation's sake—mine—I decided not to mention the bald patches.

"I hate chickens," Lenny mumbled.

"I thought you hated Toodles," I said.

"I hate Toodles too."

"How's your head?"

Lenny raised up and glared at me. "I haven't heard you complain about it lately."

I shot him a glare. "You know what I mean."

"Well, if you must know, my head is sore. That goddam chicken almost killed me."

"Harold," I said, fighting against a smile. "His name was Harold."

"Who the hell would name a rooster Harold? They should have named him Hitler. Or Manson. Or Ted Bundy. And after they named him, they should have dunked his feathery ass in a deep fat fryer all the way up to his wattles until he was nice and crisp and dead."

I couldn't hold it back any longer. I laughed.

"Glad you're amused," Lenny groused.

He plucked the bloodstained towel off his head, gazed at it a minute as if wondering how much blood loss he had actually sustained, then tossed it in a wastebasket. His head looked better without the bloody rag on it, but his clothes were still stained with chicken poop, and he still had the occasional feather protruding here and there. He still smelled too. Lenny really needed a bath.

"I've been thinking," I said. "We should hire Jamie to do some of the footwork on our missing animal cases. Like Danny's puppy, maybe. And the gerbil."

"I don't think we should let Jamie loose within 500 feet of Arthur. Jamie's at an impressionable age. I'd hate to be the one to have to explain to the kid's mother why her son is suddenly wearing ball gowns and dressing like Donna Reed."

"Maybe you're right. Still he could scrounge through the neighborhood looking for the puppy. He could keep his eyes peeled for Toodles too. It would free us up to work our other cases."

"How much are we going to pay him? We're poor, you know. We'd have to double our earnings to reach the poverty level."

"We'll tell him he's working on commission. Ten percent of any rewards or payments we receive on the cases he solves. We can afford that. Chances are he wouldn't solve anything anyway."

"This isn't a lecherous attempt to get closer to the little hottie is it? You and I have only been lovers a day and a half. You're not already seeking out fresher meat, I hope."

"Don't be stupid. He's just a kid. Meat that fresh could give us life without parole in cellblock Q. Still, he wants to help out. Where's the harm in letting him try? A couple of intelligent gay role models in his life would do him good."

Lenny gaped at me as if a palm tree had sprouted from the top of my head. "You're not talking about *us*, are you?"

I lost my momentum. "Well, yeah. Although I guess calling us intelligent role models is putting a high gloss on the facts."

"Might be a bit of a stretch."

Still, Lenny considered the Jamie question for all of ten seconds. Then he slapped his hand on the desk and announced, "I think it's a great idea! Jamie can work the cases after school and on weekends, or whenever he has some free time. He'll be an extra pair of eyes for us."

"Eye candy, more like it."

"You say that like it's a bad thing," Lenny said with a grin. Two seconds later his own eyes narrowed as his thoughts shifted.

"I've been thinking too," he said.

"Uh-oh. That can't be good."

"Shut up. I've been thinking we need to stake out the snake lady again. We should have followed her last night when she drove off. She had a couple of her animals with her, and she was dressed to the nines. What the hell was that all about? Who dons their best little black dress, slips into a pair of heels, does their hair up in a chignon, then grabs a couple of venomous reptiles and heads out for a night on the town?"

I considered that. "Hmm. I never quite thought of it that way before. What do you think she was up to? Where was she going?"

Lenny shrugged. "I don't have a clue. I think we should find out, though. I'd also like to know if, when she came home, she brought two empty cages back with her."

"You think she was making an illegal delivery of poisonous reptiles?"

"Or worse," Lenny said slyly.

"What do you mean, worse? What could possibly be worse?"

"Nothing. Just a theory I have. If I find one tiny shred of evidence that backs up the theory, I'll tell you all about it. Otherwise, you'll think I'm nuts, so I won't."

"Give me a hint."

"No."

"Just one little hint. Please."

He pulled a chicken feather out of his shirt pocket, gazed at it strangely, then tossed it over his shoulder. "Fine. Rosemary sauce."

"Rosemary sauce? That's your hint?"

"That's it."

Lenny crossed his arms on top of his chest, trying to look smug. It didn't work. It's hard to look smug when you're covered with chicken shit.

"I'm intrigued," I said.

That perked Lenny right up. "I like it when you're intrigued, Mait. Want to take a siesta in the back room?" He cast me a wink, trying to be alluring through all the Band-Aids on his face, which is no easy feat.

I reached over and plucked a feather from his ear. "Lenny," I said, "have you smelled yourself lately?"

"What's that supposed to mean?"

"It's supposed to mean we are never having sex again until you take a bath. A long one. With sterilizers and perfumes and bubble bath and quite possibly kerosene and sandpaper and one of those metal brushes they use to scrub rust and barnacles off the bottom of ships."

"Then take me home," he said.

"My home or your home?" I asked.

"I don't have a home. Remember? Neither do you. Only *we* have a home. Together. And I think we should make our home *your* place because you've got all the animals and more square footage. There's also more food in your refrigerator than there is in mine. So your apartment it is."

I tapped my heart. "So romantic. I could swoon."

"Don't," he said. "I just tried it, and it wasn't any fun at all."

"You didn't swoon," I said. "You knocked yourself out cold by running into a tree while fleeing from an irate chicken."

"Please don't ever put it that way again."

I tutted I was sorry and led him through the door. The van was right outside. We hopped in and headed for the apartment. *Our* apartment. I rolled the windows down and hung my head outside until we got there.

WITH LENNY all cleaned up and scabbed over, we leashed up Pudding Pop and Ed and took them for a stroll through the neighborhood while keeping our eyes peeled for Toodles and Fido. Pudding Pop had done his business in the cat box again, so I was thrilled. If he kept it up, I would have to decide what to do with the twenty-three bottles of 409 I had bought on sale at CVS.

While Pudding Pop had been a good little doggy, Ed had been the houseguest from hell. In fact, he had peed on the living room window. I knew it was Ed because Pudding Pop's little Chihuahua pecker couldn't reach that high. I was less than thrilled with Ed. Still, I couldn't hate him.

"What are we going to do with this monkey?" I asked. I smiled down at the little guy, who kept staring behind him as if he were being stalked by another monkey. The other monkey was his shadow. He was so cute I could hardly stand it, but still, decisions needed to be made about his future. He couldn't stay with us.

Pudding Pop didn't look as enamored of the simian as I was. He still growled and snarled and slobbered himself into an epileptic seizure every time Ed came within three feet of him.

"I've been thinking about Ed," Lenny said. "I think we should tell Jason Johns we're coming around to his way of thinking and that we'd be willing to snoop on his ex-wife instead of snooping on him like we were paid to do if certain conditions were met."

"What conditions? And what does that have to do with Ed?"

Lenny shot me his patented Hercule Poirot eyebrow wag, trying to look clever. All he succeeded in doing was looking as cute as Ed. Or he would have looked as cute as Ed if he hadn't had so many scabs on his head and holes in his hair and Band-Aids on his face from the homicidal rooster attack.

"Johns works at the zoo, Mait. We can tell him we'll help bring his wife to justice, if she really is doing something illegal, which you and I both know she probably is. Since he'd like nothing more than to get back at the bitch for ruining him in the divorce, and since he's just as worried about those animals in her care as we are, we can tell him in payment for our services, we would like him to arrange for the San Diego Zoo to take Ed."

Ed said "*Erp?*" at the sound of his name. I stared down at him.

"Lenny, that's brilliant! Ed will be with his own kind, we won't be stuck with an illegal monkey—no offense, Ed—and Pudding Pop won't be plotting ways to kill the poor little guy when we're not around."

"Just how big *was* Jason Johns's dick?" Lenny asked.

I bopped him on the shoulder. "Never you mind. What about Leroy? Your brother?"

Lenny shrugged. "I don't know how big Leroy's dick is. I haven't seen it since he was eight."

"No, dumbass. The monkey. What's he going to say if we give his monkey to the zoo?"

"Oh. Leroy'll have to suck it up. Besides, one of these days he's going to do something so far outside the law that he'll be shipped off to Chino state pen for years on end, and where would Ed be then?"

"You're right. We'll be doing Ed a favor. He'll finally have some security. At the zoo Ed'll get a proper monkey diet by experts who know how to care for exotic animals, and he might even find a girlfriend so he won't have to spend the rest of his life beating off."

Lenny grinned. "Wild monkey sex with an actual monkey partner! That's the ticket, huh, Ed? A slutty girlfriend or two? Maybe even a harem? An occasional kernel of popcorn tossed your way by some marauding child? Lounging around doing nothing but picking fleas and looking handsome for the tourists? What a life!"

Ed climbed Lenny like a tree and perched himself on Lenny's shoulder. He flung his little monkey arms wide and screeched, "*Hoo-hoo-hoo-hee-hoo!*"

"Guess that means yes," Lenny said, laughing.

At that moment—at that *precise* moment—I had an epiphany. I don't have many epiphanies, you know. It was quite an occasion.

My mind went back to Jamie. He was sixteen and a half. That meant he probably had a driver's license. And if he had a driver's license, he probably had a car. Or if he didn't have a car, I wondered if he knew how to drive a Mini Cooper and was smart enough to read a road map.

Hmm. Lenny didn't know it yet, but he and I might have just solved *two* problems instead of one.

The monkey and the gerbil.

While Lenny was busy bagging up a long winding trail of Chihuahua poop, with Ed still perched on his shoulder, I slipped behind a tree and hauled out my cell phone.

Jamie, the little hottie, answered on the first ring.

"LET'S TAKE your car," Lenny said. "My van's making funny noises."

"Your van is always making funny noises. And we can't take my car. It's—um—in the shop."

"When did that happen?"

"Doesn't matter. We've got other irons in the fire to worry about."

"Such as?"

"Such as your ass."

"Ooh, I like the sound of that."

It was midafternoon, and we were waiting for Jason Johns to get home from work after herding reptiles at the San Diego Zoo all day. Lenny and I looked a little better. Our wounds were mostly bloodless now—mine from the rosebushes, his from the homicidal chicken—and as soon as our scabs fell off, and we both removed our bloody Band-Aids, and Lenny's hair grew out in the spots where Harold had ripped it from his scalp, we would look as good as new.

"But what's wrong with your car?" Lenny persisted. "Is it going to cost a fortune to fix?"

"Doesn't matter," I said. "Don't worry about it."

Lenny opened his mouth to say God knows what, when a furious funnel cloud spun through the shop door. The funnel cloud had a bald head, hairy ears, and tossed out a debris field of obscenities for twenty feet in every direction. The funnel cloud was Lester Boggs, and he wasn't happy.

"How dare you fucking hang up on me! How dare you sit around this fuckhole of a storefront instead of searching high and low for poor Toodles! How dare you take my three hundred fucking dollars, then go prancing through the fucking park with a fucking mutt and a fucking monkey!"

"You saw us?" Lenny asked.

"Damn right I saw you! I been watching. Safeguarding my investment."

"Sneaky," Lenny said, as if he actually admired the old twit for not trusting us. Then he toned the admiration down considerably. "As for your stupid bird, we had a sighting this morning. Toodles managed to elude capture, causing great risk to my own personal welfare, I might add, but we are hopeful there will be another sighting soon. Toodles isn't exactly a stealth bomber. Since he's got a foul mouth on him—get it? Fowl mouth?—that perfectly replicates your own, what with him throwing out a 'fuck this' and 'fuck that' every five seconds, which he learned from *you*, I expect we'll hear from Toodles soon enough. No doubt he'll be strafing the city with fuck bombs any minute now as he flies over spitting obscenities and pooping on every head that doesn't dive for cover."

Boggs's face grew cherry red, and his neck bulged out like a bullfrog's. Before he started ranting and raving again, I squeezed myself into the conversation. I patted Lenny's chest to hush him up, then I draped my arm over the old man's shoulder and steered him toward the door.

"Just let us do our job, sir. Go home to your lovely wife and pray for Toodles's well-being."

"And a lovely thing the little woman is too—for a dump truck," Lenny muttered out the window.

"Like my partner says," I butted in, "I'm sure Toodles will turn up soon. He looked healthy when we saw him last, but he's a wily little guy. He misses you too, I'm sure."

"Like who wouldn't, you're so frigging charming?" Lenny sniped at a passing motorbus.

I gave him a gentle kick in the ankle to shut him up, then turned back to Boggs. "You should probably stay close to home in case Toodles decides to return of his own volition. I'm sure he misses his happy home."

"And his uglyass cast iron bird cage with the wall-to-wall parrot poop on the floor," Lenny muttered to the California sky.

"And if Toodles does return on his own," Lenny continued, mumbling to the sky, "don't expect your fee back! We've already spent it on Band-Aids and Neosporin trying to capture the little prick!"

Boggs cast a leery eye at Lenny. "What's he saying?" he demanded. "He keeps mumbling over there. Is he being snotty?"

I patted Boggs on the back and bum-rushed him out the door. "No snottiness going on here, no siree. My partner wouldn't know snottiness if it bit him on the ass. No, sir."

Boggs sputtered and frothed. "Well, I… well, I—"

And that was all he got out. I all but threw him through the door and slammed it in his face. The last I saw of Lester Boggs, he was muttering and cussing his way down the street, casting an eye skyward every five seconds, no doubt scanning for Toodles in the firmament. Good luck with that.

To Lenny I growled, sarcastic as hell, "Maybe we should put you in charge of customer relations. What do you think?"

Lenny shrugged. "The guy's a wart."

"Yes," I said. "But he's a paying wart."

"*Harrumph*," Lenny blustered. Then he rolled his chocolate eyes over me, and I saw his bluster turn to heat. The good kind.

"Speaking of biting my ass…," he said around a leer.

"No time," I said. "It's almost the hour for Jason Johns to get home. Let's run back to the apartment, grab Ed so we'll have something to bargain with, and make our deal with the guy with the big dick."

"Come on, Mait. Tell me. Exactly how big is it?" Lenny asked for the tenth time.

I rolled my eyes and dragged him to the van. "Jeez, give it a rest."

On the way to the apartment, we left all the van windows down because the vehicle still reeked of chicken poop. An occasional feather wafted out the window in the wind as we rumbled down the street. Lenny continued to cast lascivious glances my way as I drove.

I loved him for that.

We were home in no time. Before stepping through the apartment door, we heard the television blaring out the theme song from *Days of Our Lives*. I knew we hadn't left the TV on. Had we been broken into? Had a burglarizing housewife let herself in through a back window with a brick to steal the silverware and catch up on her soaps?

Lenny and I rushed through the door and were greeted by—no one. No Pudding Pop. No Ed.

It was instantly made clear why Ed didn't greet us at the door. He was the one watching *Days of Our Lives*. He was parked in my big recliner with a huge bag of Cheetos in his lap, munching away. His little hands and half his face were orange with Cheetos dust. I was afraid to look and see if his pecker was orange too.

I set off in search of Pudding Pop. He should have been at the door at the first sound of our footfalls outside, hopping excitedly around, waiting for us to step across the threshold so he could give us his usual Chihuahua kisses of hello and getting so excited he would piddle on our shoe tops. But there was nothing. No barks, no whines, no yips, no tippy-tappy toenails on the linoleum, nothing.

After going from room to room and searching everywhere, I ran back to the living room and stared down at Ed sitting in my recliner. Was it my imagination, or was he looking guilty?

"Ed," I said, "where's Pudding Pop?"

Ed hoisted the Cheetos bag and thrust it toward me, offering to share. "*Erp?*"

"No, I don't want Cheetos. Where the hell is my dog, Ed?"

Lenny dropped down to his knees in front of the recliner and gently clasped Ed's foot, getting his attention. "Where's Pudding Pop, Ed? What have you done with him?"

Ed wrapped his tail around Lenny's arm, and craning his head around, he pointed toward the front door. "*Orp,*" he said. "*Orp-eep.*"

"You didn't!" Lenny gasped.

I wasn't sure who was making less sense. Lenny or the monkey. "Are you telling me you understand what he's saying?" I asked.

"It's pretty obvious," Lenny said, and he didn't look too happy when he said it.

"What is?" I asked, my heart sinking like a rock inside my chest. "What's pretty obvious?"

Lenny sighed. He cast a sad gaze at first Ed, then at me. "He's gone," Lenny said. "Pudding Pop is gone. Ed set him loose."

"He *what?*"

"He opened the door and let him out."

I tried not to bellow, but the words came out in a screaming rush anyway. "Well, where is he *now?*"

"He's loose in the city, Mait. He must be. He wasn't on the step. He wasn't in the yard. He's loose in the city. He's lost."

Ed gave a broad innocent monkey grin and offered me another Cheeto.

I turned away and headed for the door with Lenny hot on my heels.

"Don't worry, Mait. We'll find him." Lenny snapped a leash on Ed and patted my shoulder as we raced through the door. Not feeling particularly charitable, I shook off his touch.

We searched every street and every alley in a three-block radius. We checked out people's yards and under every hedge. We peered under every parked car. I called Pudding Pop's name until my voice started to crack. Lenny was staying quiet. Perhaps he knew I was so mad that anything he said would make it worse. After all, it was Lenny's monkey that tossed my dog out of the apartment. It was because of Lenny's monkey that poor Pudding Pop was lost and scared in an environment he knew nothing about.

We expanded our search grid even as I began to grow desperate. It was starting to get dark. Pudding Pop would be so frightened out in the big city all by himself at night. He hated strangers, and he knew nothing about the dangers of traffic. That scared me more than anything.

My fear slowly morphed to anger. What kind of pet detectives were we if we couldn't find our own dog?

Two hours later, with the streetlights blinking on up and down the street, chasing away the shadows, we knew we had to give up for the time being.

As we moped our way back to the apartment to grab the van and meet with Jason Johns about our plans for handling his wife's little crime spree, whatever the hell it was, I tried to remain hopeful we'd find Pudding Pop later. But I'd seen so many lost pets disappear forever, it was hard to be optimistic.

Ed knew I was upset and continually tried to reach out and offer a comforting touch, begging forgiveness too, perhaps, hoping for a teeny show of affection, but I brushed away his attempts at reconciliation and refused to look at him.

Lenny fell silent. I suspected he was feeling as guilty as Ed.

Poor Pudding Pop.

As Lenny and I drove off in the van with Ed peering over the dashboard between us, a nagging guilt tore through me. I felt like I was abandoning Pudding Pop and leaving him to fend for himself.

My heart ached.

When Lenny reached through the darkness to lay his hand on my arm to plead for his own forgiveness, I coolly slid my arm away from his touch.

Lenny sighed in the darkness beside me, and even Ed climbed into Lenny's lap and lay morosely silent.

All I could think about was how lifeless the apartment had been without Pudding Pop in it. It no longer felt like home. No one had ever loved me as much as Pudding Pop. No one would ever love me that much again. Not even Lenny.

I gave a long shuddering sigh and told myself to get a grip. We'd race through our business with Johns, and then I'd return home and search all night if need be. Pudding Pop would show up. He had to.

"I'm so sorry," Lenny whispered.

I pretended I didn't hear.

WE MET Jason Johns at a rundown motel of individual log bungalows on the old Pacific Highway west of town. He was waiting for us outside cabin number six, sitting in a rusty metal porch swing. Stella the Rottweiler was nowhere in sight. She must have been guarding the double-wide back in the trailer park. I interpreted it as a sign of goodwill that Johns had told us where he was hiding out. It made me trust the man far more than I had ever trusted his wife.

Johns shook our hands and smiled down at Ed, whom I still couldn't bear to look at.

"Who do we have here, then?" he asked. He tweaked Ed's cheek then turned back to me. "These animals are illegal to own, you know."

"Yes," I said. "That's one of the things we want to talk to you about."

"So talk," Johns said. "What's on your mind?"

I turned away to let Lenny take over. This was his idea. Let him handle it.

"Do this quickly," I told him. "I want to get back."

Lenny nodded. His beautiful chocolate eyes were sad inside his head.

I stepped out onto the gravel driveway, mumbling something about stretching my legs. My thoughts were filled with Pudding Pop. I walked to the edge of the motel grounds and stared down from a cliff face at the beach below. It was fully dark now, and the white foam of the ocean breakers slapping at the sand glowed like phosphorous in the darkness. The smell of the ocean filled my nostrils. Memories of Pudding Pop filled my head. One was delicious, the other heartbreaking. In the distance I could hear Lenny and Jason Johns speaking softly on the porch behind me. I didn't try to piece together what they were saying. I knew the general gist of what Lenny was asking him to do.

When night sounds encroached and I no longer heard the hum of human voices, I crunched my way back across the gravel driveway to cabin number six. There was no one on the porch, but the cabin door was open. Hearing voices again, I stepped through.

The room was about what one would expect for a rundown motel like this one. A behemoth Panasonic TV sat on a metal stand by the door. The establishment hadn't upgraded to flat screens yet, and probably never would. Since there were no closets built into the room, next to the TV stood a tall wooden chifforobe. The bedclothes were haphazardly rearranged over the mattress, obviously by Johns himself. Perhaps he had left a Do Not Disturb sign on the door so he wouldn't be bothered with the housekeeper. Pretty soon I understood why.

Lenny and Jason Johns were standing before a long cage placed atop a battered bureau. It was a wire cage like the ones we had seen in Lorraine Johns's house. Ed was perched on Lenny's shoulder, looking nervous. Apparently he wasn't too thrilled with what the two humans were looking at.

I squeezed my way into the group and checked it out for myself.

There were two fat Gila monsters lying in the cage, lazily devouring a saucer of raw eggs.

"Is that…?" I asked.

"Frederick, yes," Lenny answered.

"Then who's the other one?"

"That's Rosemary."

I turned to study Johns's face. "I thought your dog ate Rosemary."

He shrugged. "That's what I told Lorraine. I figured if she thought Rosemary was dead, she wouldn't try to get her back."

Lenny gazed at me. There was still a leery look in his eyes, as if he didn't quite know how far out of my good graces he had fallen, but there was determination there too. "Gila monsters are from Nevada, Mait. Among other places."

That made no sense at all. Why was he telling me this? "So?"

He pulled an index card from his back pocket and handed it to me. There was typing on the face of the card. It was the card we had found on the table in Lorraine Johns's dining room. Nevada Tenderloin with Rosemary Sauce, the card read.

"Don't worry," Johns said, dragging my attention away from the card as he eyed me, then Lenny. "If you guys help me do this, I'll make sure Ed finds a permanent home at the zoo. I don't have much pull there, but I have a little."

"Thank you," Lenny said, shaking Johns's hand. And to me, he said, "Jason is going to help us keep an eye on Snake Woman. We're a team now. We're working together. Snake Woman is no longer a client. She's the enemy. And no, we're not refunding her three hundred bucks."

I nodded. "Okay. Fine. We can do a better surveillance if we work in shifts anyway."

"Right," Lenny said. "And now our business here is settled. Let's go find the pooch."

Johns lifted an eyebrow at that weird statement, but he didn't ask any questions about who the pooch was. Perhaps he had come to expect weird statements from us. I couldn't say I blamed him.

I stared again at the index card in my hand. Then I stared at it a little harder. Thoughts began to coalesce. Nerve endings began firing on all cylinders. Then they snapped, popped, and fizzled out completely. The next thing I knew, I didn't care anymore. Screw the card. Screw the bloody lizards.

All I could think about was Pudding Pop, lost in the big city. I didn't care about any of the other cases we were working on either. Not really. My priorities had shifted.

I could see in Lenny's eyes he knew exactly what I was thinking. He plucked the card from my hand and stuck it in his pocket. With Ed still perched on his shoulder, Lenny took my arm and steered me toward the door.

"Come on, Mait. Let's go rescue Pudding Pop."

Chapter Eleven

THREE HOURS later, Pudding Pop was still missing. Leaving Ed back at the apartment, Lenny and I had traipsed for blocks, weaving in and out of yards and backlots, checking front porches and flower beds, peering under anything we thought Pudding Pop might hide beneath if he got scared. I knew he must have been scared. This was the first time he had ever been on his own. He must have been terrified.

Lenny grew more morose as our search wore on.

There is something you should know about Lenny. He can be a doofus at times. He can't balance a checkbook or cook worth a damn or play a musical instrument, but he has a lot of good qualities too. He's funny, generous, honest, sweet, trustworthy, likes the same kind of pizzas as me, almost always puts the toilet seat up before he pees and back down after he finishes, and is forever in the mood to fool around. Speaking of which, his talent in the sexual arena is nothing to sneeze at either. Sex with Lenny is always hot. And he's gorgeous, which certainly doesn't hurt.

Lenny has one other exceptional quality. He loves me. He loves me as much as I love him.

For those reasons and many more, I realized I couldn't stay mad at him any longer. It wasn't fair. He wasn't the one who tossed Pudding Pop out in the street—the blasted monkey had done that. And frankly, I could barely stay mad at the monkey either. Ed had merely done what his instincts told him to do, which was pretty much how Lenny and I lived our own lives, so how could I blame Ed for doing the same thing?

By unspoken agreement we were heading back to the apartment, both of us shuffling our feet, depressed, despondent, heartsick. As we walked I reached out and took Lenny's hand.

"I'm sorry," I said. "It wasn't your fault. I shouldn't have blamed you."

Lenny eased closer until our shoulders touched. His fingers tightened around mine. "Thank you, Mait. But don't give up yet. He's microchipped. Even if we don't find him, maybe someone else will."

"I know. It's just hard."

"I know."

Then Lenny stopped in his tracks. We were three houses from our apartment building. He lifted his hand and pointed ahead. "Isn't that your car?" he asked.

I gazed ahead. Yep. There it was. My Mini Cooper. And sitting on the fender was our new assistant, Jamie. He wasn't wearing any more clothes than he had been wearing the first time we met him.

"Is that who I think it is?" Lenny asked, gaping. "And if it is who I think it is, what the hell is he doing with your car? I thought you said the Coop was in the shop."

"I lied."

"Say what? Since when do we lie to each other?"

I sighed. "It was meant to be a surprise. Jamie is helping us solve one of our cases. Sort of."

Lenny didn't look any less confused than he had earlier. "What the heck is that supposed to mean?"

Jamie spotted us and hopped off the fender. He raised a hand in greeting. "Hey, guys!"

The kid was all smiles and all skin. He sported a mouthful of snow-white choppers that looked like they belonged in a toothpaste commercial, along with teeny short shorts, a teeny muscle shirt, and tennis shoes with teeny ankle socks, all of which looked like they had been plucked from the wardrobe department on the set of a porno movie.

"Aren't you cold?" I asked.

He *pshawed*. "Nah, I'm used to it."

"How'd the car do?" I asked. "Did you get good mileage?"

Jamie patted the fender beside him. "The car's a dream. Your radio sucks, but everything else was fine." He dug into his shorts pocket and hauled out a couple of twenties. "I didn't have to fill up at all, so here's your gas money back."

"Keep it," I said. "And the cargo?"

"Safe and sound."

"The likeness?"

"A spitting image."

I stepped in closer and lowered my voice. "Any problems at the state line?"

"Nary a hitch," Jamie said. "I lubed my way right through."

I could feel Lenny squirming up behind me, scared to death he was going to miss something.

"What do you know about lube?" I asked the kid with a smirk.

Jamie frowned. "Not nearly enough, I'll bet."

I ignored that, because I sure as hell wasn't going to be the one to teach him. "So the mission was a success, then." I pinched his cheek like a doting uncle.

Jamie's smile exploded like a hand grenade. His teeth sparkled in the moonlight. "Beyond all expectations, Boss. Excellent rodent deception. Just like the picture. No one will ever know the difference."

I pulled him into a hug, then thought better of it and pushed him away. "You really need to wear more clothes," I said.

"No kidding," Lenny grumbled behind my back. "And would someone please tell me what the hell you two are talking about? What cargo? Where'd he take the car? Spitting image of what? What's going on? And what the hell does he mean by excellent rodent deception? What does that even *mean* exactly?"

"Show him," I said to Jamie, and the kid pulled open the Cooper's front door, reached across to the passenger seat, and hauled out a small animal carrier I had supplied him with earlier.

While Jamie did that, I gave Lenny the scoop. "Jamie made a little road trip to Yuma, Arizona, for us."

Lenny looked more confused than ever. "Why'd he go to Yuma? What the heck's in Yuma?"

"Different laws," I said. "That's what's in Yuma."

"You're not making a lick of sense, Mait."

Jamie handed Lenny the animal carrier, which was about the size of a car battery. "Maybe this'll clear it up for you," Jamie said proudly.

Lenny peered into the carrier. I peered in with him. A tiny fuzzy face with long whiskers and beady, sparkling eyes stared back.

"A rat?" Lenny said.

"No, dummkopf. A gerbil. Gerbils are legal in Arizona. You can find them in any pet shop."

Lenny blinked, still trying to get things straight in his mind. "And?"

"And look," Jamie said, handing Lenny a photograph. "Compare that gerbil with this gerbil."

Lenny gazed at the picture, moving it around until he had maximum illumination from the streetlight up the road. "This is Ethel, Arthur's missing gerbil."

Jamie tapped the pet carrier. "So is this. At least it is now."

"We'll switch 'em," I said. "Arthur will never know the difference. Hopefully neither will the gerbil's owner. I told you I had solved the gerbil case. Sort of. And now we won't have to give him his money back, and everyone ends up happy."

"How much did the gerbil cost?" Lenny asked.

"They were two for ten bucks," Jamie said with a grin. "One for six."

Lenny's face lit up. "So we made $594 profit." Then his face lit up a little more. "You never intended to give Arthur his money back, did you?"

"Of course not," I said. "What am I? Stupid? But you didn't figure our profit right. You forgot to include Jamie's cut." I turned back to the boy. "What about your parents? They must be getting worried."

Jamie grinned. "I didn't even have to lie. I told them I was with Ethel. They seemed so astounded I was out with a girl, they told me not to hurry home."

I grinned right back. "Sneaky. All parents need a little false hope now and then. You did good, kid." I reached into my pocket and peeled off a couple more twenties. "Take this," I said. "You earned it."

Jamie gawked at the four twenty-dollar bills he now held in his hand. "Wow! I like being a pet detective!"

"And you're worth every penny," I said.

I turned to Lenny. "Stay here and keep an eye out for Pudding Pop. I'm going to run Jamie home."

"Sure you don't want me to sleep over with you guys?" Jamie asked with an unholy twinkle in his eye that didn't fool me one little bit. "I could square it with my folks. No problem."

"Never in a million years, kid. You're going home to your mommy and poppy."

"And no lube lessons along the way," Lenny warned, gathering the front of my shirt in his fist and yanking me into his face.

I kissed his nose. "Oh, hush."

"Darn," Jamie said around a pout. "A lube lesson sounds like fun."

"Put the kid in the cage," Lenny said, pointing to the large animal carrier in the back of the Cooper. "I don't trust him."

"I'll be good," Jamie said with an insincere pout.

When Lenny offered up a smile, the smile was pure saccharine. "I still don't trust him."

I'm pretty sure he was kidding. Or maybe not. Frankly I didn't trust the kid any more than Lenny did, but I figured if he didn't keep his hands to himself on the ride home, I'd break his fingers like pretzels. The first time he used a lubricant, it would be to get his cast off.

Lenny took the pet carrier with the new and improved Ethel the gerbil inside. He stepped up onto the curb to wave good-bye as I drove off with Jamie in the passenger's seat beside me. Lenny stood there looking worried until we rounded a corner two blocks down. I knew because I watched him in the rearview mirror until we were out of sight. His jealousy amused me.

Then I remembered Pudding Pop, and all my newfound good cheer headed south.

I WAS up at sunrise, expanding the search perimeter, hunting for poor Pudding Pop everywhere I could think to look. Lenny had gone off searching in one direction, I in the other. Pudding Pop would be getting hungry by now. Hungry and thirsty. When dogs are scared, they run. If the little guy had panicked and took off in one direction, he could be in Tijuana by now. That thought made me want to drop to the curb and cry like a baby.

Jason Johns had taken the first shift watching the Snake Woman, as we had all dubbed her. I had spoken to Johns earlier on the phone. He was hunkered down in a rental car across the street from what used to be his house, waiting for his ex-wife to make a move so he could follow her. We needed to discover where she was taking the reptiles, and once we discovered where she was taking them, maybe we could also figure out what it was she was doing with them. Whatever it was, we all knew it couldn't be for their welfare. Then Johns spent two minutes complaining about his lawn.

"That yard used to be a showcase," he groused. "I kept it immaculate."

"I'm sorry," I said.

"Look at the hedges, look at the dead grass, look at the weeds in the sidewalk! Lazy bitch hasn't even cleaned the windows," he growled and hung up.

Two hours later, my cell phone cheeped and clicked. I had just finished changing the ringtone. *Dixie* was long gone. Now the phone sounded like a dyspeptic woodpecker when I had an incoming call. I'd probably have to change the ringtone again. This one was annoying as hell.

"Speak," I said.

It was Lenny. "Any luck?"

"No. You?"

"No. I'm sorry, Mait. Maybe we should put up flyers."

"Oh God, I couldn't bear to see Pudding Pop's little face on one of those lost-dog flyers. It would break my heart."

I could hear Lenny sighing over the phone. "I know, babe, but it might help. I'm going to head back to the apartment and post a notice on a few local websites, warning people to keep an eye out. I'll phone the humane society too. You never know. We might get lucky."

A lump had formed in my throat. Actually it had been there since yesterday. "I hate to think of Pudding Pop's safety being governed by the whims of luck."

"I know you do, Mait."

"I'm going to stop by the shop and see if we have any calls on the phone there," I said. "After that, I'll join you at the apartment, and we'll plan out the rest of the day."

"Okay, Mait. See you soon." There was a momentary pause on the line, then Lenny said, "Don't get discouraged. We'll find him. I know we will."

"I hope you're right," I said and disconnected.

I was only a few blocks from the storefront where Lenny and I had hung our Two Dicks shingle. The storefront was only a few blocks from our apartment. I headed there, still peering under every parked car and behind every tree and bush. I saw a truckload of cats and even one possum. But no frightened Chihuahuas. Nary a one.

On the stoop in front of the shop, I spotted the tiny figure of Danilo Dalisay, huddled in a despondent ball with his chin in his hands. He was obviously waiting for either me or Lenny to show up. It was Saturday morning, so he wasn't wearing his school uniform. Instead, he wore a striped T-shirt and funny little cargo pants that looked like they had seen better days. Like the average kid, his tennis shoes were filthy. One shoelace was untied altogether.

Sitting there on the stoop, he looked like he'd been crying. Morning light glittered from the dampness on his cheeks. Old tears. He didn't smile when he saw me approach.

"You didn't find him, did you," he said when I was close enough for us to speak. It wasn't a question. He spoke the words as if he had given up hope a long time ago.

"No, Danny. I'm sorry. But we're still looking."

"You look sad too," he said. "What's wrong?"

"It's my dog," I said. "He ran away."

Danny's eyes grew bigger as he let that soak in. "You must feel like me, then."

I nodded, dropping down to the first step to sit beside him. "I think I do."

He scooted over a smidgeon to make more room for me, and the faintest glimmer of a smile softened his cherubic face. "Maybe they're together. Your doggy and my Fido. Maybe they're somewhere playing." His tiny hand came out and patted me consolingly on the back.

I tried to give him a smile. "Maybe they are."

"Maybe they'll come home when they're done."

"I hope so," I said.

He frowned. "Me too."

Danny gazed down at his shoes, then back at me. "My daddy said you and your partner are nice. He met you when he was delivering your mail."

"I remember," I said. "Your daddy was nice too. Does he know we're trying to find your dog?"

Danny nodded. "He laughed when I told him."

"Why would he laugh?" I asked.

"I'm not sure. But he laughs a lot. Maybe it was just one of those times for him to laugh."

"Maybe," I said.

"I have to go," Danny said with a sigh. "I have a piano lesson. I hate piano lessons. The teacher has bad breath, and she's always covered with cat hair."

I dredged up my first laugh of the day. "She's probably been licking her cat's butt. That's why her breath is bad and why she's covered in cat hair."

"Eww," Danny said, making a face. "Really?"

"Let's hope not."

He stood and stuck out his hand for a shake like a grown-up. I took his little fist in mine and gave it a gentle pump.

"I hope you find both our dogs," he said. "It's lonely not having them around."

"I know it is. Have fun with your piano lesson."

He scrunched up his face into a tight wad of fury. "Yeah, right."

"And don't kiss the teacher," I added.

"Eww," he said again. "Cat-butt cooties. Don't worry. I won't." Then he laughed. "The piano teacher's name is Mrs. Pigg. With two g's."

"Nice name," I said.

"You think?"

"No. It sucks."

"That's what I thought," he said, and then he was gone, morosely dragging his feet toward his piano lesson, his untied shoelace trailing along behind him. Poor little bloke.

The phone inside the shop jangled, and I hastily pulled out my keys to unlock the door.

It was Jason Johns.

"She's on the move," he said without preamble. I could hear his car engine rumbling in the background. "When she gets to wherever it is she's going, I'll call you back. Gotta go. It's illegal to talk on a phone and drive at the same time."

Boy Scout. Lenny and I have been known to screw and drive at the same time. The tricky part was not blowing the horn every five seconds.

"We'll await your call," I said.

I punched in Lenny's number and told him what Johns had said. "Bring the van," I said, "and pick me up at the shop. Leave Ed at home. Bring Ethel. We don't want the damn monkey throwing the gerbil out the door too. Lock the deadbolt when you leave. That way Ed can't open the door at all. If I'd done that yesterday, Pudding Pop would still be safe."

"Okay, Mait. I'll be right there."

I wasn't sure what we were getting ourselves into, but I thought there might be a chance that other people were involved in whatever scheme Lorraine Johns had cooked up to turn a profit from the poor unfortunate creatures in her care. And since I didn't know if those other people were Sunday school teachers or slobbering homicidal troglodytes, I thought I should take precautions. I gathered up the snake grabber, the grizzly bear pepper spray, and the stun gun, after checking to make sure it was fully charged. At the last minute, I scooped up the industrial-sized Taser too, in case one of her accomplices was particularly large and mean or turned out to be a rhinoceros. Chances are I wouldn't need any of those things, but my mother always told me it's better to be safe than sorry. I didn't have any antivenin on hand or I would have snatched up a couple hundred vials of that too.

LENNY GAZED at all the weaponry I'd dumped into the back of the van. "Are we going to war?"

"You never know."

Ethel's carrier was perched on the seat between us. I peered inside. She was happily nibbling on a wedge of apple, her little beady gerbil eyes blinking merrily, her whiskers whirring. Every few seconds her back leg thumped out a staccato message in Morse code.

"Ethel's happy," I said.

"Yeah, but Ed's pissed," Lenny responded. "He didn't like being left behind."

"Tough," I said. I still hadn't completely forgiven Ed for setting Pudding Pop loose. Maybe a little alone time would help him see the error of his ways. More likely, however, he was sitting at home watching *Curious George* on PBS, scarfing down a five-dollar bag of Fritos, and playing with himself. Damn monkey.

Lenny and I remained parked in front of the Two Dicks Detective Agency corporate headquarters (it still sounded grander in my head than what it really was), waiting for Jason Johns to tell us where his wife was headed. We didn't have to wait long.

My cell phone chirped and clicked. It was Johns. "We're headed down the main drag in La Jolla. She's three cars up. I'm trying to hang back so she won't see me."

"We're on our way. Did she take any animals with her?" I asked.

"She stashed three carriers in the back of her car when she left the house. Not sure what was in them."

"Well, it wasn't puddy tats, we know that."

"What a bitch," Johns snarled.

"If you hate her so much, why did you marry her?"

"She fucks like a monkey."

"Oh, good. Maybe when this is all over, I can set her up with Ed."

"Don't do it," Johns said. "He deserves better."

We hung up.

"Head for La Jolla, Lenny. We'll get more detailed instructions once we get there."

"Gotcha," Lenny said, and we were off.

La Jolla is a well-heeled suburb of San Diego where most of the county's money goes home to die. The residents are rich, the rents are astronomical, and the streets don't have a single pothole. Even the waiters are so snooty they'll barely deign to speak to you long enough to take your order. We had just passed the La Jolla city limits sign when Johns rang up again. This time he was whispering so softly I could barely hear him.

"She's inside a private residence on Seaview Palisades. It's 2027. She took the cages in with her."

"Why are you whispering?" I asked.

I heard what sounded like the crackle of tree limbs. Either that or he'd rolled around in a bathtub filled with Cheese Nips. "Because I'm hiding in a clump of hibiscus bushes underneath a south window, trying to get a glimpse inside."

It was still broad daylight. "Isn't that a little dangerous?"

"I work with venomous reptiles. I know how to be sneaky."

"Do you know how to be invisible?" I sniped, but he had already disconnected.

Lenny and I spotted the address up ahead, so we rolled on casually by in Lenny's rusted-out clunker of a van, coughing up a trail of deadly exhaust fumes, hoping people would think we were yardmen or something. We were standing out like turds in a box of donuts, what with all the Mercedes Benzes and Rolls Royces and Range Rovers parked all over the place. As the van grumbled past the address Johns had given me, I scanned the south side of the house, and sure enough, there he was, Jason Johns, hiding behind a bush, hanging on to a windowsill by his fingernails, trying to peer inside. He was being about as unobtrusive as Lenny trying to sneak up on an orgasm. Like that ever happened. When Lenny came, the whole world knew it.

We parked in front of a rococo mansion a couple of doors up. Some old lady looked down her nose at the van as she walked by with her black pug on a leash. The black pug wore a collar of pink rhinestones and walked like it had a kielbasa stuffed up its ass. Actually so did the woman.

She hurried past, obviously fearing for her life, her blue hair sparkling in the sun. The moment she was gone, Lenny and I slipped from the van and jogged across the street. I was carrying the bigass canister of pepper spray for grizzly bears stuffed in the back pocket of my pants. Lenny was unarmed, which made him the sane one.

The home at 2027 Seaview Palisades was a Frank Lloyd Wright wannabe, or maybe it was the real thing. What am I, an architect? It was two stories, so modern it was retro, with odd angles and protuberances everywhere. But what I really liked about it was the fact that the grounds were heavily foliated. There was a lot of ground cover to hide behind. Plants, trees, boulders, bushes. It was a ninja's wet dream.

Lenny and I ducked in off the sidewalk, tiptoed between two hanging walls of wisteria—pissing off a lot of bees—then fought our way through a tightly packed stand of dwarf palmetto with a thousand palmetto blades, as sharp as hacksaws, whacking at us left and right.

"Ow, ooch, shit, aargh!"

When we reached the other side of the dwarf palmetto minefield, we found ourselves against the side of the house. Gazing along the wall, I saw Jason Johns still hanging from the windowsill and trying to peer inside.

Lenny and I crept along the side of the house toward him. What with stealth being our middle name and all, what else could we be expected to do?

We were almost upon him when I said, "*Psst!*" to get his attention and startled him so that he lost his grip and fell on his ass in the mulch with a horrendous *crunch*.

"Uh-oh," Lenny said.

Approximately three seconds later, all hell broke loose.

The window Johns had been trying to peer through slid up and a head slid out. It wasn't Lorraine Johns's head. It was a gorilla's head. At least that was my first impression. Upon further reflection I realized it was merely the head of a guy who resembled a gorilla. Which didn't make the situation any less dire, in my humble opinion.

Jason Johns took off in one direction. Lenny and I took off in another.

I don't know where Johns ended up, but Lenny and I torpedoed our way straight for the van. Lenny cranked up the engine, and we took off down the street before the gorilla could pull his head back through the window and take up pursuit.

The van grumbled and squeaked its way up to twenty miles an hour as it rumbled past 2027 Seaview Palisades, trying to build up enough momentum to flee the scene. Lenny's van could be relied on to go from zero to sixty in a little under an hour and a half. That was on a good day. As we chugged away, I turned back one last time to see if we were being chased.

While I could see no one hot on our tail, I did see Lorraine Johns standing at the curb with her hand on her hip, staring through the cloud of exhaust fumes the van was spitting out behind us. She had a hanky over her mouth, trying not to choke on the smoke.

To say she didn't look happy would have been gilding the lily considerably. She looked furious.

Two minutes later, Jason Johns called. "Did she see us?" he asked.

"Everybody saw us," I said. "We'll probably be on the evening news."

"Crap. You startled me."

"I know," I said. "Sorry."

He hung up.

I knew I was right. The Snake Woman had most certainly seen us, but I chewed my cheek all the way home wondering if she had *recognized* us. Lenny hadn't looked back, so he hadn't seen her at all. But I had. There had been a murderous glint in the woman's eyes as she watched us clatter our way down the street in Lenny's rattletrap van that I didn't care for at all. Lionesses look that way before they bite the lion tamer's head off under the big top.

Lenny pulled to the curb in front of our apartment building. I jiggled my ass around on the seat in preparation for exiting the vehicle, and the grizzly bear repellent exploded in my back pocket, squirting pepper spray everywhere.

Ethel squeaked, Lenny went immediately blind, or so he screamed, and I started gagging, eventually peeing my pants from the exertion of trying not to barf. Oxygen was instantly nonexistent. We fought our way out of the van, hacking and retching, and as soon as my feet hit the ground, I threw the canister of pepper spray as far as I could throw it.

I grabbed Lenny by the shirt collar and pulled him, stumbling and strangling, toward the side of the apartment building where the garden hose lay. As blind as one of those crabs that lives two miles down on the ocean floor, I groped around until I found the faucet sticking out of the side of the building and cranked the water on, fattening the hose. I pulled

Lenny against me and aimed the spray directly into our gasping faces, hosing us down from head to toe, washing away the pepper spray and the tears and the snot, and in the back of my mind, I was glad we were drenched because now no one would know I'd peed in my pants.

It took a while, and though the snot was still running, we were finally able to breathe and even see a little bit by squinting through bloodred eyes. When we decided we might actually survive, we turned the hose on poor Ethel, who was still reeking and squeaking in outrage inside her cage. After a couple of minutes in the spray, I thought she looked a little perkier, so we turned the water off before she drowned. The three of us stood there staring at each other, still gasping for a breath of air, shivering from the cold water, and spitting out a torrent of saliva that kept building up every two or three seconds or so, like each and every one of us had popped an O-ring on our runoff valves.

I gazed up with tear-filled eyes at my living room window and saw Ed. He had his little fuzzy fist against the glass, giving us the finger.

I guess he was still mad we'd left him behind. After seeing the state we were in, you'd think he would have been grateful. What a dumbass.

Chapter Twelve

INSIDE THE apartment, Lenny and I tore off our soggy, stinking clothes, grabbed a gallon of milk from the fridge, and jumped into the shower. Taking turns, we bathed our eyes with milk to remove the last vestiges of pepper spray, then we soaped each other down. Although we were naked and rubbing each other from head to toe—legs, balls, butts, you name it—being pepper-sprayed with grizzly bear deterrent was such a crappy experience, we didn't even *consider* having sex. That was most certainly a first.

When we were as free of the stench of pepper spray as we were ever going to get, we dried off, dressed, and collapsed at the kitchen table with a couple of beers.

Ed studied us from the top of the refrigerator. I supposed his sense of smell was a tad more acute than ours, and to him we still reeked to high heaven. I also supposed that was his problem, not mine. Besides, I was still unhappy with the buggery bastard.

My gaze drifted to the floor where Pudding Pop's water dish and food bowl sat empty and forlorn. I sighed, and Lenny's hand came out to stroke my cheek. He knew what I was thinking.

Forcing myself to get back to the business at hand, I sprayed my cell phone with disinfectant and topped it off with a layer of Febreze to get the smell off. It had been stuffed in my *other* back pocket at the time of the unfortunate incident with the grizzly repellant, so it got a pretty good dose of pepper spray too. As soon as I could hold it to my cheek without puking, I punched in Lorraine Johns's number. I immediately received a notification that her cell phone had been turned off. I wasn't surprised. She was probably regrouping with her cohorts, wondering what they should do next. Move their crime scene to a new location? Come gunning for Lenny and me? Open up a GoFundMe account online to buy us a new van?

I was about to call Jason Johns when the cell phone chirped and clicked in my hand. Johns had beaten me to the punch.

"Yo," he said. "You guys still alive?"

"Barely," I said. "So what are we doing? Where do we go from here?"

"I think it's time to call the police and get them involved. I'm worried about the reptiles. I don't feel comfortable leaving them with her another minute. I had no idea she had so many animals in her care until you guys broke into the house and found them. Now that I know she's not the only one involved in whatever it is she's doing—did you see that ape-looking fucker at the window?—I have to think the reptiles are in imminent danger. They need to be rescued."

"The authorities may not be too pleased that Lenny and I broke into our client's place of residence, even if it was for a good cause. Maybe we can find a way to leave that out of the story."

"No problem. I'll tell them I peeked through the window when the cow—I mean my ex-wife—wasn't home and saw the reptiles there. They'll believe me. I'm a herpetologist. But I will have to tell them Lorraine hired you guys to get Frederick back. You were probably seen at the house in La Jolla anyway. The police will want to know why you were there. I'll tell them the truth about everything else. You started working for the scummy twat—I mean my ex-wife—but when you realized laws were being broken, you switched your allegiance to me, and we've been working together ever since."

I nodded, then I realized we were on the phone. He couldn't see me nod. I wondered vaguely if pepper spray destroyed brain cells. "All right," I said. "Lenny and I will support you on all of that."

"Good. I'll call you back, Mait, when I find out what the police want to do. I appreciate you guys helping. You and Lenny. I want you to know that. You've done a good thing. Most people think venomous reptiles deserve whatever fate dishes out. But it's not true. They are God's creatures too, and sometimes they need protection like we do. And as for Ed, we'll get him into a safe environment soon. Nobody takes better care of their animals than the San Diego Zoo. Ed won't have to worry about a thing for the rest of his life."

"You're a good man," I said.

"With a really big dick," Lenny whispered. I shushed him with a snarl.

"I heard that," Johns said. "You found my pictures when you snooped around my trailer."

"Maybe," I said, trying to be evasive but failing miserably. "Lenny hasn't seen them. Just me."

"Sounds like he's interested in photography," Johns said with a smile in his voice. "I'll send him a couple of my better poses to show my appreciation for all his help."

I laughed. "Lenny will love you forever. I mean, from a distance. You can't have him. Lenny and I are an item."

"I thought you might be. Not that you're obvious or anything. Plus you don't need to worry. I'm straight."

"If you say so," I said. "Okay, Jason, we'll wait for your call. And be careful. I don't trust the bitch—I mean your ex-wife—any more than you do."

"Don't worry," he said. "Her days are numbered."

"Let's hope so," I said and hung up.

I turned to Lenny, who was watching me with wide, curious eyes.

"He's calling the cops," I said. "When he meets with them, he wants us with him."

Lenny nodded. "I figured. Why will I love him forever?"

"He's sending you a picture of his dick."

"Well, isn't that sweet."

"He also promises to take care of Ed. He hasn't forgotten."

Lenny twisted around in the chair and studied Ed, who was peering into the kitchen cabinet above the refrigerator. He had a pot lid in his hand like maybe he thought we needed to reorganize our cupboards.

"You're going to get laid, Ed. We've found you a home with other monkeys."

Ed gazed at Lenny, then at me. "*Hoo-hee?*" he asked.

"*Hoo-hee* your ass," I grumped, and we settled in to wait for Jason Johns to call back. I wondered what Snake Woman was doing now. She had to know the jig was up, that we suspected her of wrongdoing, or why else would her ex-husband and the two pet detectives who were supposed to be working for her be following her around, glued to her ass like carbuncles?

Lenny and I were on our second beer when Ed dropped a cast iron skillet off the top of the fridge and gave us both a heart attack.

Ed said, "*Oop erp*," by way of apology.

Lenny peered out the kitchen window a little too casually. "When do you think the mail will get here?"

"Pecker pictures take longer to process," I said. "The post office stamps them by hand. Probably won't come until next week. And by come, I mean arrive."

"That's disappointing," Lenny pouted, making me grin.

A moment later the phone rang. It was Johns.

"Meet us in La Jolla," he said. "We're on our way there now."

"You and the cops?" I asked.

"Me and the cops and animal control."

"Okay. We're out the door."

THE LA Jolla mansion where Jason, Lenny, and I had flushed out the gorilla-looking dude was situated in the eye of a storm. The storm consisted of four police cruisers, two trucks from animal control, a News 8 van with a bigass antenna poking off its roof, a panel truck with Forensic Team painted on the side, and a roach coach. Apparently the driver of the roach coach had seen the activity and pulled into the midst of it all thinking he might make a few extra bucks. And he was right. Two policemen were ordering sandwiches, and one of the animal control guys with a big net on his shoulder was slurping at a humongous ice cream cone while waiting for a couple of fish tacos. The TV reporter, a bimbo-looking blonde with more makeup than Tammy Faye, was interviewing the guy with the ice cream cone, presumably because the police wouldn't talk to her.

If I had secretly harbored the idea that maybe we had been imagining it all and no crimes were truly being committed, the hubbub in front of me convinced me otherwise.

Lenny was almost speechless. He kept muttering, "Holy smoke, holy smoke, holy smoke."

Jason was hovering around the mansion's front door, speaking to a police officer who looked like he had consumed a few too many donuts during the course of his career. When Jason saw us, he waved us forward. I heard him say, "These are my partners, Officer," as Lenny and I approached. To my surprise the fat cop stuck out a huge paw and welcomed us to the proceedings. Lenny and I weren't used to being welcomed by the authorities. Usually we were either looked on as outsiders, or else we were actually the ones being arrested.

There was no smile on Jason Johns's face, which bothered me. "Did they catch her?" I asked.

He shook his head. "Lorraine was gone. She got away."

"What about the animals?" Lenny asked. "Did you guys get here in time to save the animals she brought with her?"

Jason and the cop exchanged glances.

"Go ahead," the cop said. "Show them what we found. Just don't let them touch anything. We'll be fingerprinting the joint soon. Probably tomorrow we'll have you three come down to the station to answer some questions and make an official statement." Another cruiser pulled up out front and the fat cop announced, "There's the chief. I need to talk to him. Animal rights people are going to be all over this like stink on a cow pie. Best give the chief a heads up before the pie hits the fan. You guys go on inside."

He waddled off. I hoped he would make the acquaintance of Jenny Craig soon before he keeled over dead from a donut-induced stroke. In the meantime, Lenny and I followed Jason Johns through the mansion's front door and into the middle of an honest-to-God crime scene investigation.

Techs from the forensic lab were already beginning the process of collecting evidence. They were joking with each other while they did it. Maybe they were relieved to be dealing with animals for a change instead of a dead human. Still, they appeared extremely careful when they searched dark corners and under low furniture. The fact that venomous reptiles were, for all they knew, loose on the premises, kept them watchful. Couldn't say I blamed them.

The mansion was furnished with pissy art deco stuff, fat overstuffed furniture, lots of doodads sitting around. Crap everywhere. Dusting for fingerprints would be a bitch. We followed Jason through the entryway, the living room, a den with about a gazillion books stacked on shelves to the ceiling, and from there into a formal dining room. There were techs and cops and animal control people scattered around in every room, either searching or shooting the shit or simply standing around waiting for their shifts to end. I could tell by the nervous expressions on their faces they were all keeping an eye peeled in case an errant reptile came slithering out from among the knickknacks and table legs. A guy shaking a pair of maracas could have caused about ten heart attacks without even trying. It might have been funny if it wasn't so sad.

In a hallway leading out of the dining room, I spotted our gorilla friend. He was dressed in white pants, white shoes, a white T-shirt, a blood-stained white apron, and strangely, he had a white chef's hat perched on top of his ugly head. His hands were handcuffed behind his back. He appeared big and surly and uncooperative, like Chef Boyardee on steroids with an attitude problem.

"The cook," Jason Johns said as we passed, which made no sense to me at all. Why would they arrest the cook?

Lenny, however, mumbled, "I knew it," which made no sense to me either.

I saw the gleam of stainless steel ahead. Black-and-white tile floors, white walls, copper pots and pans hanging from an overhead carousel in the middle of the room. A gas stove as big as a Volkswagen stood against the wall. A refrigerator you could have held a cotillion in stood next to it.

This was the mansion's kitchen.

I plucked at Jason's shirtsleeve. "Where are the animals? Did they find them?"

Johns shook his head. "We were too late."

"What do you mean? Were they gone?"

"No, Mait," Johns said. "They were dead. A seven-foot Indian cobra. A six-foot spitting cobra, probably the one you and Lenny saw at the house. And a slightly smaller African tree cobra."

"And they were all dead? What happened to them?"

"I'll show you."

Jason led us to what I quickly realized was a walk-in freezer. There were shelves inside containing cases of frozen meats, vegetables, desserts. In the back of the walk-in unit, hanging from hooks on the wall, were the flayed bodies of three snakes, two of them as long as I was, the other longer. They weren't quite frozen yet, so they hadn't been hanging there long. Their throats were pierced by hooks, their fangs exposed, their rippled flesh unmoving. Each of the snakes had been slit open from gut to tail to remove the organs.

I stood there in shock staring at them. It took me a minute to realize Lenny had my arm in a death grip. He was obviously in shock too.

"I didn't expect this," Lenny said.

Jason Johns gave a sad nod. "Who would?"

I was beginning to shake from the cold. At least I think it was from the cold. Johns noticed and quickly led Lenny and me out of the freezer, carefully latching the door closed behind us when we left.

"Were those the cobras?" I asked.

"Yeah. Freshly slaughtered," he said. I noticed he had a handkerchief in his hand to prevent himself from leaving fingerprints on the door handle.

"At least the twelve-footer wasn't here," Lenny said. "That big guy was spared at least."

"Thank God for that," Johns and I said in unison.

My head was spinning. I still didn't understand. "What was the point of killing them and hanging them in a freezer? How could your wife make money from dead, frozen reptiles? Wouldn't they have been worth more alive?"

Johns leaned against the stove and folded his arms across his chest. He studied his shoe tops as he spoke, as if shutting out his surroundings entirely. His forehead was furrowed. He was not happy.

"Apparently Lorraine and the gorilla in there found a niche for themselves in the designer food market. For a truly substantial fee, and offered by invitation only, of course, a bunch of sicko nut jobs were invited to dine on some of the earth's deadliest creatures. It gave them a sense of power, I suppose. It gave them a thrill. Like ingesting rhino horn or lion steak. Reptile meat is actually a delicacy. The Indians ate rattlesnake often. The ancient Egyptians consumed asps and crocodiles. Supposedly, the wiliness and cruelty of such creatures can be absorbed into the bodies of those who eat them. That's the market Lorraine tapped. And she was making a fortune at it. Cobra meat was on tonight's menu. The cops will lay a trap for the diners later. They don't know it yet, but dinner's been canceled."

Lenny stared at me while I tried to comprehend. I finally turned to study him.

"And you knew," I said.

He shrugged. "I suspected. There's a difference."

I turned back to Johns. "That picture we found of your ex entering an unknown building. What was that all about? Why was it so important?"

"That's where they used to serve the dinners. It was a storefront up the coast in Del Mar. I think she knew I had tracked her there, so she moved the enterprise immediately. One of her clients offered her the use of this mansion, according to the chef in there, who pretty much stopped talking after sharing that tidbit of information. The owner is currently abroad, but he'll be in a world of trouble the minute he returns. Maybe even before. Interpol has his number too. These are serious charges."

Johns turned his eyes toward the voices we could still hear in the distance. The voices of two police officers continuing to interview the gorilla in the chef's hat. The gorilla wasn't saying much. Mostly growls and snarls. Johns was right. The guy had apparently decided to clam up.

I was having a hard time believing it all. "Let me get this straight. She's running a restaurant for select clients with only venomous reptiles on the menu."

Lenny bumped me with his hip. "Bingo. You're catching up, Mait."

"Maybe this will help," Johns said around a grim smile. Dipping into his shirt pocket, he pulled out a folded card. "Tonight's menu," he said, offering it to me. I plucked it from his hand. Lenny moved in closer to gaze at it alongside me.

The card was on creamy paper, nicely embossed with a coiled snake on the front. It looked rich. It looked classy. The only writing was on the inside.

Braised Cobra Fillet the card read in ornate golden letters, tasteful as hell. With Small White Potatoes and White Sauce.

"Holy crap," Lenny breathed in my ear.

I remembered the other card. The simple index card we'd found on Lorraine Johns's dining room table. The card that read Nevada Tenderloin with Rosemary Sauce. A menu that hadn't been printed yet? Two Gila monsters would have comprised the ingredients, I suddenly realized. Frederick and Rosemary. If Jason hadn't stolen them, they would already be dead. Dead and eaten. Yuk.

"I think I'll skip lunch," I said. "Maybe for the rest of my life."

The fat cop who had been standing at the door with Jason Johns tromped his way through the kitchen like a bull elephant crashing a tea party. He approached us as Johns plucked the menu card from my hand and stuffed it back in his shirt pocket.

"She eluded us," the cop said, his words directed at Johns. "She wasn't at the house. Her car is gone. She'd been there, but she was in and out before we arrived."

"What about the reptiles?" Johns asked, his voice tight, his eyes steely. "She had dozens of creatures caged up inside that house. What happened to them? Were they there?"

The cop frowned. "All gone. Disappeared. Every last one of them."

"What a bitch," Lenny muttered.

The rest of us, even the cop, nodded our heads in agreement. It was the opinion of all present that Lorraine Johns was indeed a bitch. Not a dissenting vote among the lot of us.

I thought of the poor flayed snakes in the walk-in freezer and longed for a bottle of Maalox. Johns and Lenny looked like they wouldn't have minded one themselves. The fat cop looked like he'd rather light into a box of eclairs.

Lenny obviously didn't care that a cop and a herpetologist with a big dick who was a little too insistent he was straight was standing there beside us. He took my hand and leaned in to say, "Take me home and make love to me, Mait. I don't much care for the snooty part of town."

Chapter Thirteen

LENNY AND I were lost in our own private thoughts on the long ride home. Still we were never physically unconnected. While I drove, his hand rested on my thigh the whole way. The van's windows were down because the vehicle still smelled vaguely of grizzly bear repellant.

"I wonder how many reptiles she killed?" Lenny finally asked after a couple of silent miles rolled beneath our wheels. His voice was sad. I've never known anyone who abhors cruelty to animals more than Lenny does. I suddenly realized it was one of the reasons I loved him.

"I don't know," I said. "We'll probably never know. I wonder what she charged for a serving of cobra fillet."

Lenny didn't bother answering. He merely shook his head as if it was all incomprehensible. His fingers tightened on my leg. "How could she do it, Mait? She must have loved reptiles at one time in her life. Loved them enough to study them and become a—you know."

"Herpetologist," I prompted for the four hundredth time.

"Yeah. That. How could you love something one minute, then turn around and start tossing them in a skillet and serving them up for dinner two minutes later?"

It was a question I had been trying to work out in my own head for a while now. It was also a question I was pretty sure I would never be able to answer no matter how long I pondered it.

My cell phone chirped and clicked. Spastic woodpecker. I flipped it open, almost grateful not to have to think about the reptiles another second. "Speak," I barked.

It was Arthur. "Hello, Maitland, dear. You sound grumpy. Hope you're not irregular. That can make anyone feel grumpy. Umm—my friend gets back into town in a couple of days. He's going to kill me, you know. He'll never trust me again. I hate to disappoint people. I feel *horrible* when I do. So, love, on the off chance the fates have decided to bless me with a favor for once in my miserable life, I wanted to call this very last time to find out if maybe, just maybe—" Here he sucked in a long shuddering breath before finishing up. "—maybe there had been an Ethel sighting. I know it's a longshot, sweetums, but—"

"As a matter of fact, Arthur, yes, there has been a sighting," I said. "A sighting and a capture. We have Ethel in custody even as we speak." I waited for a lightning bolt to shoot down from on high and incinerate my ass for lying, but nothing happened. Maybe God was busy incinerating some other liar's ass and didn't have time for me just then. But I was pretty sure I was in the queue.

Arthur gasped into the phone. I heard a series of bumps and thumps and scrapes like maybe he had almost dropped the phone and spent the last two or three seconds juggling it back into his grip. Then I heard a horrendous crash. He must have dropped an earring.

"You what? You *what?*" Arthur cried, insanely jubilant. I imagined sequins and feathers flying everywhere. "Good lord, where was she? Wherever did you find her?"

"Yuma" I wanted to say, but didn't. What I did say was, "We'll see you later."

Arthur was still screaming. "What? How? Where? Talk to me, dammit. *What?*" As a last resort, he bellowed, "Try Metamucil, love! That should do the trick. I was irregular not two weeks ago. That stuff is like Drano!"

On that cheery note, I snapped the phone shut.

Lenny was smiling when I laid the phone on the seat between us. "You hung up on him," he said around a grin.

I had to admit it. "I did. I really did."

My cell phone chirped and clicked again. This time I scooped it up and read the readout before answering, and thank God I did. It was Lester Boggs. Lenny leaned in to check the readout too.

"Oh, no," he said. "Not him. I'm not in the mood for any more fuck-yous today—unless they come from you. Either disconnect or throw the damn thing out the window."

Cell phones are expensive, so I disconnected.

During all this, Lenny's hand had been gradually creeping higher and higher along my thigh until now his fingers were planted squarely on my crotch, and my crotch was rising to the occasion.

I was grinning inside, but on the outside I was trying to sound appalled. "Not here, Lenny. Stop playing with my dick or we'll end up wrapped around a light pole. Oh, God, that feels good. Stop it. Oh, lordy."

Then suddenly it didn't feel so good. Lenny's tender ministrations to my expanding pecker turned in a heartbeat to a death grip when his fingers tightened around my cock like a vise and I heard myself scream, "Yeeouch! Stop it. Let go. What the hell are you doing?" The van swerved as I squirmed around trying to free my crotch from his grip.

Lenny was barely aware that I was screaming and writhing in pain and panic beside him. He was too busy pointing with his other hand to our apartment building up ahead.

"Holy cow, Mait! Lookit! Lookit who's waiting for us."

I pried his fingers from my dick. Said dick still seemed to be attached to my person, so I was grateful for that; don't think I wasn't. I wiped the tears from my eyes and peered ahead to where Lenny was pointing. I leaned over the steering wheel and peered closer. It couldn't be. I could feel my face stretching wide in a most remarkable smile. A smile the likes of which I hadn't felt on my puss for heaven knows how long. Even my heart was getting in on the act—gaily hammering away inside my chest, banging against my ribs like a squirrel hopping around in a barrel. Somewhere farther south, my gonads were starting to do a rumba. That was a new sensation for sure. Especially when two seconds earlier they had been running for their lives.

At the apartment building, I slammed on the brakes and launched myself out of the van with Lenny hot on my heels. We raced across the front lawn, for there, sitting on the front stoop, was…

…Pudding Pop!

He was dirty. He had burrs stuck to his coat, and I thought I saw a few extra ribs poking through like he hadn't been eating all that well lately, but he was clearly glad to be home. His tiny tail was flipping back and forth like a metronome, his eyes as bright as ever. He was lying on the top step, watching Lenny and me through wide brown eyes, and underneath his chin was tucked a stuffed animal he had picked up somewhere. It was a toy dog that looked like it had seen better days. About the same size as Pudding Pop, it was brown with black ears, and it had a tail that might have once been white.

Pudding Pop gave himself a shake, rose to his feet, and came running toward me. He leaped into my arms while tears sluiced down my cheeks. Lenny scooped us both into his arms, and the three of us stood there on the lawn, laughing and crying and hugging and whimpering, and I had never known a better homecoming in all my life.

I held Pudding Pop up between us and buried my face in his belly. He didn't smell so good, but I didn't care. Apparently Pudding Pop didn't care either. He stuck his tongue in my ear to give it a good washing, and while Lenny and I *oohed* and *aahed* and fawned over the little guy, Pudding Pop *oohed* and *aahed* and fawned over us.

"Where you been, boy?" Lenny kept asking. "Where you been? Where you been?" But Pudding Pop wasn't saying.

I gave them both a kiss between the eyes, first the dog, then Lenny. Arm in arm, with Pudding Pop cradled between us, we headed up the stairs to the apartment door. We didn't get more than two or three steps up when Pudding Pop wiggled out of my grip, took off down the stairs and back outside. Once there, he clamped his teeth around the stuffed toy and whirled to awkwardly galumph back up the stairs in our direction, dragging the stuffed animal between his front legs like a leopard dragging a dead goat up a tree.

He had obviously made a friend while he was off on his adventures. And any friend of Pudding Pop's was a friend of mine. I lifted them both into my arms, and together the four of us—me, Lenny, Pudding Pop, and Pudding Pop's stuffed guest—all sauntered toward the apartment together.

Lenny used his key to open the door, and we froze.

There were pots and pans everywhere. Ed had indeed been reorganizing cupboards. He was sitting in my best spaghetti pot in the middle of the living room floor with a saucepan on his head when we peeked in the door. He had the good grace to look guilty. Then he saw Pudding Pop in my arms, and I could have sworn he looked even guiltier.

"*Hoo-hee?*" Ed asked, scratching his nuts.

"You know who he is," Lenny groused. "And don't you be bothering him. Pudding Pop's had a rough couple of days, thanks to you."

"*Erp?*"

"Yes!"

Lenny scooped up my spaghetti pot with Ed still in it. I wondered vaguely if he had been beating off in there but was afraid to ask. Lenny deposited them both on the bedroom floor. He rejoined Pudding Pop and me after closing the bedroom door behind him, locking the monkey out.

Lenny gave a great big theatrical sigh, emoting all over the place. He was being motherly, glad we were home, glad Pudding Pop had found his way safely back to me. I gently placed Pudding Pop on the floor and he ran around in circles, dragging the stuffed animal along with him.

"Our family is together again at last," Lenny said, walking into my arms. With Lenny still clamped around me like an octopus on a stalk of coral, I took off for the kitchen, dragging Lenny along for the ride. I filled a plate with Pudding Pop's favorite food. Raw hamburger. I cracked an egg and dumped it over the meat. I filled his water bowl. Lenny and I then stood back, watching Pudding Pop go to town on what must have been his first decent meal in two days.

Lenny tucked his head into the crook of my neck, and I pulled him close. We watched, entranced, while Pudding Pop cleaned his plate.

The stuffed toy dog sat silently by, waiting. I guess he wasn't hungry.

LENNY LAY naked in my arms. It was still daylight. Our hearts were pounding down to a rhythm that didn't promise an aneurysm anytime soon, unlike the way they had been pounding a few minutes earlier. I could still taste Lenny's juices on my lips, and I was pretty sure he could still taste mine.

As in days of old, Pudding Pop was curled up in a snoring little ball at our feet. His stuffed doggy was tucked under his head like a pillow. We had locked ourselves in the bedroom, and now Ed was locked out. He wasn't happy about it either. We could hear him still rearranging the pots and pans in the kitchen. Actually he had gone beyond the "rearranging" phase. Now he was lobbing them about like hand grenades and making an unholy racket doing it. Until I met Ed, I never knew what a pain in the ass monkeys could be.

Lenny's hand was lazily stroking circles on my bare belly. We were both in that contented postorgasmic state where the nerve endings were still buzzing like electrodes and lazy petting and possessive cuddling were still required activities. I closed my eyes, enjoying Lenny's touch, basking in Lenny's scent and heat. I leaned in to bury my face in his chest, and I was about to mutter a few romantic words when he pulled away and sat up in the bed.

I opened my eyes to see what he was doing and caught him staring at Pudding Pop. Just staring.

"What is it?" I asked. "What are you thinking?"

"I just had a palophony," he said.

I laughed. "You mean an epiphany?"

"Yeah. That's what I said."

Lenny in the throes of an epiphany was something I never thought I would see, but I tried not to let him know it. No point in being insensitive, right?

"So what is this epiphany concerning?" I asked, leaning in to lick away a smear of something glistening on his left pec—as if I didn't know what it was. Still I thought I'd lap it up and find out for sure.

Lenny shuddered beneath my tongue just as I had hoped he would. He held me against him and absentmindedly stroked the back of my head. While he was doing that, he lifted his other hand and pointed toward Pudding Pop at our feet. "Lookit that dog," he said.

I tore myself from the task at hand and looked. "You mean Pudding Pop?"

"No, Mait. The other one."

I was so comfortable, it took a couple of grunts before I could pull myself up to a sitting position alongside Lenny. When I finally managed it, I looked down the length of our naked legs to where Pudding Pop was still softly snoring at the foot of the bed.

Lenny reached down and gently eased the stuffed animal out from under Pudding Pop's head. Pudding Pop gave a teeny growl in his sleep, but he never woke. He must have been really exhausted.

I stared at the stuffed doggy in Lenny's hand.

"Look at this thing," Lenny said. The toy was limp, dirty, and one of its glass eyes was loose, hanging by a thread. It was a beat-up old toy. Nothing more.

"I'm looking," I said, still confused as to what he was getting at. "What am I supposed to be seeing?"

"Remember Danny telling us about his missing dog?"

"You mean Fido?"

"Yeah. Fido. Remember how he described him?"

"Yeah," I said. "Brown with black ears and a white tail."

"Like this one," Lenny said, holding up the toy, dangling it in my face.

"About the size of a cat," I added. "That's what the kid said."

"Right," Lenny agreed, still dangling. "Again like this one."

I was beginning to have an epiphany of my own. "And with a scar on its back from when Danny's dad accidentally nailed it with a Weedwacker."

"A scar," Lenny said in a hushed voice as if he were in church. "A scar like this one."

And there it was. I saw it for the first time. Or I should say, this was the first time I really *looked* at it. For I had seen it there earlier. It just hadn't rung any bells. Well, it was ringing them now.

Across the stuffed dog's back was a line of stitches, not particularly well sewn, where someone had repaired the animal's cloth back. Danny's mother, probably. Or maybe his dad. The mailman.

"You don't suppose Danny's missing doggy was a toy all along, do you?"

"My God, it must have been."

"Maybe that's why Danny said his dad laughed when the kid told him he had hired us to look for it."

"Maybe it was."

"But where the hell did Pudding Pop find it?"

"I'm pretty sure we'll never know the answer to that question, Lenny, since Pudding Pop sure can't tell us."

We both stared at Pudding Pop.

"We have a dilemma," I said.

"What dilemma's that?"

"Do we give the brokenhearted kid his stuffed doggy back and break Pudding Pop's heart in the process? Or do we keep the stuffed doggy for Pudding Pop and break the kid's heart?"

"Oh, crap. That *is* a dilemma."

"No, it isn't," I said. "It's not a dilemma at all. We have no choice. We have to return the toy to Danny. He's our client. We promised."

"I know."

"And he's just a little kid."

"I know. I know."

"And he promised us ice cream cones if we found his dog."

"Well," Lenny said. "That settles it, then. I could use an ice cream cone. Let's go tell him now."

WE DIDN'T have to look for Danny Dalisay. We found him where we usually found him—sitting on the stoop in front of the Two Dicks Detective Agency. The only difference about the other times I spotted him there and this time was the fact that he wasn't moping. He was laughing.

He was laughing because of the golden retriever puppy he had tethered to his wrist at the end of a brand-new bright red leash. A real puppy. Hair, guts, happy little clacky toenails, flappy tail, and a bright pink tongue, which was at that moment giving Danny a thorough face wash. Thus the laughing.

Lenny and I stood looking down at the kid with broad smiles on our faces. I mean, come on, who *doesn't* smile when they see a kid playing with a puppy?

Danny came out from under the smothering pink tongue long enough to spot us there, and his face got even happier.

"You guys!" he cried. "Meet Rover! Daddy bought him for me! Ain't he great?"

The kid apparently wasn't particularly creative when it came to naming his pets. Fido. Rover. But neither Danny nor the pup seemed to mind much. I squatted down on my haunches and Rover flew into my lap and started giving *me* a tongue bath. Then he went after Lenny. Puppies are equal opportunity lickers. It's one of their charms.

"He's kind of friendly," Danny said while still wiping the dog spit off his face with the tail of his shirt. "Daddy told mommy if I was desperate enough to hire pet detectives to find my stuffed animal, then maybe it was time to move up from a toy dog to a real one. So we answered an ad in the paper, and look what we found!"

"So Fido was a toy, huh?" I asked, eyebrow arched, trying to look all mortified and offended.

"Well, sure," Danny said. "Did I forget to tell you that?"

I shot him a glower, which didn't affect him much. "You might have failed to mention it."

Lenny steered Rover and his tongue back to me so he could reach into his back pocket and pull out the missing toy. "That's great, Danny, but look what we found."

Danny's eyes got as big as saucers when he saw what Lenny was dangling in front of him. "Oh, man," he cried. "You found him. You really found him. You guys are *good*!"

Rover heard his master's voice and flew back into the kid's lap. A boy and his dog. A dog and his boy. The tongue bath resumed.

"We didn't find him," Lenny explained, getting a wily look in his eye. "Mait's dog found him. Pudding Pop's the hero, not us. Pudding Pop loves this little guy like you do. But the toy is yours. Here. You take it. It's only fair. Rover won't mind if he has to share you with Fido."

I knew what Lenny was doing, even if the kid didn't.

Danny's face sobered as he glanced at the stuffed animal Lenny was holding up. Then his gaze traveled down to the real live puppy, who was at that moment in the process of chewing on the kid's chin. I could see Danny's little mind working, and two seconds later he made an executive decision.

"You know what? I never knew Fido *wasn't* real until Rover came along. Ain't that funny?" His face scrunched up in concentration, then all of a sudden it lit up like a neon sign. Yep. An executive decision. Definitely. "Let Pudding Pop *keep* Fido," he declared. "He found him. Maybe he thinks he's real like I did."

"Pudding Pop loves him," I said. "And I've got a sneaky hunch he *does* think he's real. Are you sure you don't mind giving him up?"

"Naw. It's okay. I think I've pretty much got my hands full with Rover."

No kidding. The kid was covered in dog hair and dog slobber, and I'd never seen him look happier. He hugged Rover close, more to evade the puppy's tongue than anything else, but again I saw his expression grow solemn as he gazed up at Lenny and me.

"Guess I owe you guys an ice cream cone."

"We'll collect later."

Danny looked relieved. "That's good 'cause I've only got three cents. I spent all my allowance on puppy biscuits."

I reached over and tousled his hair. "Another time, then. Good luck with your new friend," I said. "Treat him good."

Danny grinned. "Don't worry. I will. Daddy said he'd shoot me if I didn't. I'm pretty sure he meant it."

Lenny gave the kid a fake punch on the chin. "I guess there's always the risk of going postal when you're a mailman."

The last we saw of Danny, he was headed up the street at full tilt, Rover galloping along at his heels, nipping at his pant legs, tripping him up every third or fourth step. We could hear Danny laughing even after he turned the corner toward his house and we couldn't see him anymore.

Looking smug, Lenny stuffed Fido back into his pocket and nudged me with his hip.

"Am I smart or what?" he asked.

"You da bomb," I said. "The kid didn't stand a chance."

"Don't I know it." Lenny smirked.

Side by side we headed home.

Chapter Fourteen

IT WAS a perfect day. Sunny, warm, glorious. It had California summer written all over it in big, sunshiny gold letters. Resisting the urge to fling our gayness in people's faces, Lenny and I didn't hold hands as we strolled along, although I knew we both wanted to. We merely let our shoulders bump now and then in a companionable sort of way. That seemed to be enough contact to get us by for the moment. Later I had other plans. Those other plans included full naked body contact and the swapping of bodily fluids. For now, I made myself satisfied simply having my lover close.

My lover. Just thinking that five-letter word made a smile creep across my face.

For lack of anything better to do, I scanned the skies for Toodles. Nothing. He was probably winging his way across his homeland by now, soaring high on a thermal over Zululand, maybe, or plucking bugs out of a baobab tree in Botswana, cussing up a storm at the wildlife below.

So be it. More power to him. I was content knowing I had a lover. A real, honest-to-God lover.

Lenny knocked the smile off my face by asking, "What do you think happened to Snake Woman, Mait? Where do you think she's gone?"

Good question. "Hiding out, I guess. The farther from us, the better."

"Think she'll try to exact some sort of revenge with us for partnering up with her ex?"

"Nuh-uh," I said. "At this point she's probably too busy trying to elude the law to worry about a couple of two-bit pet detectives with a lousy sense of loyalty."

I didn't know it yet, but I was about to be proven wrong. With bells on.

"I hope you're right," Lenny said on a sigh. Then he snagged my attention by adding, "Uh-oh."

We were standing at the apartment door and Lenny had his hand on the knob.

"Uh-oh, what?"

"It's unlocked."

"The door?"

"Yeah. Did we deadbolt it?"

"I don't remember."

We warily squeaked the door open and peeked inside. The joint was still a mess with pots and pans scattered all over the place, so it looked normal to me. The first inkling of danger came when we stepped across the threshold to find Ed perched in the branches of the cheap plastic apartment-grade chandelier that hung over my crappyass dining room table.

Pudding Pop was nowhere in sight. *Oh no*, I thought. *Ed's let him out again.*

Ed cried "Whoop!" and then let out with a series of high-pitched *Eeps* and *Orps*! and *Erps*. He hung from the chandelier by his tail and madly swung back and forth, doing his best Tarzan impersonation. Plaster dust sifted down from the ceiling. Ed screamed upside down for a minute, then he righted himself and went at it in that position for a while. Ed had made a lot of noises since he came to stay with us, but I had never heard him sound like this. It took me a few seconds to figure it out, but I finally settled on the fact that he sounded terrified.

Ed was one scared monkey. But scared of what?

"Get down here," I said, jabbing my finger at the floor like a distraught father down to his last ounce of patience.

Ed ignored me and kept whooping. His little monkey eyes were as big as Ping-Pong balls.

I glanced into the kitchen and saw Ethel on the counter by the sink. She was peering out through the window of her car-battery-sized carrying case, whiskers whirring, tail upright, wondering what all the hubbub was about. I gave her a grateful finger waggle of greeting—since she was so blessedly silent—before turning my attention back to the damn screeching monkey.

Because he was being so annoying, I decided I should chew Ed's head off, but before I could really get primed up with outrage—you have to be in the mood for that sort of thing—Lenny called out from the bedroom. "Hey, Mait, come and take a gander at this!"

Oh, Lord, what now?

I stepped into the bedroom and found Lenny pointing to the bed. There was a lump underneath the bedclothes about the same size as Pudding Pop. The lump was trembling.

"Pudding Pop?" I ventured. "You in there?"

A soft growling rose up from beneath the blankets. Then a whimper. It was Pudding Pop all right. Ed screamed and screeched in the other room. I heard a chunk of plaster land on the crapola dining room table. The chandelier wasn't going to last much longer.

What the hell is going on?

I took a step closer to the bed and the growling deepened. The lump twisted first one way, then the other. Pudding Pop started howling. Wolves couldn't have done it better. I stopped in my tracks. Goose bumps climbed up the back of my neck, and my hair stood on end. If Lenny's hair hadn't been so curly, his would have stood on end too. As it was, his mouth gaped open and his eyes popped wide like Ed's.

"Listen," he breathed. As soon as he said it, Pudding Pop and I both froze. In the sudden silence, I heard a breathy, rasping sound. I didn't like that sound one little bit. Two seconds later I understood why.

A flat, hooded head rose up from the other side of the bed. It was the size of my hand, the neck as big as my wrist. Black and menacing, the creature spun its head first to me, then to Lenny. As it stared at us, it slowly rose higher and higher on its long stalk of a body until it hovered two feet higher than the bed.

Pudding Pop lay silent now, frozen in terror. He was still trembling, but he'd quieted his howling and whimpering. I had a feeling the need for self-preservation had kicked in. He was trying to fly under the radar, hoping he would go unnoticed. Good luck with that.

The king cobra, for that's what it was—and a *big* one—hissed a sibilant hiss and shot its tongue out, testing the scents on the air. It knew we were there. This was a predator with perfect eyesight, excellent depth perception, and no qualms about showing everybody present who was boss. He was. I knew it, he knew it, we all knew it.

"It's the twelve-footer," Lenny whispered. "I think I'm going to faint."

"Don't you dare," I whispered back.

I started quivering, and the balls of my feet were suddenly barely touching the floor. That's how ready I was to run. I slowly reached out and clasped Lenny's hand, knowing I'd drag him along with me if it looked like we needed to make a hasty retreat.

But before I could do that, I had to rescue Pudding Pop.

"The bitch did this," Lenny whispered, his lips barely moving, doing his best ventriloquist impersonation so as not to attract the attention of the cobra. Or, heaven forbid, piss it off. "She dumped this snake in here to kill us."

For some reason I was feeling sarcastic. "Duh. Gee, Lenny. You think?"

"What a vindictive cow."

"No kidding."

"No sense of fair play at all."

"Not an ounce."

"I sort of wish she'd cooked this one now."

"Me too."

As if things weren't bad enough, we suddenly heard a rattling sound.

Lenny gasped, whirling left and right, trying to locate the source of the noise. "We can't be unlucky enough for that to be what I think it is."

My knees were knocking. "Why? What do you think it is?" As if I didn't already know.

"Rattles," Lenny moaned. "And not the kind a baby shakes."

Sure enough, two seconds later a fat triangular head poked out from beneath the pillow at the head of the bed. Brown and mottled, this snake too had its tongue extended, gathering information on everybody's whereabouts. It flexed its jaws wide, exposing two long fangs. A drop of venom appeared at the tip of each pointed tooth, sparkling in the light.

"Oh lordy," I breathed, trying not to pass out.

The rattler glided forward, homing in on Pudding Pop right away. Unfortunately for the snake, it didn't appear to consider a gigantic king cobra in full attack mode two feet away a matter of any great concern. Big mistake.

And speaking of big, the rattlesnake was at least four feet long and as big around as my ankle. As it slithered its full length out from under the pillow, the fat rattler twisted itself into striking posture with its rattles standing straight up and clattering away in the center of its writhing, tightening coils. Every ounce of its attention was centered on the trembling lump in the middle of the bed.

Then the cobra struck.

Taken by surprise, the rattler struck back, both animals ignoring Pudding Pop completely.

"Holy shit," Lenny hissed. "There's something you don't see every day."

The two venomous beasts coiled about each other as the cobra's fangs sank into the throat of the rattler. While they were duking it out, writhing and spitting and rattling for all they were worth, I saw a chance to save Pudding Pop, so I made my move.

I took a slow, easy step toward the bed, and just as the cobra spun to train its beady little eyes on me, even while it was waiting for the rattler to die in its jaws, I took a fistful of the bedclothes and flung them across the bed, burying the snakes completely.

Fully exposed on top of the bed now, Pudding Pop saw me hovering there and made a diving leap into my arms. As soon as I had him safely in my clutches, I grabbed Lenny by the shirttail and dragged him out of the room, slamming the door closed behind us.

I thrust Pudding Pop into Lenny's arms and ran to the kitchen, where I snatched up the throw rug in front of the sink. Racing back to the bedroom door, I stuffed the rug under the bottom of the door, hopefully sealing the cobra inside. I didn't figure I had to worry about the rattler much. It looked like it was on its last legs, so to speak, even before we left the room.

"Holy shit!" Lenny screamed when Ed leaped off the chandelier onto his shoulders, scaring him to death. Lenny was clutching Pudding Pop and clutching his heart and clutching Ed all at the same time. He was running out of hands to clutch with, and he was so scared he had almost gone white.

"Call Johns," I said. "No, I'll do it. You're busy. Where's the phone? Oh, it's in my hand."

I was shaking like crazy, and I thought I felt a rope of drool dangling off my chin.

"Call him, call him, call him!" Lenny wailed.

I slapped my forehead with the heel of my hand and damn near knocked myself out. It took me three tries to punch the right buttons to make the call.

While I tap-danced around waiting for Johns to pick up the stupid phone, Lenny rushed into the kitchen, presumably to retrieve poor Ethel, who was still probably wondering what the hell was going on. Gerbils always seem to have a hard time keeping up.

When Johns finally answered, I didn't bother with pleasantries. "Your wife's been here, and she dropped off a couple of snakes!" I yelled.

He didn't sound amused. "What kind of snakes?"

"A king cobra and a rattler!"

Johns growled. "Holy shit."

"That's what Lenny keeps saying!"

"What's your address? I'll be right there with my equipment. Get the hell out and lock the doors behind you. Don't call the cops yet. They won't know what to do. Somebody might get bitten. What's your address?"

I told him.

"I'm on my way."

"Good," I said to an empty line.

I heard Lenny mumbling something from the kitchen.

"We gotta go," I called out. "Get the pets and let's get out of here. Johns is on his way."

Lenny didn't respond. He merely kept mumbling whatever he was mumbling. It sounded like a chant. What was he suddenly, a Buddhist?

I peeked around the corner to see what the hell the holdup was and saw Lenny squatting in the kitchen sink of all places. It was something you don't see every day—a six-foot-tall black man cowering all hunched over in a kitchen sink. For one brief insane moment, I sort of wished my cell phone had a camera function. This was a Kodak moment for sure.

"What the hell are you doing?"

Lenny was still chanting. "Red touch yellow, kill a fellow. Or is it red touch black? Black touch yellow? What was it? I used to know!"

"What are you doing?" I bellowed. "What are you jabbering about?"

Lenny didn't have any free hands to gesture with since he was holding a monkey, a Chihuahua, and a gerbil, so he bellowed right back at me without pointing to what he was bellowing about.

"I'm trying to remember if that fucking thing is deadly!"

"What thing?" I shrieked. "*What* thing?"

Lenny had rivulets of sweat running down his face. Ed's tail was wrapped around Lenny's throat, Ed's little monkey hands were buried in Lenny's hair, Pudding Pop's apple-shaped, snarling head was poking out of the neck of Lenny's shirt, and Ethel, still in her carrying case, was dangling from Lenny's one free hand. All four of them were staring at the floor in front of the refrigerator.

"*That* thing!" Lenny spat, slinging saliva everywhere.

I looked to where all eight eyes were aimed and where most of the spit had landed.

A three-foot-long coral snake was slithering around in front of the fridge. It was a pretty little thing with its red, black, and yellow bands, but I was beyond seeing beauty by this point. All I saw was fangs. Or I imagined I did. I screamed. Then I screamed again. I sounded like a banshee. Then I rediscovered the ability to form words and construct sentences.

"Jesus H. Christ! It's a coral snake! Of *course* it's deadly. It was dumped here by the cow who cooks only venomous reptiles for dinner. What do you think it is? Harmless?" I couldn't seem to shut up.

"I was afraid of th-that," Lenny stammered. "And you don't have to be so snippy."

I gnawed on my lower lip. "Sorry. I'm a little stressed."

Lenny's eyes bugged out and he snarled, "Gee, I wonder why."

I reached down and picked up the cast iron skillet Ed had dropped off the refrigerator earlier and threw it with every ounce of force I could muster directly at the coral snake's pretty little head. I didn't wait around to see if I nailed the bastard or not. Instead, I grabbed Lenny's arm, yanked him out of the sink, and dragged him and all his cargo out into the hall, slamming the apartment door behind us. I ripped my shirt off and stuffed it into the crack under the door—I was getting pretty good at this—and when that was finished, I tugged Lenny and friends down the stairs, across the lawn, and into the van parked out front, where we proceeded to slam the doors shut, hit the door locks, roll up the windows, and seal ourselves inside like we were astronauts in a rocket ship getting ready to blast off into outer space. I even snapped the air vents closed. Don't ask me why. Overkill seemed like a good idea at the time.

Ed unwrapped his tail from around Lenny's neck, worked his fingers out of Lenny's hair, and crawled into my lap, still trembling and "*hoo-hooing*" in terror. I pried the handle of Ethel's gerbil carrier out of Lenny's cramped fingers and set it on the dashboard.

"Uh-oh," Lenny said softly, his chocolate eyes boring into mine.

"Oh God," I groaned. "What now?"

"Pudding Pop's peeing inside my shirt."

"Can't say I blame him," I said.

Lenny grunted. "Actually neither can I."

JASON JOHNS arrived while Lenny and I were still jabbering senselessly in horror. He appeared unafraid as he strolled into the apartment and went calmly to work. I decided on the spot that herpetologists were nuts. There was no other explanation for it.

The rattlesnake was dead, of course, and the coral snake had been flattened by a cast iron skillet flung by a panicked homosexual. Me. The cobra, however, was still very much alive. And not in a good mood. After a few nervous minutes—nervous for Lenny and me, not him—Johns gathered up the cobra by slipping a noose around its neck from the end of a long pole and dropping it into a bag, which probably didn't improve its mood much. Not that I cared. I just wanted it gone.

Lenny and I spent the rest of the afternoon being interviewed by cops and recording statements and wondering if there were any other venomous reptiles lurking among the nooks and crannies of our little love nest. Formal charges were filed against Lorraine Johns for attempted murder, reckless endangerment, animal cruelty, running an illegal restaurant, and God knows what else. If she wasn't on the lam before, she most certainly was now.

In the meantime, Lenny and I had a business to run.

We were still debating whether to move since we didn't know if our apartment was now snake central or not. We rattled the pros and cons back and forth as we stood outside Arthur's apartment door in the Belladonna Arms with Ethel's gerbil carrier dangling from Lenny's hand like a rat-infested evening purse.

Arthur answered on the second knock, ending our discussion on the spot. He was dressed in a square-dance skirt with a series of galloping horses appliqued around the hem and what looked like twenty or thirty petticoats stuffed underneath. The skirt stood out perpendicular to Arthur's massive body like a gigantic tutu. It rustled and swayed when he moved. Over the skirt he wore a lacy blouse under a fringed suede vest that had enough leather in it to hold a cow together. On his head sat a bigass cowboy hat with a little string tucked under and among his three chins to hold it in place atop the humongous pink wig he was wearing. The cow motif was amplified by the fact that Arthur's voluptuous hairy bosoms were squeezing through the front of the suede vest like a couple of milk-fattened udders. He had on clunky high-heeled shoes with big bows on top and metal taps underneath that made him sound like a machine gun when he walked.

Lenny and I stood there blinking in amazement, which Arthur took as a complement.

He did a dainty spin, like one of the ballet-dancing hippos on the Disney backlot.

"You like?" he simpered.

Speechless, I simply nudged Lenny to get his attention. He clapped his mouth shut. He had been gaping again.

Lenny stuck out his hand and thrust the Ethel imposter in Arthur's face. Always the gentleman, he said, "Here's your fucking gerbil."

Arthur squealed. "Oh my God, oh my God, oh my God! It's her. It's really her!"

It wasn't her at all, of course, but there was no point telling Arthur that. All Lenny and I had to do was keep our mouths shut and Arthur would be happy, Ethel would have a new home in a brand-new state, and Arthur's friends would not think he was a twit for misplacing their stupid gerbil. Oh, and Lenny and I came off looking like a couple of clever pet detectives who never lost a case. It was an all-around win-win situation.

Arthur poked his fat hand into the cage and hauled Ethel out by her tail, holding her up to his nose and studying her closely. Lenny and I held our breath. This was the moment of truth. Would he suspect he was being duped?

Arthur wrinkled his nose. "This gerbil stinks."

"It's grizzly repellant," Lenny said before I could stop him.

Now it was Arthur's turn to blink in surprise. He stared at Lenny, then me, then back to Ethel.

"Well, well, well," he cooed to the gerbil. "You've had *quite* the adventure, now, haven't you? Grizzlies and everything."

He studied Ethel a little closer. "She appears to have shrunk."

"She's had a rough two weeks on short rations," I said. "She lost a little weight. It happens."

"Her hair is lighter," Arthur said, turning Ethel this way and that, still dangling her upside down by her tail in front of his eyes.

"She turned gray from the shock," Lenny offered. "Or maybe it's old age. She's been gone awhile."

Arthur batted incredulous eyes at Lenny. "Oh, please. She hasn't been gone *that* long."

Arthur hoisted Ethel even higher. Ethel's little feet were going a mile a minute. I suspected if Arthur didn't flip her upright soon, she would barf up the Ritz cracker I had fed her for breakfast.

"Did the shock also make her grow balls?" Arthur asked.

Lenny and I jumped. "Say what?"

"Ethel used to be a girl gerbil. Now she's got testicles. Cajones. You understand what I'm saying? She's got gerbil nuts."

Lenny decided it was time to surpass himself. Even I was astounded he would attempt such a feat. He cleared his throat like Carl Sagan about to explain the universe to a bunch of third graders. "Ahem. It's common knowledge that under stressful situations, Arthur, gerbils have been known to spontaneously change sexes. It's a matter of survival, don't you know. Rather like the Teutonic tree frog on the upper Danube or the Guatemalan salamander on the banks of the lower Amazon who go from male to female to male again, as if by whim. Clever little chaps. Tits, twats, tallywhackers. They've got it all. Nature is a grand and wondrous mystery, don't you think?"

Arthur wasn't buying it. "I hate to break this to you, but the Amazon goes nowhere *near* Guatemala."

Lenny tapped the side of his nose. "Or so they would have you believe."

Arthur rolled his eyes so far up into his head he could probably read his hat size. He had Ethel still dangling by her tail in one hand and his other hand was stuffed into folds of fat at his hip. His eyeballs reappeared like cherries on a slot machine, and he stared at Lenny like he had never seen such an amazing bullshit artist in all his life.

As well he probably had not.

"How dumb do you think I am?" Arthur asked.

"Just dumb enough?" Lenny replied, looking hopeful.

Arthur considered that while I gazed around for a hole to climb into. But soon, Arthur let out a whoop of laughter, yanked Lenny into his arms, and hugged him so hard Lenny's ears swelled up like balloons. Then he did the same to me.

"I don't care how you did it," Arthur announced. "I'm just glad you came through. Thank you, boys." Ever the businessman—or woman as the case may be—Arthur asked, "Are we square, then? Is my bill paid in full?"

The man had just doled out six hundred dollars for allowing us the privilege of delivering into his hands a six-dollar gerbil. Seemed square to me.

He dropped Ethel back in her cage, shoved a platter of brownies at us, and gave us both a juicy kiss on the cheek to speed us on our way.

"Ta-ta," he cried as we ambled away. "Ta-ta, boys! I'm glad you finally admitted you love each other!"

That stopped us in our tracks. We turned and stared back at Arthur, who was eyeing us with tears streaming down his cheeks.

"How'd you know?" I asked.

Arthur swept his hand through the air, encompassing all before him. Sort of like God. "Love pollen," he said. "Like I told you."

Lenny took my hand, and with his other hand, he blew Arthur a kiss. Arthur went through the motions of grabbing it in midair and slapping it to his heart.

"Let's go home," Lenny said, turning back to me and stuffing a brownie in his mouth.

"Yes, let's," I replied grandly, snatching a brownie for myself.

Chewing happily, we clutched hands and hustled off to the car.

WE HAD a few more errands to run before we could get down to the task of settling into a cohabitative lifestyle.

The first thing we had to do was stop by the apartment and pick up Ed. When we entered he wasn't screaming from the chandelier, so we took that to mean the apartment was probably reptile free, which was a nice change.

A detente of sorts seemed to have been struck while we were away tending to Ethel's needs. Pudding Pop and Ed were lounging around on the sofa watching Bugs Bunny cartoons. They were sharing a bag of Fritos, eyes glued to the television. Fido was stuffed into the cushions between them. His loose eye had disappeared altogether. I prayed to God Pudding Pop hadn't swallowed it with a Frito.

Pudding Pop, ever loyal, came running when we walked through the door, yipping merrily. Ed yawned and gave us the finger. Fido just lay there, stuck between the cushions, one eye open, one eye gone.

"Up and at 'em, Ed," Lenny crooned. "Time to get laid."

Ed said, "*Orp?*"

To which Lenny answered, "You bet your sweet monkey ass, *orp*."

I laughed and patted my shoulder, beckoning him to come. Ed said, "*Eep, oop*," and bounced across the room, scattering Fritos everywhere. Leaping to my shoulder, he wrapped his fuzzy tail around my neck for balance and gripped my hair in his tiny, clever hands.

Lenny hugged Pudding Pop. He scratched Pudding Pop's ears, gave him a smooch on top of his head, and gently set him back on the sofa. "Stay," he said. "Hold down the fort. Don't let any homicidal snake women in. We'll be right back without the monkey."

If only Pudding Pop could have understood that statement, I'm sure he would have done a cartwheel. As it was, he merely cuddled up to his stuffed buddy, Fido, and refocused his attention on Bugs, who happened to be in drag at the moment, not unlike Arthur, singing an operatic duet with Elmer Fudd. And they say there's no culture on television.

"Bring the rest of the Fritos," I said to Lenny, and the four of us— Lenny, me, Ed, and the Fritos—headed for the door.

We were barely outside when my cell phone rang. It was Lester Boggs.

"I called the fucking Better Business Bureau, I'll have you know. I told them you guys are as worthless as tits on a screen door. Then I entered fourteen one-star reviews about you fucking creeps on Yelp, and spread the rumor across town that you both have crabs. Ha! What do you think of that?"

"I think you're consuming too much caffeine."

"Where's my *parrot*?"

"You know, Lester. With the proper medication you might not be such a raging asshole."

"Yeah," Lenny interjected, leaning into the phone to be better heard. "Then you'd just be a *regular* asshole."

"What'd he say? What'd he say?"

My God, Lester's voice was piercing. Even Ed stuck his fingers in his ears.

I gleefully disconnected in the middle of his upcoming rant, and the three of us were off. We took the car this time, since the van still reeked of grizzly repellant. Ten minutes later we were standing at the service entrance of the San Diego Zoo, waiting for Jason Johns to usher us inside.

He showed up with a broad smile on his face and wearing a khaki zoo uniform with short pants and a zoo emblem sewn over his left shirt pocket.

"Nice legs," Lenny muttered under his breath. "Wonder if he mailed the pecker pictures yet."

"Hush up," I muttered back. "Mine is the only pecker you need to be ogling."

"Oh, yeah. I forgot."

We followed Johns along a winding path through the guts of the zoo, far from the places where tourists usually visited. Johns had taken

Ed from my shoulder and placed him on his own. Ed seemed to know he was in for an adventure. He stared at everything with wide, excited eyes, clutching Johns's index finger and vibrating with excitement. Every once in a while, when something caught his attention, he'd squeak.

Johns stroked Ed's arm as we walked. "We lost one of our male capuchins a few months ago, so the curator of monkeys is giving Ed a holy dispensation. After a few weeks of isolation, once they've run some tests and concluded he's healthy, of course, Ed'll be integrated into the capuchin group. Hopefully, Ed will find everything he needs there. Companionship with his own kind, proper medical care, and enough tactile stimulation to keep him happy and interested."

"By tactile stimulation I'm assuming you mean monkey pussy," Lenny said. "Ed's really looking forward to some monkey pussy."

Johns laughed. "I'm sure he is. Mature capuchin males enjoy their trysts. Sex is a big part of their lives. I'm surprised he isn't beating off right now."

"He probably just finished," I said. "Give him a minute. His recuperative powers are disconcerting, to say the least."

Johns led us to a redbrick building shaded by banana trees with a sign over the door that read Quarantine. He punched in some numbers on a keypad at the entrance, and the door beeped open. Johns waved us in.

In glass booths along a circular walkway, sundry animals watched us passing by. A cassowary. A trio of meerkats. A young bison being fed from a gigantic baby bottle by a male worker in zoo garb like Johns was wearing, only Johns's legs were cuter. Each of the animals had a nameplate in their window. The cassowary was Steve. The meerkats were Hewey, Dewey, and Louie. And the bison was Bisontennial.

Just past the bison's enclosure was an empty booth. A little card taped to the glass said Ed.

His new home was waiting for him.

Johns slipped around to the back of the booth and entered through another door. He freed Ed and sent him scurrying into his temporary living quarters. There were stuffed toys and hanging ropes in the enclosure to keep Ed occupied while he waited for his first piece of ass. In a metal bowl on the floor was a pile of fresh fruits and vegetables. Beside the fruit sat a bowl of water. Ed picked up a peach, perched himself high on a platform at the front of the booth so he could see us through the glass, and chomped into the peach, squeezing his eyes shut in bliss. Poor bastard. He'd probably never see another Frito for as long as he lived.

Johns came back and shook our hands. "You've done a good thing, guys. Ed wouldn't have survived much longer without proper diet and care. You saved his life."

"Actually," I said. "We couldn't stand to be around him anymore. He was driving us nuts."

Lenny tapped the glass and Ed laid his hand to the spot as if saying good-bye. Lenny's eyes misted up. "Speak for yourself, Mait. I, for one, am going to miss the little guy. It was nice having another sex fiend in the family. Made you and me look almost normal."

Johns watched Lenny with a gentle smile on his face; then he cleared his throat.

"I've got news, boys. Lorraine is in custody in Tijuana. The cops called earlier. They caught her entering Mexico with a shitload of venomous reptiles in the trunk of her car and a box of recipes in her purse."

"What a bitch," Lenny said, and we all nodded. No argument there.

"So the reptiles are safe, then," I said.

"Yes. They'll be dispersed to various zoos and reserves. They're off the menu."

Lenny rested a hand on my shoulder. "Thank goodness."

From farther along the circular hallway, we heard a familiar voice, raucously loud, scratchy and piercing and annoying as hell. It was actually more a squawking screech than a voice.

"Blow it out your ass!" the voice screamed.

Johns rolled his eyes and sighed. "Oy," he said.

Lenny and I tensed beside him. It couldn't be.

"I know that voice," Lenny said. "I'd know it anywhere."

He took off down the hall with me hot on his heels. Four booths down we saw a lone bird perched high on a fake limb behind a sign that said John Doe. "Holy shit!" Lenny exclaimed. "That's not John Doe. That's Toodles!"

Johns came up behind us. "You know this bird?"

"Yeah," I said. "We know him. What the heck is he doing here?"

Johns tapped at the glass trying to get Toodles's attention. He got it.

"Eat me," Toodles said.

Johns sighed again. "We captured this guy stealing food from the flamingos. He's obviously someone's pet, but the zoo doesn't have funds in its budget to advertise lost animals, so we decided to try to incorporate him into life with the other African greys we have on display. Problem is, the San Diego Zoo has a lot of kids tromping through, and every other word out of this parrot's mouth is a word kids don't really need to hear. Their vocabularies are extensive enough already."

Lenny was grinning like a fool. "We've been chasing this bird for days."

"You know who he belongs to?"

"Sure. We just got an obscene phone call from the guy. He talks just like Toodles."

"Figures," Johns said. "Parrots imitate their owners. If the owner's an asshole, the parrot's an asshole. The keepers are ready to ring his neck."

"Don't let us stop them."

Johns shuffled his feet. "Well, we're not really supposed to murder any of the animals in our care, no matter how annoying they are. If you'll just inform the owner we're holding the little bastard, we'll be more than happy to turn him over. He's cured, by the way. He had mites and ringworm and all sorts of avian skin afflictions. His feathers should be filling in soon. Maybe the owner will be kind enough to reimburse us a little something for his bird's care."

"Yeah," Lenny said, chortling. "Good luck with that."

I gazed at Lenny fondly. He's really cute when he chortles.

"Stupid pissants!" Toodles squawked, taking me out of the moment.

"You can take him with you now if you like," Johns deadpanned, and this time we all chortled.

I turned back to the glass enclosure with Ed inside and found him with his little face smooshed up against the pane, staring out at us. I could have sworn he had tears in his eyes, but I knew that was not empirically possible. At least I didn't think it was.

I gently stroked the glass where Ed's cheek lay, and he closed his eyes as if he could feel my touch. Lenny sniffed.

"He'll be fine," Johns said softly. I nodded. Lenny sniffed again.

It was a somber threesome that trooped back toward the entrance. At the door, Johns said, "Please don't forget to come back for the bird."

In the distance a high-pitched voice screamed out, "Fucking Republicans!"

"Guess Lester's a Democrat," Lenny said, rolling his eyes.

"So it would seem."

"I still don't like him."

"Neither do I."

Just before we exited the building, Lenny gazed back to the distant glass partition where we could see Ed, pressed to the window, still watching us, wondering where we were going maybe. Wondering why we weren't taking him with us.

"Poor little guy," Lenny sighed.

"He'll be fine," Johns said, patting Lenny on the back. "You've done a good thing today."

A tear slid over Lenny's lower lash and skittered down his cheek as we stepped out into the afternoon sunshine. We heard laughter somewhere on a distant path, and a constant hum of excited voices echoing among the treetops. The tourists were having fun. The smell of popcorn and churritos lingered on the air. Life went on.

We said our last good-byes to Jason Johns. When that was over, I took Lenny's hand and led him toward the car.

By the time we got back to town, Lenny was smiling again. His beautiful smile lasted until we stepped through the apartment door to the sound of the telephone ringing.

While Pudding Pop pranced around my ankles, welcoming me home and begging for attention, Lenny picked up the receiver and hit Speaker. "Two Pet Dicks," he blithely answered.

"I need help!" a female voice wailed. "My beloved Marion is *gone*! And all her babies are missing too!"

Lenny shot me a thumbs-up as if to say "Another live one!"

"Yes, ma'am," he responded, all pompous and snooty. "Of course. I understand completely. You're distraught. Well, let me tell you, you've come to the right place. Now, then, just for our paperwork, what species might Marion be, if one might be so bold as to inquire?"

The woman's voice crept up another octave. "I've had her forever! She's like one of the family!"

"Yes, yes, of course," Lenny replied. "I understand. We all become attached to our animals. You miss her. You want us to find her. I get it. But I need to know what sort of creature she is. Pussycat? Puppy dog? God forbid it's a thirty-foot anaconda. We just went through an ordeal with snakes, and frankly I'm not up to facing another one of those motherfu—"

The woman chuckled nervously. "Oh no. Nothing like that. Marion is a tarantula."

Lenny's voice went flat. Lenny hated spiders. "A tarantula."

"Yes. She's missing. And so are her babies."

His voice went flatter. "Her babies."

"Yes. Every one of them."

"How many were there?"

"Sixty-three."

"Hold please."

Lenny's face fell void of all emotion as he calmly handed the phone to me. There may have been the slightest tremor in his hand, and I wasn't entirely sure, but I thought I detected a glimmer of panic buried somewhere in the back of his chocolate-brown eyes.

"It's for you, Mait. Have a nice life. Stay well. I quit. I'll be working the deep fryer at McDonald's if you need me. I'll see if I can get you a discount on onion rings."

"Oh, hush," I said, and pulled him into my arms. I slung the phone cord over my shoulder while planting a kiss at the base of his throat.

"That feels good," Lenny muttered, his cock lengthening against my leg. "Oh yeah. That's the spot. Kiss me there, just above my Adam's apple. Ooh, yeah, use your tongue. I like that. Hmm. Maybe I won't quit after all. Maybe we'll just—ooh, yeah, do that again—maybe we'll pawn the tarantula case off onto the walking hormone."

"You mean Jamie?"

"Who else?"

Lenny's throat lay hot against my mouth. His pulse was pounding faster. So was mine. He tasted heavenly. "We could do that," I said. "Jamie won't mind."

A few seconds passed before Lenny muttered, "That's good. Kiss me there again," in a languid, dreamy voice. I seemed to have sufficiently distracted him enough that he forgot what we were talking about. I smiled to myself. I still had the touch. Yessir.

Lenny moaned, and his head fell back as I continued to graze at his throat. He slid his hands under my shirt, pulling it over my head at the same moment as I dropped to my knees in front of him. The phone clattered to the floor.

"Hello? Hello?" the woman cried, her voice tinny with distance. "Where'd you go? What's going on? What's that moaning sound?"

Lenny reeled in the cord and placed the phone gently on the cradle, cutting the woman off completely. A moment later his pants slid to the floor.

"That's the ticket," Lenny gasped when my tongue found his belly button and my arms curled around his long, naked legs.

"I thought it might be," I said, enjoying the tug of his trembling fingers digging through my hair, pulling my mouth ever closer. His knees were knocking against my chest.

I figured knocking knees was pretty much a green light, so without further ado, I abandoned his belly button and happily headed south. Lenny graciously mapped out the route and guided my mouth along the way.

I don't mind telling you, no matter how many times I traveled that road, it was still a lovely, lovely trip.

Stay tuned for an excerpt from

Sunset Lake

By John Inman

Reverend Brian Lucas has a secret his congregation in the Nine Mile Methodist Church knows nothing about, and he'd really like to keep it that way. But even his earth-shattering secret takes a backseat to what else is happening in his tiny hometown.

Murders usually do that.

Brian's "close friend," Sam, is urging a resolution to their little problem, but Brian's brother, Boyd, the County Sheriff, is more caught up in chasing down a homicidal maniac who is slaughtering little old ladies.

When Brian's secret and Boyd's mystery run into each other head on, and Boyd's fifteen-year-old son, Jesse, gets involved, all hell breaks loose. Then a fourth death comes to terrify the town, and it is Brian who begins to see what is taking place in their little corner of the Corn Belt. But even for a Methodist minister, it will take more than prayer to set it right.

www.dreamspinnerpress.com

Chapter One

HERE IN Nine Mile, kinship still shapes daily life. Familial bonds are strong, and the ties of friendship are lifelong and rarely broken. We seem to possess the tattered remnants of a pioneer culture, with all the spirit and cohesiveness that entails, and at the same time, we find ourselves coexisting with satellite dishes and microwave ovens and shiny computer-driven automobiles that beep and boop and flash annoying little lights at us every time we do something stupid.

The people here are good, most of them. Kind, simple country folks. Many are farmers, and like good farmers everywhere, they have an undying, tongue-in-cheek faith in the ability of God or government, or both, to somehow mangle the next harvest and render it worthless.

In reality, these people haven't changed as much as they might think they have. Their accessories have, certainly, but not the people themselves. Like the pioneers before them, their hearts are strong with reverence for country, family, friends, and church. And the land, of course. With citizens such as these, it is always the land that comes first. Always.

Put simply, they are nice, decent people. On the whole.

Exceptions, of course, can always be found.

And on this, the last day of her life, Grace Nuggett would meet one of those exceptions face-to-face.

It wasn't the sort of day one would choose for the last day of life if one's options were open. The rain had not yet come pelting down, but by the look of that dismal gunmetal sky above our heads, I figured it was only a matter of time before it did. From the occasional grumble of distant thunder, it seemed a safe bet Someone up there agreed with me.

Being the only Methodist minister in Nine Mile, and knowing full well the farmers were scanning the sky for the least little promise of rain to ease the long drought they had been enduring (God did it to them this time, since they couldn't very well blame the government for the weather), I should have sent up a grateful prayer of thanks that the withered crops in the fields would finally get some much-needed moisture. But in reality, all I did was lean against the outside wall of my church, cross my arms, stare balefully at the sky, and sigh. If I were a farmer in need of sunshine, I would have had the pleasure of blaming God for this outrage, but being a preacher in need of sunshine in the middle of a drought, I didn't quite dare. Not that I wasn't tempted.

After two long months with nary a hint of moisture in the air, today, of all days, the sky had finally decided to open up. Sam had warned me, of course. He always does. About everything.

Sam is my go-to guy for all things mechanical, since I'm about as useful as a box of sick hamsters. Sam is also my best friend. We have known each other since we were kids growing up in this one-horse town. Looking at us, one would think we were polar opposites. Sam stands about five foot six, and I'm six four. Sam is well built, and I'm a beanpole. His hair is reddish blond while mine is black. The only thing we truly have in common, other than friendship, is the fact that we are both single. Which, of course, opens up a whole new can of worms since every woman at the church is constantly trying to set us up with a female relative or two. Or three. But so far Sam and I have held on to our bachelorhood with tooth and claw.

But that's another story altogether.

"Give the farmers a break, Brian," Sam told me. His voice was a booming, sonorous echo because he had his head buried in the church's old upright piano. He had his head stuck in the piano because he was trying to tune the thing himself since the church couldn't afford to pay an actual piano tuner to do the job.

I didn't say anything, but it sounded to me like he was getting questionable results as far as the tuning went. His words, however, would later prove to be right on key.

"Set the date for the annual basket dinner," he said. "That's the only way the poor farmers'll get any rain, and you know it."

He must have heard my derisive snort, for he poked his head out of the piano and gave me a glare. A dust ball the size of a mouse was stuck in his hair. "Just wait. You'll see. And while you're waiting, hand me that velvet hammer. The one in the toolbox."

I handed him the hammer, and here I was, two weeks later, propped against the side of the church like a tired wooden Indian, the back of my neck heating up, remembering how I had scoffed at Sam's prediction.

Well, to make a long story short, I did see. All too well. As I watched, the good ladies of my congregation, with their starched Sunday dresses flapping like flags about their legs, tried rather unsuccessfully to place tablecloths and napkins atop the plank-covered trestles arranged in rows beneath the elm trees at the edge of the churchyard. Unsuccessfully because as soon as someone neatly spread a tablecloth, the wind would come along and flip it into the grass. Or happily toss the napkins into the air. Or simply poof the poor lady's skirt up around her ears until she was forced to drop everything in an attempt to maintain her dignity, and the moment she did, the wind would take everything—tablecloth, napkins, paper plates and cups—and gleefully scatter them to hell and back.

At my back, through the walls of the old church, I heard the sweet voices of the Methodist choir practicing, yet again, one of the hymns they had chosen for this occasion. Behind the emphatic lead of the ancient upright piano—which still wasn't tuned right, dammit—I heard the choir sing the old familiar lyrics I grew up with.

Shall we gather at the ri-i-iver,
The beautiful, the beautiful r-i-i-iver.

Before the verse was finished, a particularly energetic gust of wind rattled the elm branches, and rain began to splatter the sidewalk at my feet and plunk against the tall windows of the church. Then something a bit more insistent began plunking at the window beside me, and I turned to see Sam tapping at the glass from inside the chapel and pointing to the ladies out there beneath the trees as they frantically gathered up the tumbling paraphernalia of our ill-timed basket dinner. With squeals of laughter, they began scurrying, light-footed, through the wet grass toward the church to seek shelter from the quickening rain.

As luck would have it, the food was already in the basement.

"Just in case," Sam had said earlier, with a wary eye on that ugly sky overhead as the ladies began arriving with dishes upon pots upon containers of every sort, filled with heaven knows what but all smelling so wonderful it sent saliva dribbling off the end of my chin as if the gaskets in my mouth had dissolved from the sheer splendor of it all.

As my nephew Jesse, fifteen years old and looking uncomfortably spit shined on this summer afternoon, and his friend Kyle, looking equally clean and miserable, ran past me to help the ladies do what they had to do, I realized it might not be a bad idea if I helped them a bit myself. They weren't paying me to prop up the church. I was supposed to be the man in charge.

Before I could set off to assist the ladies of Nine Mile, a loud crack of thunder made me jump straight up into the air and bang my head on the underside of the electric meter nailed to the side of the church.

One of the ladies squealed in mock terror as she ran for the door, trailing a tablecloth over her head to protect her hair from the rain. Manly enough not to squeal, or so I hoped, I caught one last glimpse of Sam's laughing face in the window as I sprinted for the door myself. Rather than mowing the good woman down in my haste to escape the now cascading sheets of rain, it seemed a bit more gallant to grab her arm and lead her safely, but hurriedly, up the church steps and into the vestibule. There we shook ourselves off like a couple of wet dogs and laughed at the silliness of the situation.

Never one to miss an opportunity to embarrass me, as old friends always seem to do, Sam gave me a good-natured ribbing as I stood in the vestibule, dripping. "Good Lord, Brian! It's raining cats and dogs out there. Let's have a picnic, shall we?"

Sam's aunt Mrs. Shanahan, a rotund lady of eighty-some years with blue finger-waved hair that rolled across the top of her head like a corrugated tin roof, and possessing a voice that could crack obsidian, came to my rescue. Not. Mrs. Shanahan and I were adversaries from way back. She used to chase me out of her scuppernong arbor back in my youthful, barefoot days, and she had been chasing me one way or another ever since.

"Now, Sam. Mustn't pick at the poor man just because he chose the worst day we've had in six months to hold our annual basket dinner. We'll get by. We always do. Old Reverend Morton, now. He knew how to pick 'em. Always chose the prettiest day of the year. I asked him once how he managed to do that year after year, and he said he asked God to set the date for him. Now, there was a man of faith!"

He was also a pompous old windbag who inevitably smelled of garlic and cheap aftershave, I thought, rather uncharitably, I suppose, for a Methodist minister. Especially when referring to the man of God who had preceded me at my post for nigh on fifteen years. But it was true nevertheless. Reverend Morton was the dullest man to set foot on this planet since the conception of time, and if he ever spoke directly to God, and God actually deigned to answer, then I was a Kurdish camel driver on the road to popedom.

"But never mind," Mrs. Shanahan yammered on, giving Sam a wink and me a snarl. "We'll eat inside. Lord knows we haven't had to do that for ages. Kind of defeats the purpose of an outdoor basket dinner, don't you know. But what the hey? The food's good. That's what counts. Right, Jesse?"

A hand the size of a thirty-dollar pot roast came out of nowhere and slapped Jesse on the back. I could hear the boy's teeth rattle from the impact. The poor kid looked vaguely appalled at being thusly singled out for an opinion, but he carried it off well enough. "Suppose so," he mumbled to no one in particular. At the same time, he rolled his shoulder around to get some circulation back into it. "I like the rain."

Mrs. Shanahan enthusiastically pounded his back again, this time nearly driving the boy to his knees, which elicited a snicker from his friend Kyle. She appeared oblivious to her own strength. "Of course you do, Jesse!" her voice boomed out. "You and everybody else within shouting distance come from good American farm stock. Ain't a farmer been hatched yet that don't like the rain. In decent doses, that is."

The woman stuck her great arm through mine and dragged me toward the basement steps. "Come on, Reverend. Let's get the tables set up downstairs. Gotta work before we eat, you know."

Sam stood on the sidelines, watching this exchange with laughing eyes and a heart, I'm sure, that soared with happiness. Nothing amused him more than my own embarrassment. If you get to really know Sam, sooner or later he'll tell you about the time I peed my pants in first grade. But let's not get into that.

JOHN INMAN has been writing fiction since he was old enough to hold a pencil. He and his partner live in beautiful San Diego, California. Together, they share a passion for theater, books, hiking and biking along the trails and canyons of San Diego or, if the mood strikes, simply kicking back with a beer and a movie. John's advice for anyone who wishes to be a writer? "Set time aside to write every day and do it. Don't be afraid to share what you've written. Feedback is important. When a rejection slip comes in, just tear it up and try again. Keep mailing stuff out. Keep writing and rewriting and then rewrite one more time. Every minute of the struggle is worth it in the end, so don't give up. Ever. Remember that publishers are a lot like lovers. Sometimes you have to look a long time to find the one that's right for you."

E-mail: john492@att.net
Facebook: www.facebook.com/john.inman.79
Website: www.johninmanauthor.com

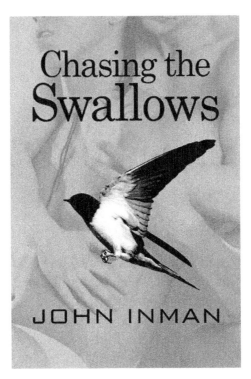

Sometimes an entire lifetime can be spent in the arms and heart of one person. It is not so with imaginations, for they go anywhere they wish.

David Ayres and Arthur Smith are about to find that out. When they meet as young men within the garden walls of the Mission of San Juan Capistrano, one man from one continent, one from another, an uncontrollable attraction brings them together. But it is something stronger than attraction that holds them there. It is love. Pure and simple.

After forty years, when the fabric of their existence together finally begins to fray because of David's imaginary infidelities, it is with humor and commitment that they strive to remain in each other's heart.

And turning fantasy into reality, they find, is the best way to do it.

www.dreamspinnerpress.com

A Belladonna Arms Novel

Barney Teegarden knows what it's like to be alone. He knows what it's like to have a romantic heart, yet no love in his life to unleash the romance on. With the help of a friend, he acquires a lease in a seedy apartment building perched high on a hill in downtown San Diego. The Belladonna Arms is not only filled with the quirkiest cast of characters imaginable, it is also famous for sprinkling love dust on even the loneliest of the lovelorn.

At the Arms, Barney finds friendship, acceptance, and an adopted family that lightens his lonely life. Hell, he even finds a cat. But still true love eludes him.

When his drag queen landlord, Arthur, takes it into his head to rescue a homeless former tenant, he enlists Barney's help. It is Barney who shows this lost soul how to trust again—and in return Barney discovers love for the first time in his life.

It's funny how even the hardest battles can be fought and won with laughter, hugs, friends, plus a little faith in the goodness of others. All it takes to begin the healing is the simple act of coming back.

www.dreamspinnerpress.com

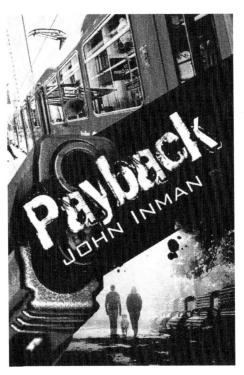

When Tyler Powell's life is torn apart by an unspeakable crime, the need for vengeance takes over. Every moment of every day, as he tries to pull his shattered existence together again, it's all he can think about—revenge.

Will he give in to his rage and become the very thing he hates most? A killer?

Only with the help of Homicide Detective Christian Martin, the cop in charge of his case, does Tyler see the possibility of another life beginning—the astounding revelation of another love reaching out to him. A love he thought he would never know again.

Will he let that love into his life, or is he lost already? Is payback more important to Tyler than his own happiness? And the happiness of the man who loves him? Tyler is determined to find a way to exact his revenge without sacrificing all hope for a future with Christian, but it will be difficult—if not impossible—and in the end he might be forced to make an unbearable choice.

www.dreamspinnerpress.com

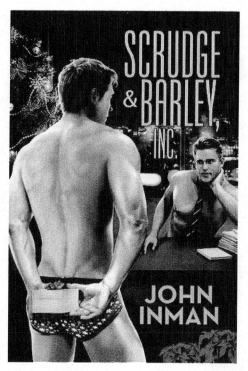

A classic tale takes off in sexy new directions! Poor Mr. Dickens must be twirling in his grave.

When E.B. Scrudge, putz extraordinaire and all-around numbnuts, is visited by his dead ex on Christmas Eve, he can't imagine how his life could sink any lower. But the three ghostly spirits that come along after are even worse! Good lord, a dyke, a drag queen, and rounding out the trio, a big, hunky bear with nipple rings and a butt plug! What's next?

What's next is a good deal of soul-searching and some hard lessons learned with a dash of redemption thrown in for good measure.

And love too, believe it or not. Love that had been simmering all along at the heart of Scrudge's miserable existence, although he was too selfish to see it—until a trio of holiday beasties pointed his sorry ass in the right direction.

www.dreamspinnerpress.com

FOR **MORE** OF THE **BEST GAY ROMANCE**

DREAMSPINNER
PRESS

dreamspinnerpress.com

CPSIA information can be obtained
at www.ICGtesting.com
Printed in the USA
LVOW03s1200240517
535498LV00039BB/1767/P